THE WRONG NEIGHBOUR

CALEB CROWE

INKUBATOR
BOOKS

Published by Inkubator Books
www.inkubatorbooks.com

Copyright © 2024 by Caleb Crowe

ISBN (eBook): 978-1-83756-402-6
ISBN (Paperback): 978-1-83756-403-3
ISBN (Hardback): 978-1-83756-404-0

Caleb Crowe has asserted his right to be identified as the author of this work.

THE WRONG NEIGHBOUR is a work of fiction. People, places, events, and situations are the product of the author's imagination. Any resemblance to actual persons, living or dead is entirely coincidental.

We make our friends; we make our enemies;
but God makes our next-door neighbour.

G.K. CHESTERTON

PROLOGUE

Whoever said a dog is man's best friend never came across this fucking monster. One hundred and forty pounds of muscle, sinew and teeth. A killing machine on legs.

The air is split by an eerie high-pitched screaming. It's hard to tell whether the awful sound comes from the woman watching it happen, or the man pinned to the ground while the brute of a dog rips into him. The beast shakes him like a ragdoll, allowing the teeth to razor deep into the man's flesh. The man jerks his arms upwards to protect his face, but any movement only spurs the dog on to greater ferocity. The jaws clamp onto his right arm so hard you can hear the snap of bone from twenty feet away, his forearm cracking like firewood. Dots of red spatter the ground. This thing wouldn't let go even if you caved its skull in with a baseball bat. You'd have to prize its jaws apart with a crowbar.

The only thing that could possibly stop it now is its master giving the right command.

But its master isn't saying anything.

PART 1

1

DREAM HOUSE

If I never see another caravan I'll die happy.

Only a couple without kids would be dim enough to make a trip to the seaside during Easter school break. We haven't bargained for this slow-moving holiday traffic, and the drive over from Manchester takes far longer than expected. Nick keeps accelerating too hard up to the backs of caravans blocking his view, but what's the point of fighting stuff you can't change? You have to accept things as they really are. I learnt that from Tiffany, my yoga instructor. That said, even Zen Buddhists might get a bit wound up by the tailback on the A55.

I chill Nick out with a playlist I have on my phone, the one I put together for our party this Christmas, just after we met. I unwrap a couple of mints and pop one into his mouth as he drives.

"Thanks, Meg."

He gives my leg a little squeeze. That's better. We're just on a day trip out. No hurry.

It's only when we notice the road signs are in two

languages we realise we've crossed into Wales. No big fanfare. No "Welcome to Wales" signs. We drive for another half hour or so, then the road crests the top of a hill and there it is – the sea. We both get excited then, like we're little kids, on holiday ourselves. I can't help giggling as Nick puts on a terrible Welsh accent and tries to say all the unpronounceable names of the towns we drive through. *Dwygyfylchi. Llanfairfechan. Abergwyngregyn.* He's hilarious, and utterly shameless.

"Stop it," I laugh. "You're spitting."

"I know. If I say any more we'll need windscreen wipers on the inside."

We drive into Menai and cross the pretty bridge onto Anglesey. Eventually we come to our junction and turn off. The roads narrow to lanes, and the lanes dwindle to tracks. The hedges push in closer on either side and funnel us towards our destination, which has now appeared as a checkered flag on the screen. *Bae Breuddwyd.*

Nick turns hard into a gap between the hedges. We bump along a narrow lane with two thin, undulating gravel wheel tracks separated by tufts of bright green grass.

"Wow. Jesus." Nick slows to a stop and we stare ahead.

And there it is.

It's absolutely and unquestionably the most beautiful house I've ever seen.

It's even more lovely than it seemed in the photos. A vast, modern building, with crisp clean lines of white-rendered walls, like some incredible millionaire's mansion transplanted from somewhere exotic and dropped into this little corner of the wild Welsh coast. I realise my jaw has dropped open.

Nick crunches the car up the gravel drive past beds of

pretty geraniums, and parks next to the sort of bashed-up VW estate car only rich people own. We get out. I can hear the seagulls calling as they wheel overhead. The cool sea breeze sweeps over me, like throwing open the windows of a musty house and having a refreshing breath of air blow through.

I've only seen the front of the house and I already know I love it.

The front door opens and Peter and Gavin come out to greet us, Peter hovering in the entrance and Gavin striding towards us, arms open expansively, drawing us in, like old friends.

"Megan, Nick, welcome, welcome!"

In fact, we only met Peter and Gavin a week ago. We were at a house party thrown by Pippa, my oldest friend from school. Gavin was loud and overbearing, while Peter seemed much quieter. Somehow, the conversation turned to where they lived in Anglesey, a place overlooking the sea, which they'd designed and built in a tiny little cove called Bae Breuddwyd, which translates roughly as Dreamer's Cove.

Gavin got his phone out and showed me and Nick the map. I couldn't be sure, but I got a sudden flash of famil-iarity, a memory of a deserted beach I once visited as a child before my parents passed away. I had a really warm feeling. Then Gavin showed us photos of the amazing house.

My God, we were awestruck. It was unbelievable. The sort of place you could only own in your wildest dreams. Gavin scrolled through more gorgeous photos while Peter stood by silently – probably modest about having created this incredible building. Gavin explained they were having to sell the house, for personal reasons. If Nick and I liked it, we should come down and visit.

Later that night, as we were lying in bed, we couldn't let the subject drop. We kept flirting with the idea that we should go and take a look, that we could actually live in a house like that.

I knew it was all just idle, excited, drunken chatter. But the following morning Nick brought the house up again over breakfast and said he'd texted Gavin and arranged a trip to Anglesey next weekend. It was just a look. No commitment. What harm could it do?

IF ONLY I had known then what I found out later. Then I would have been able to answer Nick's question:

It could do a *lot* of harm. More harm than either of us could ever possibly imagine.

2

JUMP

"It's my parents."

Gavin is filling us in on why they have to move.

"They're getting too old to do everything themselves. And it's just too far to drive all the time, isn't it, Peter?"

Peter says nothing, just gives a thin, sad smile and offers round a plate of biscuits.

"I get it," I say. "It was the same for me when my mum got ill. My dad had died by then and I'm an only child. It's too much sometimes."

Gavin gives me a sympathetic look. "I'm so sorry, Megan. What was wrong with her? Do you mind me asking?"

"Cancer." I take a breath. "She passed too, I'm afraid."

That was only nine months ago. I still find it so hard to talk about it without getting upset. It brings the past crashing back into the present.

Gavin squeezes my arm.

"I'm so sorry to hear that. How terrible for you." He pauses. "My mum has cancer too."

I feel a sudden bond of empathy with Gavin. A connection. It's a relief to share what I'm feeling with someone who understands.

I see Nick shift awkwardly and give Peter a little look. Nick's amazing in so many ways, but he never knows what to do when I bring this up, a thing he can't do anything about. I think he just feels useless. Maybe Peter feels the same because he doesn't meet Nick's gaze; he just drifts away to wash the coffee cups.

Gavin gives us the guided tour. Through the enormous open-plan lounge, up the wide staircase of floating wooden treads and onto the galleried deck above. Nick strides around with his customary confidence, as if he owns the place. He chats away easily with Gavin, friendly and warm. I love watching how he is with people, putting them at ease, making them feel like the centre of his attention, winning them over with his magnetic charm. While they talk, I peek into all the rooms, uncluttered and calming. I feel like it isn't quite real, like it's something from a dream.

"We have to move fast," continues Gavin as we walk. "We thought she was recovering, but she's relapsed. We've got to go as soon as possible. That's why we're willing to drop the price so much. We need to move by July."

I imagine what it must be like having to leave this beautiful house, all marble and oak, polished concrete and glass, like a page torn straight out of some interior design magazine. We head downstairs and out into the vast garden.

That view. That incredible view. Cove of Dreams.

It's a lovely spring day, bright and fresh. I stand on the grass and breathe in the crisp, salty air. The garden ends at a low fence with a small gate, through which a private path

THE WRONG NEIGHBOUR   11

zigzags its way down the cliffside to a beautiful beach of smooth yellow sand, totally empty. The sunlight shimmers and sparkles off the sea in the distance.

The only other building I can see is a glimpse of a house about a hundred metres away, mainly hidden behind a tree. Aside from that it's clear all along for about five miles to where the coast bends round at a rugged outcrop of rocks and a picture-postcard blue and white striped lighthouse. I close my eyes and listen to the seductive crashing of the waves.

Nick and Gavin are already talking about prices and timetables. I can't help thinking things are moving absurdly fast. This was supposed to be just a fun day out to the seaside. Gavin must see my expression because he stops talking.

"I'm sorry. I'm being pushy," he says.

There's a slightly awkward silence.

"Look," says Gavin, "why don't you take a moment alone in the garden? Have a chat amongst yourselves about it."

"DID you hear how little they want for it?" Nick's face is lit up like an excited child's. "It would be insane not to say yes, Megan. We should be ripping their arm off."

It's all he can do to stop leaping around the garden in his excitement.

How have we got to this point? It's our six-month anniversary next weekend, but here we are, talking about upping sticks, buying a house together.

I try to keep a level head. "This is mad, Nick. We can't just up and... It's insane."

"Yes, we can!" he says emphatically.

He strokes his floppy fringe away from his face and beams at me with his beautiful eyes. The sun behind him picks out the red in his chestnut hair and makes it glow like a halo. This is typical Nick, all boyish energy and puppy-dog enthusiasm. In contrast, I'm like a nervous bungee jumper clinging to the railings.

"But what about work?" I ask, trying to be practical.

"Forget work!" says Nick. "I can get something down here. And you can do your jewellery as easily here as in Manchester."

Nick turns to me and fixes me with a serious gaze. He strokes away a hair where it's blown across my face. The back of his hand brushes my cheek.

"This house, this could be *our* place. I could sell mine. You've got your money. This could be the start of a whole new adventure."

Something in what he's saying resonates with me. I can almost hear Tiffany telling our class *opening yourself to risk lets you discover new possibilities and deepen your understanding of yourself and the world.* That's what I want for myself after the struggle and tears and turmoil of the last year. This could be the proper start of our story together. I let myself imagine what it would be like to live here. There's more room for my workshop. So much more to inspire me... I take another look at the sea, sparkling like the diamonds in a bracelet or necklace I might make.

As I'm looking, a wild rabbit hops out of a hedge by the side of the garden and skips across the lawn as if he doesn't have a care in the world. The whole place is full of spring and the promise of something new. I don't want to be limited by caution.

But something keeps holding me back. It's taken so much out of me, Dad's death, Mum's illness, and then Mum dying too. Then my divorce, all so messy. I feel like I've only just got back on track. I couldn't cope with any more nasty shocks and surprises.

Nick takes my arms gently and turns me towards him.

"Do you trust me, Meg?"

He looks deadly serious.

"You know I do."

"Then trust me now," he says. "This is right for us. I *know* it. I don't have any doubts whatsoever. I know you think it's a risk, but if you hadn't taken a risk and left Niall you wouldn't be with me, would you? D'you remember what I told you then, the old trapeze artist's motto?"

I smile.

"You have to let go to find the hands that are waiting to catch you," I say. He told me that in our favourite restaurant, holding my hands across the table. That was the night I went home and told Niall about Nick, that I wanted a divorce, that I was leaving.

Nick grips me tighter by the shoulders.

"That's right. Sometimes you just have to jump."

I feel myself swept up on the sea of Nick's enthusiasm. Maybe *this* is what I should learn from losing Mum and Dad. Life's too short to be cautious. You need to take the moments when you see them. You just have to jump.

And then I really am jumping, leaping up and down in the garden, throwing myself into Nick's arms, hugging him.

"Yes! Let's do it! Yes! Yes!"

The startled rabbit scurries back into the hedge as we spin round laughing and laughing. We only come to a halt when I spot Gavin and Peter staring at us through the glass of the patio doors. Gavin's face is glowing with a wide, beaming smile. Peter's expression remains fixed, a blank inscrutable nothing.

What I should realise at this moment, but only find out far too late, is that taking a wild jump into the unknown can be fatal when you're perched on the edge of a cliff.

3

_____

BUTTERFLIES

We watch as the removal van bumps its way down the narrow gravel path and out of sight round the hedge. It felt like an omen this morning when I realised today's date, the 21st of June, is the first day of summer. It's definitely the start of something new for us. Nick's arm is around my waist and he gives me a little squeeze. I can tell he feels what I feel. We've moved. It's official. This house is now our home.

We go inside, giggling. We share a look, like co-conspirators embarked on some mischievous adventure. I love how cheeky he looks when he smiles. His eyes light up, looking at me. Laughing, we hurry up the stairs, throw ourselves on the bed, pulling each other's clothes off. We make love, quickly and playfully, excited because the house seems alien to us and at the same time it is ours.

"Well," Nick says at last, "at least we've christened the place."

He rolls onto his side and looks at me. He is staring into my eyes. The intensity of it is almost too much.

"What?"

"I love you, Meg. I really love you. I can't believe how lucky I am to have you."

I feel so happy I could burst. The adventure we've chosen to embark on together gets more exciting day by day. I feel it flutter inside me, a stirring in my stomach like the stirring of butterflies I felt when I met Nick and he pursued me so relentlessly that it made my head spin, sweeping me off my feet in a matter of weeks. Why is it that love and excitement and nervousness all feel the same?

I hug him tight to me and he buries his head in my hair. I feel his lips touch my ear.

"We're going to be so happy here," he whispers.

WE DRESS AND GO DOWNSTAIRS.

The house seems even larger now than when we first saw it, the rooms empty of clutter, the spaces stripped and echoing. I notice the bits of dust around the edges of the floor, the crumbs on the kitchen work surfaces. I spent ages cleaning Nick's house once we'd packed, leaving it spotless, but it seems Gavin and Peter haven't extended us the same courtesy. It is as if they've loaded up as quickly as possible and hurried off with unseemly haste.

I set to work on the grimy surfaces, while Nick bashes around the living room with the hoover. After a couple of minutes Nick's phone rings and he stops vacuuming. He looks at the phone and grimaces.

"Work. I need to take this."

He drifts off to a far corner of the house. I can't hear what he is saying, but I detect his frustrated tone. It was the same just before we left Manchester – animated, fractious calls to his office, no doubt because we moved so fast that he's leaving with the minimum of notice, and they are angry with him. Whatever the cause, there has clearly been some kind of falling out.

I resist the urge to listen in by picking up the hoover and carrying on where Nick has left off, letting the hum of the machine drown out his call.

It isn't long before I have everything clean for our new start. I dig out the kettle and a couple of mugs, and the plastic bag I've kept with me in the car, with tea bags, milk and biscuits. I make us both a drink and go out to look at the garden. The unpacking can wait.

I sit on the wooden decking and take in the view. The grass is lush and there are a couple of cheeky rabbits nibbling away at the far end. The sun is bright, and as I lean back the wood feels warm under my palms. The last couple of months have been insane – rushing around to get everything sorted for the move. Nick took charge of most of the practicalities, bustling around the house, making calls to banks and phone people, utility companies and broadband suppliers, arranging a mortgage, finding estate agents, booking furniture movers and chasing solicitors. He thundered through tasks at breakneck speed, as if his life depended on it. It's completely down to him we've got here so quickly.

Thank God that's over.

I hear the patio door slide open and Nick comes out and sits down next to me, picking up his tea and a couple of biscuits.

This view is what it was all for. The sea. The sound of its ebb and flow across the sand seems to wash all those stresses away as easily as I just washed away the biscuit crumbs and tea stains on the worktops. Clean. A clean start.

"Fuck it."

Nick is trying to hook half a biscuit out of his tea mug. He must have dunked it and it snapped off.

"Bloody Rich Tea."

He slams down his mug, spilling a puddle of tea across the decking.

"Is everything okay?" I ask.

"It's this bloody work stuff. I think I'll have to go back for a few days."

He stares out at the sea, looking resigned.

"Oh no. When?"

"Tomorrow. Sorry. I know it's shitty timing."

I put my hand on his arm.

"It's okay," I say. "It's all happened so fast, there's bound to be a few loose ends."

"Yeah." He sounds deflated.

I give his arm a little squeeze. He smiles, then looks back at the sea. Nick waits for me to finish my tea. He heaves a weary sigh.

"Right, let's crack on with the unpacking. If we get our heads down we can break the back of it tonight."

This isn't the start I was hoping for. The tide is coming in and the breeze has picked up a bit. When the sun ducks behind a large bank of clouds it gets suddenly chilly. I pull my cardigan around me. Nick picks up the mugs and the remaining biscuits and goes inside. It's just me and the sea and the puddle of spilt tea on the decking.

4

AWAKENING

What's that?

I've woken up suddenly. My heart is thumping in my chest.

My head is still foggy from sleep. I try to work out what's happening. It's dark, and it takes me a moment to remember I'm in the Anglesey house. I reach out across the bed for Nick, but he's not there. Then I remember he went back to Manchester yesterday. I'm alone.

It was a noise that woke me, like a bomb going off.

I stare into the gloom, trying to get my bearings in the unfamiliar room. There's an expanse of dull light on one side. I haven't had a chance to put curtains up yet, and thin moonlight creeps in at the uncurtained window. It must still be the middle of the night. I work out the bathroom is ahead of me, and the bedroom door on the wall opposite the window.

And the noise. I can make it out now I'm more awake – the *thump, thump, thump* of loud dance music. It must be

Nick, having driven back from Manchester through the night. But why the hell has he come in and started clubbing at Christ knows what o'clock?

I get out of bed and hurry to the bedroom door.

I expect to see light from downstairs, but the rest of the house is also in darkness. I realise the music isn't coming from inside the house but from outside. This isn't Nick. This is something else.

I flick the landing light on and make my way down the stairs. Crossing the kitchen, I look at the clock and see it's just after 3.30 a.m. I go to the patio doors and press my nose against the glass, cupping my hands around my face and staring into the murky darkness to work out where the music is coming from. The glare of the landing light is reflecting on the glass, making it impossible to see out, so I unlock the door and slide it open. The crisp night air hits me immediately and I regret leaving my dressing gown upstairs.

I take a step out onto the deck, wondering if it could be people partying on the beach. But I can't see anything out there other than the inky black void of the sea and a few twinkling lights on the headland miles off. The light from the lighthouse sweeps across the water and scatters dimly onto the beach below – once, pause, once. Then it's dark again.

The music isn't coming from the beach. It sounds nearby – possibly at the front of our house. I close and lock the patio door, and shiver as I walk across the cold stone of the kitchen. Maybe it *is* Nick, in his car in the driveway, with his radio on too loud.

But when I open the front door, the only car on the driveway is mine. Nick is nowhere to be seen.

The music is louder here though – nasty, cheap, monotonous techno, hammering away like an angry pile driver, thumping away and reverberating off the side of the building. It echoes round the front garden. *What the hell?* I slip my coat over my nightdress, pull on some wellingtons, grab my house keys and step outside, pulling the door closed behind me.

Walking up the path, I begin to think the music must be coming from the house we can see from the back garden. There's been no sign of any neighbours, and Peter and Gavin said the house was unoccupied when we came for our first visit. We assumed it was an empty holiday home and thought no more about it.

I come to the point on the drive where the path splits into a Y and begin to walk towards the other house. The music is louder, and I can hear voices. There is light too, just over the crest of a small rise. I come round the hedge at a curve in the path and see where the noise is coming from.

A car, a big black showy four-by-four, parked outside the neighbouring house. The car has all its doors open, and the music is blaring from the radio inside, but there is no one in sight. The door to the house is open, and lights in all the rooms are on, dazzlingly bright. The house is as large as our own, but nowhere near as stylish – a redbrick new build, like something from a soulless suburban estate, but pimped up with incongruous turrets and crenelations like a child's drawing of a castle. A grotesque monstrosity.

Then a man comes out through the front door and I instinctively duck out of sight behind the hedge. He begins to unload boxes from the boot of the car. He looks in his forties, a clinically obese, balding thug of a man wearing a scruffy tracksuit in football colours of some team or other. The boxes he's shifting are big, but he moves them easily. He looks out of shape, but clearly he's strong. He hefts another couple of boxes onto his drive, then slams the boot shut. He stands there, catching his breath and staring at the tower of boxes, considering his next move.

A woman emerges from the house, about the same age as the man, not as fat but certainly overweight. She has a shock of straggly bleached-blonde hair scraped up on the top of her head in an untidy nest. She comes over to the man and says something inaudible, but whatever it is makes him laugh, a gruff bark carrying over the volume of the music.

Then out of nowhere, he lunges for the woman, grabbing hold of her and making her shriek, her shrill laughter acting as the soprano to his bass.

He starts to spin her around, presumably in some sort of dance, and they both shuffle awkwardly around to the music. Then he pulls her into a bear hug, making her shriek again.

"Ron, you pillock, let me go!" I can hear that over the music. She's laughing, but I don't think she's enjoying it.

"Ron, let go."

She isn't happy. She is wriggling, but he doesn't let her go, pawing away at her, grabbing great handfuls of her flesh, kneading her breasts and arse like huge mounds of dough.

The woman is pushing him away and still laughing, but I really can't tell whether she is enjoying her mauling or genuinely objecting. Is this a game? Or is he doing all this against her will? Either way, the man carries on and begins to hoick the woman's dress up, exposing her large pale thigh like a side of meat in a butcher's window, baring her flesh to the punishing cold.

I feel suddenly cold myself, and strangely exposed in my thin white nightdress. I am unsettled by the ambiguous scene I'm witnessing, half playful romp, half molestation.

I've seen as much as I can bear. I step further back into

the shadow of the hedge, then turn and retreat down the pathway. I can still hear just the woman over the sound of the music. I can't tell if it's laughter or something else. I quicken my step as I approach the safety of the house. My hand hurts, and I realise I'm clutching the key in my fist so tightly it's practically cutting into my fingers. I fumble at the lock, unsure if a sound I hear is something in the music or the half-giggle-half-scream of the unknown woman drifting across the dark landscape.

I hurry into the house, double-lock the door, then scamper up the stairs, turn off the landing light, go into the bedroom and slide into bed, pulling the cold duvet up under my chin. I can't hear the voices now, just the *thump, thump, thump* of the music.

What should I do? Does she need help? Should I phone the police? I'm not even sure what I'd say I've seen. If I phone 999 and then find out it was just people larking about I'll feel ridiculous.

But I'm still unsettled. I can't not report it. Did she consent? What if something bad happens? I decide on a compromise and call the police non-emergency number. I dial 101. I get a holding message. I wait for five minutes. Ten. I rehearse what I'm going to say when someone answers.

After about half an hour, the music stops. There is silence again. There aren't any voices. All I can hear is the crackle of the phone and the eerie back and forth of the sea outside on the beach.

I stay on hold for another five minutes and then I hang up.

I'm sure everything is fine. I'm sure it is.

I lie in bed, unable to get back to sleep. I look at the dull light through the window and try to work out whether the room is brightening and the dawn is coming, or whether my eyes are merely adjusting to the darkness.

I lie there for what seems like an eternity, praying for it to get light.

5

CLIFF

I don't hear anything else from next door the whole of the following morning. It's as if they appeared in the middle of the night, like characters in a bad dream, and have vanished into the ether.

I unroll my yoga mat and start my asana practice. I try to do this every morning if I can. I'm a relative novice, and my body still struggles with some of the postures that Tiffany gets into with ease. I started yoga just after Mum died. I was plagued by awful nightmares and was constantly distracted, and after one particularly teary session in the pub, Pippa put me on to Tiffany's classes. She explained how focussing on mindfulness and breathing and my own body could help with my troubled thoughts. I was sceptical, but it really did. Pippa only went every now and then, but I couldn't get enough of it. It was like an anchor to hang onto while everything around me was caught in a storm. Plus, I'm not at all religious, but I find something comforting in the philosophical aspects of it all, how it helps you roll with the punches.

But this morning it isn't working. I keep picturing the

couple cavorting on the lawn. I can't fully shake the image of the man grabbing at the woman, and her protesting as he wouldn't let go. Probably they were just having fun, larking about. It was probably just horseplay. If Nick was here he'd tell me I am overthinking things.

I did try to call the police. I did. But no one answered. It feels too late to call them now.

I venture out at lunchtime and tentatively poke my head around the hedge to their driveway, but their car isn't there anymore and all the curtains of the house are drawn closed. I can't even tell whether they're inside or not. Maybe they've mothballed the house and gone away again.

I skulk back home, none the wiser.

THEN LATER THAT day I hear activity outside. There's a clashing metal noise and the sound of raised male voices. I peer tentatively through the top window at the front. A flatbed truck is negotiating its way down the narrow lane. It's a scaffolding lorry. The neighbours must be having some kind of building work done. Whatever I imagined might have happened to that woman, it can't be that bad if they've got the builders in – unless the husband's burying her under the patio! Then, as if to confirm how ridiculous I'm being, the wife appears from her driveway and starts waving at the truck, directing it towards her house. They all disappear from view again behind the hedge.

Relieved, I throw myself into tasks: putting up curtains; rearranging the contents of the kitchen cupboards; chucking out things we packed in haste and brought over but will never actually use. After a couple of hours, I need a break and take a coffee out into the garden, but the irregular clank of scaffolding keeps puncturing the silence, and when the wind changes direction I can hear the workmen's voices drifting across the breeze, or the woman, cackling, offering them endless cups of tea. It's not as restful as I'd hoped. I look down the garden towards the sea. There is no sign of the rabbits on the lawn anymore. They must have been scared off by the noise.

The builders are bound to knock off soon. Meanwhile, I decide to explore.

Crossing the garden to the gate at the end, I look towards the neighbours' house, hoping to find out what work is going on, but a slight rise in the level of the land makes it impossible to see, and I don't want to be caught staring. I zigzag my way down the steep path to the beach.

Turning to my left and walking for fifty metres or so brings me to where the neighbouring house has its own way down the cliff. But while our path simply opens out onto the pebbles, the other house has installed concrete posts and a metal gate, heavily padlocked, and with a sign in crudely painted red capital letters that reads:

PRIVATE PROPERTY. NO ENTRY.

The tide is out, and I walk towards the line where the sand meets the sea, then look back and crane my neck to try and spot the workmen. But their house is set too far back from the cliff edge for me to be able to see anything.

I stay on the beach and take a long walk around the rugged coast, looking for interesting stones and shells, and sit on rocks or sand dunes or under the shelter of the craggy cliffs and sketch design ideas for jewellery in my notebook. I film the sun shimmering on the sea, and the lace-like foam where the waves meet the sand, and cut them together as reels for my Insta account, with shots of a spiderweb silver necklace I made last week.

I already miss Nick, but I look at the vast empty coastline and decide I should try to approach being alone here as an opportunity. When I was younger I went straight from home to university, and from university into my marriage with Niall. Then I moved out from Niall and immediately in with Nick. I've never really ever been on my own. So this is something new. I can come and go as I please, stay out for as long as I want, answerable to no one.

In the evening the building work stops and I rejoice in the silence. I make an effort to reclaim the house as my own. I cook something simple for myself, and open a bottle of wine, and go outside into the garden, and sit on the decking, huddled up in my coat and a couple of thick blankets against the chill, listening to the crash of the waves upon the shore, and watching the sun dip down behind the horizon. I tell myself I'm fine.

But I'm not really.

That night I have a terrible dream. In it, Nick and I are driving from Manchester to Anglesey, and when we arrive the house isn't here. Everything else is the same. The garden is here, but no house. I am really upset, but Nick is fine about it. I go to the edge of the cliff and look down and the house is all smashed on the rocks.

The house has fallen off the edge of the cliff, I say.

And Nick says, *don't you remember, that's what it's supposed to be like?*

Then I wake up.

6

CATERPILLAR

The building noise is getting worse. Now the penetrating screech of power tools has been added to the orchestra of sounds. Every time it goes quiet and I think they might have finished, it starts up again. It isn't even the volume of it – it's the fact that I know it's there, just on the edge of my existence, just out of sight.

Nick is still tied up in Manchester and I've been here for nearly a week now, on my own.

I start the day attempting some yoga, but it's more of a stretching session really, as I can't concentrate on it properly with the noise. I admit defeat and spend the rest of my morning setting up my workroom at the top of the house. I put my workbench near the window with an amazing view of the sea. I have a commission for a necklace I have to complete, for use in an editorial spread in *French Vogue*, which I'm incredibly excited about. But the sound of building work next door underscores everything and makes it impossible to concentrate on this as well. I find playing music too distracting, and noise-cancelling headphones have always made me claustrophobic, like being smothered with a pillow. Finally, I give up and go out.

I head to Beaumaris. It's a busy town at first sight, but there's only so much time I can kill here before I run out of things to do. I try to spin this to myself as part of my great opportunity to explore the benefits of being alone. Tiffany told us all about a retreat she went on, and how *solitude is an opportunity for introspection, self-reflection, and deepening one's understanding of the nature of reality.* So I force myself to stay out, drinking coffees I don't need and eating cakes I don't want, hanging on over the empty cups and plates as long as I can before getting up and finding some other way to fill my time.

I've been round the castle, walked up and down the high street and eaten my greasy fish and chips on a bench near the lifeboat station. I'm now standing on the pier watching kids fishing for crabs, while angry gangs of seagulls wheel menacingly overhead. There's a wooden sign at the end of the pier that tells me I could take a cruise around Puffin Island. That might fend off my boredom, but it's the wrong time of year for puffins, or for the seals that sometimes bask on the rocks, and the sea is beginning to look decidedly choppy, with dark clouds louring just offshore and bad weather coming in.

I feel bad about just giving up and heading home, with another two hours still to run on my ticket in the car park. So I grit my teeth and wander back up the high road to explore a few of the side streets I haven't looked at.

As with most seaside towns, anything of interest is on the front itself, and I rapidly find myself in a clutter of dull residential roads with terraces of bland, anonymous houses. As I come to a corner with a takeaway, a hairdresser and a tiny bookshop, the drizzle starts. I take shelter in the bookshop, hoping the rain will pass quickly.

The walls of the shop are covered from floor to ceiling with shelves, each one heaving under the weight of books rammed in at all angles. Over in one corner, a man is wedged behind a counter reading a newspaper. He doesn't look up as I come in.

I immediately know without a shadow of a doubt there isn't anything for me here. The shop has the unmistakable fusty smell of damp and yellowing, brittle mildewed pages. I scan the second-hand spines in the fiction section and it's as uninspiring as I expect, rammed with several identical tattered copies of the same four or five airport potboilers from a few years back.

I go to the window to check on the weather, hoping the rain might be clearing, but if anything it is getting heavier and I don't fancy heading out into it. I'll be soaked by the time I get to the car and I have a good half-hour drive home.

I look down and see I'm leaning on the "Mind, Body & Spirit" section. I scan it to see if there's anything on yoga from Tiffany's reading list, but it's loaded with books on self-help fads, crystals, Tarot cards and decluttering, all the proclaimed routes to a happy, better life. It can't be a great advert for the effectiveness of any of them if they've all been thrown out to a second-hand bookshop.

Then a tattered hardback catches my eye. *Hidden Wisdom: Your Dreams and How To Decode Them.* It's not the title that draws me, but the picture on the cover, a photograph of an idyllic coastline, cliff and beach. I pick the book up and inspect it more closely. The dust jacket is ripped at the edges, and the photograph is faded, probably because it has been sitting in this window for years. Even so, the coastline looks familiar and I'm almost certain it's a photograph of Bae Breuddwyd, our own Dreamer's Cove. I guess it would make sense to put a place called Dreamer's Cove on a dream-interpretation book. I look for a photo credit, but the part of the dust jacket where you'd expect one is torn off.

"FIVE POUNDS," the man says when I take the book to the counter. There isn't a price on the book. Maybe he just looks at the customers and estimates what they'll be willing to pay. Anyway, he's pitched it right with me. I take out my debit card and touch it against the machine.

"I'm not really into dreams," I say, "but I think this is where I live."

"Right," replies the man in a bored tone. He doesn't give the cover a second look.

It's still raining when I leave the shop. I have a plastic bag in my coat pocket, so I put the book in it and hold it over my head as a makeshift umbrella. I run back to the car, but I'm still wet through by the time I throw myself into the driver's seat. As I drive home, I can't avoid thinking about the builders back where I'm headed, and my mood hangs as heavy as the dark clouds overhead. Nick won't be home until tomorrow evening. It'll just be me on my own in the house again.

As I pull into the drive, I can see there's some kind of package on the doorstep. The postman must have called while I was out. It's probably the new business cards I've ordered. Just my luck they've come today. They'll almost certainly be ruined in this rain.

I take the box inside. I take off my waterlogged coat and hang it over a chair to dry, then go into the small toilet off the hallway and use the hand towel to rub my ratty wet hair. Then I come out and open the box to inspect the damage.

But it isn't my business cards. Sliding the contents out of the box I see it is a cake on a tray, covered with a clear plastic lid. A caterpillar cake, with a hard chocolate casing and decorated with multicoloured Smarties, the sort of thing you'd buy for an infant child's birthday party. I look at it, sitting incongruously on the worktop, its boggling chocolate eyes staring up at me, its red icing tongue lolling out of its stupid grinning mouth.

I notice there is an envelope in the box. I take it out. There are four words scrawled on the front in the same crude handwriting as the sign down on the beach:

Welcome to the neighbourhood.

7

WELCOME

"Wait."

Nick and I are standing at the fork in the path. Nick has stopped walking and called me back. He looks serious.

"We do hellos all round, one quick drink and straight home, okay?"

"Fine by me," I say. I'm not that keen to meet the new neighbours either. Probably less keen than Nick, given that I've already witnessed them cavorting on their drive in the middle of the night.

NICK LEFT Manchester at lunchtime earlier today to beat the Friday rush hour. I heard the crunch of tyres on the driveway from my workroom and hurried down to the front door to greet him. We kissed, and I helped him unload his bags. He paused at the doorway before going inside, stopping to listen to the revving of a circular saw from next door.

"Shit, I see what you mean. That could get on your tits if it was going all day."

"It *is* going all day."

Nick dumped his bags in the hallway, kicked off his shoes and collapsed onto the sofa.

"Christ, what a week."

He flopped his head back onto the cushions and stared vacantly at the ceiling. He was like a marathon runner who'd paced himself perfectly, crossing the finish line without a drop of energy left. He puffed out a long sigh and sank further into the furniture.

"I'm going to park my arse here for a bit, then go up and immerse myself in a bath of beer."

I considered telling him about the note then, but he was frazzled from the drive and clearly needed a few minutes to unwind. So I moved his discarded shoes to the rack by the door and went to the kitchen to put the kettle on. I got mugs, tea bags, and milk, and brewed the tea. When I came back five minutes later, he hadn't moved a muscle.

"Tea."

"Thanks."

He made no effort to take the cup, so I put it on the side table. He let out another weary sigh.

"Listen," he said, his voice already strained in an apology, "I know I haven't seen you all week, but are you okay if we stay in tonight? Get a takeaway or something?"

There was no point in me avoiding it any longer, so I took the envelope from my pocket and passed it to him. "We've had an invitation."

Nick leaned forward and took it. His face sank.

"Oh, Jesus, not the noisy bastards?"

He opened the envelope and took out the sheet of paper inside.

"Hello, neighbours!" he read. *"Sorry we haven't said hello*

before now. We're from the house next door and we'd like to have you over. How about 6 p.m. for a drink this Friday night? See you then, Ron and Jackie."

He let the paper drop and looked at me pleadingly.

"Really? Do we have to? Tonight?"

"Yes, we do. We're new here. And anyway, they sound much better than I was expecting. Maybe I *have* got them wrong."

"No, I'm sure you're right," said Nick with a sarcastic twinkle. "From what you've told me, they sound absolutely delightful."

I laughed and threw myself onto the sofa next to him, cuddling into him.

"They could be nice," I said. "It's a nice thing. It's neighbourly."

SO NOW HERE WE ARE, on the drive of the house next door. As we approach the door, Nick looks critically at the tasteless architecture and the two carved stone lions standing on either side of the porch. He pushes the doorbell. Deep inside the house chimes ring out, a thin electronic version of "Land of Hope and Glory", like a demented ice cream van.

Nick smirks at me. "Ooh, that's nice. We should get one of those."

We wait for some time before the door is finally thrown open.

There he is. Ron, a vast bear of a man in flip-flops, loose linen shorts and a stained t-shirt pulled horribly tight across his girth, so you can see each roll of fat. His head is shaved, and wiry stubble coats his scalp, making it look like undercooked pork skin. He fills the entrance. Beads of sweat pepper his face, which is ruddy and grinning. He leans into us and growls a welcome.

"Alright. Let's get shitfaced."

8

WHISPER

"Here you go."

Ron passes us a can of beer each. He has his own on the go. He must have made an early start of it because several empty cans already litter the kitchen worktop.

"Jackie'll be down in a minute. She's just upstairs, titivating, making herself even more beautiful."

He wipes his hand on his t-shirt and extends his arm towards Nick.

"I'm Ron."

"Nick."

They shake hands. I've always thought of Nick as solid and manly, but his hand looks feeble clasped in Ron's massive paw. They both keep hold. It's in danger of looking like a dick-waving competition. Nick digs in for long enough to look macho and then extricates himself. He flexes his hand and introduces me.

"And this is Megan."

"Nice to meet you," I say. I put my own arm out for a handshake.

"Oh fuck that," says Ron effusively, grabbing my wrist and pulling me into a hug. I'm squeezed between his flabby arms and the rolling hills of his fleshy body. I can feel the heat coming off him, and smell the musty dampness of the sweat that is soaked into his t-shirt. It's horrible, like being trapped on the Tube in summer rush hour.

"Jesus, what will the wife say!" Ron exclaims, letting me go and stepping back laughing. He's made this little joke for the benefit of Jackie, who arrives down the stairs.

"Oh Ron, you are a silly bugger." Jackie giggles.

I see Nick transfixed at the sight of her sashaying down the staircase. Where Ron appears dressed for a camping holiday in Skegness, Jackie is dolled up like she is off to Ascot races, done up to the nines in a fuchsia dress and jacket like the bride's mother at a wedding. She also wears a fascinator in the same colour, which looks utterly ridiculous here in the kitchen, next to the washing machine and the fridge freezer.

If the outfit *was* from a wedding, it was a wedding a few years back, before Jackie gained twenty pounds. It feels rude to notice, but I can't help it. She isn't straining out of her dress as much as Ron is out of his t-shirt, but it's not far off.

"Hello, luvs. I'm Jackie."

She totters over to us, wobbling on the uneven stone flags in shoes that are clearly too high for her, and gives me and Nick a hug each. I notice her hands. Every one of her fingers has a ring of some sort, a traffic light assortment of rubies and topaz and emeralds.

"Sorry I'm late," Jackie goes on. "I couldn't get this pissing thing to balance on me head. I don't look a tit, do I?"

I look at Nick's face. He obviously thinks she looks a complete tit, but he's too polite to mention it.

"Not at all. You look lovely," he says.

"Ooo, you're a charmer. You'll have to watch this one, Ron," chuckles Jackie flirtatiously.

Ron looks Nick up and down. "I *am* watching him."

I don't know why, but I immediately feel myself liking Jackie. Maybe it's the relief of knowing she hasn't been murdered by Ron, that she's here in the kitchen and not dead in a freezer in the garage. Also, she seems hilariously direct. I've demonised these people in my mind, but they're just an ordinary couple. A couple very different from us, but ordinary nonetheless.

Jackie's at the fridge, removing several platters of buffet food, great mountains of sandwiches and sausage rolls, pork pies and scotch eggs. She deposits them on the kitchen worktop and peels the cellophane covers off the trays.

"Well, we won't starve to death anyhow," she cackles.

Nick's shoulders slump a bit. It's clear from the excessive amounts of food we won't be escaping after just one drink.

"We'd normally do a barbecue on the lawn," says Ron, taking a huge chunk out of a pork pie, "but we're having work done in the garden."

"Oh yes?" says Nick, with what I detect as a hint of mischief. At least he hasn't launched into an uncomfortable conversation about building noise five minutes into meeting them. We stand smiling awkwardly, watching Ron chew his mouthful of meat.

"I feel bad we weren't here to help when you moved in," says Jackie, offering round a plate of prawn things on crackers. "We were away for a few months."

"Oh, anywhere nice?" I ask. I chance a prawn thing. The sauce on the prawns has made the cracker unpleasantly soggy.

"It was lovely," says Jackie. "A three-month cruise. Can't

you tell from my tan?" She puts her hands coquettishly under her chin and does a little twirl.

"Three months," says Nick. "That's one hell of a break. Where did you go?"

"Oh, all over. Miami. The Bahamas. Barbados..." Jackie tries to remember. "Egypt. Trinidad? Um, Jamaica..."

"Jamaica?" I say, genuinely interested. "A friend of mine from university is from there. It sounds amazing. What was it like?"

"Too fucking hot, luv." Jackie curls her lip. "To be honest, I don't really like the stops, so I don't get off much. I only go for the ship. The food is unbelievable, and the entertainment is out of this world. It's like the best hotel you've ever stayed in. They treat you like royalty. I don't understand why anyone would want to leave it just to walk round a pile of old ruins or gawp at a church."

"That *does* sound great," says Nick.

I think Nick is hilarious, but I'm beginning to feel he's in danger of taking the piss too obviously. Ron isn't saying much and I sense he's trying to get the measure of us. Maybe he really has got his eye on Nick. Whatever, he doesn't look like the sort you'd want to get on the wrong side of.

"What was your favourite place, Ron?" Nick continues.

"Oh don't ask him," Jackie jumps in. "He can't remember a bloody thing."

Ron purses his lips and says nothing, just cracks open another can of beer for himself.

Nick looks round the kitchen. It's garish compared to ours, fitted out in a kind of olde worlde country cottage style, with thick oak cupboard fronts and turned iron handles. There are a couple of gnarled wooden beams in the ceiling which are clearly more ornamental than structural. It looks very new, and at the same time like it's been transported here from the 1950s.

"So how long have you had this place?" asks Nick.

"A bit less than a year," says Ron. "We were in Liverpool, and got lucky with a lottery win, didn't we, Princess? We both loved Wales, so we found a patch of land and built this house. Our dream place."

"Did you notice all the castle oojits when you arrived?" asks Jackie proudly. "Ron designed those." She gives Ron's fat arm a squeeze.

"Really? Wow," says Nick, in a voice that feels like it's straying into sarcasm. "They look fabulous, Ron."

"Thanks," replies Ron flatly, not taking his eyes off Nick.

He looks like he is sizing Nick up. I get the horrible feeling Nick is in danger of getting himself in trouble. He has this reckless streak, where he'll make his own amusement, not respect the boundaries, and take things too far. Ron doesn't look like the sort of man you want to take the piss out of. Now feels like a good time to make a tactical withdrawal.

"It was so nice of you to invite us," I say, "and we'd love to stay longer, but I have a work thing in the morning. We just came to say hello."

"Oh really?" says Jackie, disappointed. "I haven't even put out the mini quiches."

"'Fraid so," I continue, looking pointedly at Nick. "I have a project I'm sooo behind on because of the move. But now we've met each other let's not be strangers. We could get you over to us next time maybe…?"

Nick catches on and nods. He makes a sort of sad face, like he's upset about us leaving. Even that's over the top, so I'm relieved to be getting him out of there before he has another beer and says something silly. I feel bad about all the food though. I see Ron looking at it with a slight frown. Jackie sees me looking at it too.

"Don't worry about the food, luv," she says warmly. "Ron will polish that lot off for his breakfast."

"You cheeky bitch!" exclaims Ron. He slaps Jackie hard on the arse, and the clap of his hand on her ample flesh echoes around the kitchen. They both chuckle.

"Next week maybe?" I ask, shifting my body weight towards the door to make it clear we're leaving.

"Or the week after," Nick cuts in. "Next week's a bit tricky for me. I'm away all week again. Sorry."

"What's your line of business?" Ron asks Nick.

"Financial stuff. Stocks and shares, all very boring," Nick replies.

Ron looks unblinkingly at Nick. It's impossible to tell what he is thinking. Finally, he speaks.

"We're sitting on a lump we need to invest somewhere, aren't we, Princess? We should have a chat."

"Sure, okay," says Nick brightly. "Maybe in a couple of weeks when I'm here? As I say, I'm back in Manchester next week."

"Then you're a bloody idiot," says Ron, unexpectedly forcefully. It almost makes me jump with surprise. "If I had a lush beaut like yours, I wouldn't be swanning off to England and leaving her on her own."

Ron grabs Jackie and pulls her into a hug. She leans awkwardly in her high heels and I see the buttons on her dress straining as Ron compresses her flabby body with his. She looks like a big fuchsia balloon about to burst.

"I wouldn't leave my Princess for a single minute, unless I had to. You know that, don't you, Princess?" Ron's voice is quivering with emotion. Maybe it's an excess of beer that's made him so sentimental.

"I know, baby," says Jackie, hugging him back as best she can in his tight grip. "I know you wouldn't."

Ron and Jackie cuddle and kiss each other enthusiastically. I get a glimpse of Ron's tongue as he slips it into Jackie's mouth. I pray they're not going to start up an encore of the spectacle I witnessed the other night.

"So we'll be off then," I say.

"Right you are," says Ron, thankfully letting go of Jackie.

But to my horror, he immediately catches hold of my hand and pulls me in close to him. I feel the sheer brute strength of him and know I couldn't resist even if I wanted to. Not that I struggle. I don't want to make a scene. I don't move a muscle.

Ron's voice drops to a whisper.

"Just remember, if old soppy-bollocks there is stupid enough to run off and leave you on your own, you know where I am."

I can feel the heat and the bulk of him again, can smell the sweat and the beer on his breath. His arms are holding me and the picture flashes into my mind of his hands grabbing away at his squealing wife's fleshy body. I feel trapped and powerless. Ron isn't playing the joker for the room now. This is all for me. He draws me closer and puts his mouth right against my ear. He's barely audible.

"If you need anything, you come to your Uncle Ron."

PART 2

9

LIFT

I'm visiting the building I worked in for a couple of months after uni, for a design company in Canary Wharf. I haven't been here for years, but it still feels familiar as I stand in the empty lift travelling up to my old office on the forty-fifth floor.

The lift is painfully slow. It seems to stop at every floor for people to get on. I don't recognise any of them. As they enter, I get pushed further to the back. That's fine for the first few floors, but soon the lift begins to fill up, and I have to step back to make more room. Everyone faces the doors. I'm staring at the dark woollen suit of a man's back. No one speaks to anyone.

The lift stops again, and more people get in. It must be at capacity now because the back of the man in front is pressed hard against me, and I'm pinned between him and the hard metal of the lift wall.

The lift stops again and more people try to get in.

"Excuse me. I think the lift is full," I protest with polite desperation.

But people keep pressing in.

I really am squashed now, and the lift is getting hot, and my chest feels compressed and I'm struggling to breathe. It feels like I'm going to have a panic attack. And the more I panic, the less I'm able to catch my breath.

Past the shoulder of the man in front, I can just see the illuminated floor numbers above the door. 32, 33, 34... The lift is no longer stopping at any of the floors. It seems to be climbing in a terribly laboured way. Above me, I can hear the clank of metal and I'm worried that the workings might give way under the strain. There must be more people in here than the lift is designed for.

37, 38, 39... The stifling, clammy lift continues to grumble and clang its way up the building.

There's a sickening jolt and it stops dead, between floors.

I'm panicking now. My breathing is quick and urgent. Nobody speaks. My face is pressed into the scratchy black suit material.

Then the light goes out. It's utter darkness.

There's a horrible, silent, suspended moment. I'm not panting now. I'm not breathing at all. I'm holding my breath.

Suddenly, the lift begins to fall.

I need to do something, to move, to shout out, but I'm crushed, pinned, with nowhere to go. 29... 23... 17... 12... The numbers race by in a flash. Oh Christ, we're going to hit the bottom. 8... 3...

I JOLT.

I am awake, in bed, in my room.

A dream.

I'm still breathing quickly, and my hands are clammy.

I'm startled for a moment that someone is in the bed next to me. But of course, it's Nick. It's just taken me by surprise momentarily, after sleeping alone for the week. He is sprawled diagonally across the bed, all odd angles, as if he's been dropped from a height and lies where he'd landed. He's in a deep sleep, exhausted from another week away in Manchester.

It's early, but I can see through the curtains that it's already shaping up to be a beautiful day. I push the covers back gently and swing my legs out of bed. I slip on my dressing gown and step quietly downstairs.

Thankfully the anxiety from my dream is subsiding now. I put the kettle on and while I'm waiting for it to boil I go to the bookshelf and take out my new book, *Hidden Wisdom: Your Dreams and How To Decode Them*. Not, if I'm honest, that the dream I've just had takes a genius to decode.

I look up *suffocation; claustrophobia; lifts and elevators; falling; sudden death.* Each section pretty much says what I expect: *Feelings of being overwhelmed... Situations or relationships causing emotional or psychological distress... Feeling trapped... Invasion of personal space... Intrusive individuals... Loss of control... Significant change... Transformation, or the unknown.*

Or more concisely: Ron.

It all comes back to Ron. His unsettling arrival in the middle of the night, the noise of him, the constant disruption never allowing me to relax in my own home. And that horrible powerless feeling of him grabbing me, his lips against my ear, his flesh-crawling offer to be helpful that felt more like a threat.

I find a pen and a notebook, grab a blanket from the back

of the sofa and take my notebook and coffee out onto the deck.

I vividly remember having a nightmare as a child, going crying into my parents' room, and Mum taking me back to bed. She laid me down and got me to tell her all about the dream, every detail I could remember. Mum said what scared me the most was the unknown. I couldn't be scared of monsters under the bed anymore if I looked under the bed and saw there weren't really any monsters there. She said if I could describe my dream in as much detail as possible, then it wouldn't be unknown anymore, and it couldn't scare me.

The nightmares went away for years. But since Mum died six months ago, they're back. I thought once I'd got past the funeral they'd go, but they didn't. They were there through all the stress of Niall and me splitting up. The meditation works in the day, but it doesn't stop them coming at night. Even moving in with Nick didn't stop them. I hoped I'd leave them behind in Manchester, that the move to this house, the calm of the sea, would put them to rest. But they've come with me.

I sink into a chair and begin to jot down all I can remember about my lift dream. After fifteen minutes, I've filled a page with as much detail as I can recall. I close my notebook and put it down with my pen, pull my blanket around my shoulders and sip my coffee, looking out to the sea.

The dream of death encourages the dreamer to embrace change, let go of the past, and welcome new beginnings. So says my book anyway. But every section in it tries to put a positive spin on all the negative elements of dreams. It assumes that reliving all the bad stuff inevitably gets you to a good place.

But what if that isn't true? What if I'm not able to embrace this change and welcome this new beginning? What if Ron's arrival isn't remotely the sort of new beginning it is sensible to embrace? I still feel anxious. But maybe I'm *right* to be anxious.

What if you awake panicked and anxious and sweaty, and look under the bed because you are scared of monsters, and what you find there isn't nothing?

What if you find a monster for real?

A monster even more terrifying than the one in your dream.

10

LIGHTHOUSE

It's Monday morning. It's early. Barely light.

There is more for Nick to do in Manchester than we anticipated. His boss is being difficult about him leaving and he's having to pull long shifts to manage a handover to his replacement. On top of that, there's been some hiccup in the sale of his house, and the buyers have got cold feet at the last minute. So he's got to start that whole process again. I feel so sorry for him as he disappears down the drive, obviously tired and stressed, at the crack of dawn. We've been here for three weeks, and Nick has only been here for the weekends.

I'm alone once again.

I unroll my yoga mat and start to go through my sequence of poses and concentrate on my breathing. I haven't been doing it for longer than ten minutes before the familiar screech of power tools drifts over from Ron and Jackie's. I decide to stop. I'll meditate later, when the builders have knocked off for the day.

I sit at the breakfast bar and pick up the handwritten

note which was pushed through the door sometime last night:

Ron's away this week and I think Nick said he was away too. If you're at a loose end, come over for girlie drinks on Tuesday. I'm free any time from 5 o'clock. Just send me a text to let me know. Jackie xxx

I haven't bothered to put the number at the bottom of the note into my phone. No way am I going round there again if I can help it.

The drilling, banging and sawing continues. Something in the mix seems to hit the reverberating frequency of the house itself because the walls hum and the windows rattle. I'm honestly not sure how much more of this I can cope with. I have no idea what the hell they are doing over there, so who knows how long the work and noise might go on for. It could be months.

"They're not so bad."

Nick's voice echoes in my head. That's what he said, once we'd got back home from the awful drinks.

I didn't agree. "She seems alright. But I don't like *him*."

Just thinking about Ron made my flesh crawl.

"Oh, he's okay. He's a character."

That was Nick's contribution. Why is it men have this weird attraction to blokey blokes, like it's a token of their masculinity to be a part of some grunting, testosterone-fuelled pack? I'd watched him do it the day we moved here, shifting boxes awkwardly and trying to be all matey with the removal men.

I make myself some toast and try to think it all through properly. *Am* I overreacting? Just being paranoid about Ron?

I feel threatened by him. How he made me feel when he grabbed me. His whispered offer to help me. I'm not a nervous person by nature, but he makes me feel insecure.

No. More than insecure. Scared.

I'm afraid of him.

I take a shower. As I let the water stream over me, I imagine what Tiffany would tell me. *Holding on to negative feelings only perpetuates suffering and hinders personal growth and spiritual development.* I whisper it to myself over and over, like a mantra. I wipe the steam from the mirror and have a long, hard look at myself. I've gone through plenty of tough experiences in my life and I'm still here. I'm a fighter.

I GET DRESSED and head up to my workroom to do more design work on the necklace for *Vogue*. They've sent me images of the other designers they're featuring, and I'm aware the ideas I've had so far aren't as good as I need them to be. They seem woolly and unfocussed. I sketch for a while, hoping I'll get lost in the work like I usually do, but I can't zone out the noise from next door.

I go out into the garden. It is a beautiful day and the sun is dazzling as it reflects off the sparkling sea. It strikes me just how lucky I am to be here, and I refuse to let a couple next door and some temporary building work take the shine off this experience. I look at the lighthouse in the distance and decide I should make a trip out to take a closer look. Maybe I'll find focus and inspiration there.

This isn't running away from the house and the noise, I tell myself. This is a positive decision to explore my new home.

. . .

I THROW A PACKED LUNCH TOGETHER, and as I head off in my car, I feel much better than I have for a while. I channel my inner Tiffany and open myself up to new possibilities and experiences. I decide it'll be more fun if I don't use the satnav. So long as I head in roughly the right direction, and keep the sea in view on my right, and don't drive into the water, I should be able to travel round the coast and get to my destination. It's fun.

But I soon find that the road keeps pushing me inland, and if I turn off to be closer to the coastline, I keep heading up tracks that come to houses and dead ends. After I've done this about ten times, what started as an adventure rapidly becomes frustrating. I try to tell myself it's still fun, but all these bumpy tracks and three-point turns and going back on myself are just annoying.

It takes me ages, but eventually I arrive at the empty car park for the lighthouse. By now the weather has changed. The sun has gone in, and anyone with a bit of sense has headed home, but I refuse to give up now. I haven't dressed properly for the conditions, especially now I'm down on the windy coast. I totter precariously across the huge pebbles towards the lighthouse itself. The pebbles give way to rocks, which are slate grey and uneven, wet and covered with veins of bright green seaweed that is slippery underfoot. At one point I slip and fall, spilling the packed lunch I've made and banging my knee heavily onto the stone. I extend an arm instinctively to break my fall and land hard on my hand, which jars and makes my wrist throb.

I press on, determined to make a go of it now I'm here. I pick a flattish rock I can sit on, ignoring the dampness. I look up at the towering lighthouse. It had seemed so pretty from a distance, but now, up close and in this flat light, it looks bleak and imposing. How lonely and isolated it must have been to be the lighthouse keeper here. I look around the empty rocks I am on and it strikes me how lonely and isolated *I* feel. I get out a sandwich and chew on it miserably, wiping the fine sea spray off my face as the wind tugs at my hair.

This isn't an adventure. Who am I kidding? This is shit.

I'm reminded of the summer before university, setting out on an Interrailing holiday with Pippa. We'd mapped out our route on a pin board in my bedroom, plotted a careful itinerary of everywhere we wanted to see. But only three days into the trip the plans fell apart in Paris when Pippa hooked up with a German guy in a hostel and suggested we head up to Holland with him and his friends, as opposed to Italy as we had agreed. I had no intention of spending a month third-wheeling it around Europe like an awkward hanger-on, so we decided I would carry on as planned and Pippa would meet up with me in Rome in a week.

I'd felt pretty bloody annoyed the following day when I hauled my rucksack on to continue my trip alone. But as I explored the calling points on my journey, Chartres and Orléans and Lyon, Venice and Padua and Florence, I vowed to embrace the romanticism of being alone, telling myself that the vulnerability and sadness of loneliness were part of something that connected me more profoundly to the places I passed through.

But that was bullshit.

Being alone might be enriching for some people, but I just found it intense and overwhelming. I was unhappy the whole time. Then I arrived in Rome and met Pippa, and said nothing about how thoroughly miserable my last week had been, and we carried on as planned.

When I came home after a month, and people asked me what I had most enjoyed about my trip, I thought it would sound impressive to say it was that week when I had been on my own. But that was a lie, and really, I had just found it lonely and upsetting.

And that's exactly how I feel now in Anglesey, on these rocks, in the cafes, rattling around that big empty house on an unfamiliar island on my own. Maybe that's why I've gone from uni to Naill, and Naill to Nick with no gaps. Maybe I am incapable of being on my own. Maybe there's something wrong with me.

I get up and stumble back to the car. I use the satnav to plot the quickest route and speed home. I come through the door, kick my shoes off and pick up the note. Copying the number, I type a message into my phone.

Thanks, Jackie. Tomorrow would be great. See you at 5 p.m. Megan x

11

GOOD BOY

"Let's have these outside."

Jackie drops two slivers of lime into the biggest gin and tonics I had ever seen, and passes me a glass so voluminous you could keep a goldfish in it. Maybe this will be a never-to-be-repeated disaster, but I'm going to try out the experiment. This might make a welcome change from spending the evening alone, and maybe Jackie will be decent company without Ron. Perhaps the two of us could even become a rather unlikely pair of friends.

We cross the kitchen and Jackie pulls a length of ugly blue tarpaulin away from the back door so I can pass through.

"It's a bloody eyesore, but it stops the dust getting in all me pots and pans."

I slip through the gap and into the garden.

It's immediately clear why the last few days have been so noisy. The garden has a massive assortment of building materials piled up to one side, huge sleeper-like beams of wood, and several pallets of tiles and ornamental stone bricks. There's even a small digger.

We stand on a plinth of decking on the back of the house, quite similar to ours, with bench seating covered in long chintzy cushions. At the far end of the garden, another seating area is in the process of construction, which presumably will catch the sun in the morning and give a closer view of the beach and sea. The rudimentary framework for a wooden canopy is already erected over the area to be tiled.

"Ron calls that my princess pergola."

The back of the house is as tasteless as the front, with weird turrets and crenelations at the top of the walls. A complex web of scaffolding surrounds what looks like a new construction attached to the rear wall of the building, a large, drab cell of breeze blocks with small barred windows, probably some kind of shed or outhouse for storing garden equipment.

"You've been busy," I say.

"It's Ron's little project. He's always having ideas. He'd have a pond and a maze and all sorts. Yesterday he started talking about a swimming pool."

I look at the space they have left. "Is there room for that? Can you dig down like that on a cliff?"

"Oh don't ask me, Megan luv. I leave all that with Ron. He's the boss."

I sip my gin and enjoy the gong of the ice against the glass, like frozen wind chimes. It's only early July, but it's been a lovely day and promises a blistering summer. I close my eyes and enjoy the warmth of the evening sun on my face. I tilt my head to one side, stretching my neck. I can feel the tension in it beginning to relax. When I open my eyes, Jackie is looking at me with a wry smile on her face.

"That's it, luv, you let all that shit go. It'd be a crime not to with that view."

I smile and look at the sea, listening to it rake gently back and forth across the shingle, until the sound of it gets louder and I realise it isn't the shingle I can hear, but the sound of tyres on the gravel. Someone is coming up the drive.

"Oooh, that'll be Ron. I didn't think he was back until later."

Ron? I feel myself panic. I wouldn't have come here if I thought Ron was going to be around.

"Back in a minute..."

Jackie lollops off across the grass. I try to work out what to do now. I could make a break for it across the lawn to the back of my house, but that would look strange, and I don't want to make a big thing of it. Better to play it cool, finish my drink with as little fuss as possible, and not make the mistake of coming over again.

I hear the doors of a vehicle opening and then the sound of dogs, barking and whining, and a man's voice shouting something indistinct. It sounds like a lot of dogs.

Jackie comes back up the side of the house, giggling girl-ishly as she skips across the lawn towards me.

"It's my babies. My babies are back. You're going to meet my babies."

Ron appears not far behind her, holding a thick leather lead in each hand. At the ends of the leads are two enormous muzzled dogs, yelping and barking excitedly, tugging hard.

I like dogs normally. But not these. These seem exactly the sort of muscle dogs a man like Ron would have, more wild than pets, something you'd see on the news about dangerous breeds getting banned. They are barely under control, over-excited and unpredictable. Even Ron, with all his bulk, has to lean backwards to prevent them from dragging him along.

Ron is laughing.

"That's right, boyos. You know where you are, don't you? Alright, Meg?"

No one calls me Meg except Nick. It feels horribly overfamiliar coming from Ron.

A young boy holding another two muzzled dogs follows Ron along the side of the house and into the garden. He is pale and painfully thin and can't be more than eighteen years old. One of the dogs he holds is broad and beefy like the ones Ron is holding; the other is a large, sleek, athletic animal, svelte and beautiful, jet black, with black eyes and a long, pointed face. The boy has to use all his strength to stop himself from being dragged away by the yanking animals, leaning back against the strain and digging his heels into the grass.

"Welcome home, babies!" coos Jackie, as if she is talking to an infant in a pram, while the dogs writhe and tug at their tethers, barking and snapping at each other in frustration.

The dogs are pulling towards the end of the garden as if they want to escape to the beach, but Ron and the boy haul them back and somehow drag them into the breeze block structure on the rear of the house. A lot of yelping and growling and clanking of metal comes from inside. I realise this must be a kennel and the dogs are being put in cages. It must be physical work getting the reluctant beasts in, and after a minute Ron and the boy emerge red-faced and puffing. The dogs are still howling.

The whole thing raises even more questions about Ron. What the hell does someone need a pack of savage dogs like that for?

"The babies sound upset, Ron," says Jackie in a concerned voice.

"They've been cooped up in the van all day," Ron says. "They need a bit of exercise."

Ron turns to the boy. "With me, you."

He heads into the back of the house, picking up a couple of long cushions from the benches as he goes. The willowy boy follows in silence.

"We had to send the boys away while we were on holiday," explains Jackie sadly. "I did miss them. A house isn't a home without pets, is it?" she continues over the savage barking.

I've never seen pets like these. I consider finishing my drink and leaving, but I've still got half a gallon of gin in my fishbowl. Jackie makes small talk while I consider how I'm going to get away.

After a few minutes Ron comes out of the house leading the boy. It's an extraordinary sight. The boy's limbs and torso are wrapped in yellow foam duct-taped into tubes that make him walk unsteadily with unbending limbs. His pipe-cleaner-thin body is now a parody of his fat boss. He has a crash helmet on with a face guard, the sort that van security guards wear to deliver money to banks. Under other circumstances it would be comical. But I sense something bad is about to happen.

Jackie spots the boy and leaps to her feet in a flap.

"Ron Evans! What have you done to my cushions?"

"Sorry, Princess. I'll get you some new ones."

Ron leads the boy awkwardly to the middle of the lawn.

"Stand there, you."

The boy stands like a scarecrow while Ron goes into the kennel block. My horrible feeling about what is coming next gets stronger. I wish I had left earlier, but it is too late now. Then Ron comes out with one of the dogs, the thin beautiful one, no longer wearing a muzzle. It is sleek and solid, all chiselled bone and hard muscle, its back as high as Ron's hip. Its short dark hair shines in the evening sunlight.

Ron is leaning down, talking to it, mumbling something under his breath into its ear, much like he whispered into my ear the other evening. The dog isn't pulling or struggling now. It seems focused and attentive. I get the feeling it knows that playtime is over. Now it's on duty.

I look at the boy. He hasn't moved or made a noise, but his eyes are fixed unblinking on the dog. His face isn't red anymore. It is deathly pale.

Ron stops mumbling and stands up. He takes the lead off. The dog stares at the boy. It doesn't move.

The anticipation is excruciating.

"FASS!"

The second he shouts the word, the dog explodes across the lawn towards the boy. It leaps the last few feet and hits him like a train, knocking him hard to the ground. The boy yells in terror as the dog snaps at the metal guard over his face, then rips away at his torso, before grabbing his right arm in its jaws. With a firm grip it begins to shake him, making terrible growling noises as it does so.

I'm frozen, as if I am watching an accident in slow motion, unable to look away. I can hear Ron laughing.

The shaking is savage, and in less than ten seconds the tape at the armpit end of the boy's arm is torn loose and the foam opens up round his wrist like a huge cone. The dog goes immediately for his exposed limb. The cries of the boy turn from yells of terror into high-pitched screams of pain. The dog keeps shaking. Its jaws clamp tighter and there is a sickening snap which I assume to my horror must be the boy's arm breaking.

Jackie is screaming now too.

"For Christ's sake, Ron!"

"LASS ES!"

Ron shouts the command, and as instantly as the dog has begun the attack it breaks it off, stepping back, slightly hunched, still staring at the sobbing boy on the ground, ready to start on him again if allowed. The fur around its mouth is red with blood.

My heart is racing. I feel lightheaded and a cold wave of nausea sweeps over me. I have to steady myself with one hand on the back of a chair.

Ron walks across the lawn, and I assume it's to go to the aid of the injured boy, writhing and bleeding on the grass. But when Ron gets to the dog he stops. He takes something from his pocket and lets the dog eat it from his palm.

"Good boy."

Ron takes the dog by the collar and, without looking once at the injured boy, leads it calmly back to its kennel.

12

STANDOFF

I call Nick the instant I get home and tell him about my horrific evening. He's brilliant. He listens to my concerns, calms me down and promises he'll move his meetings around to leave early and be back tomorrow night. Then he rings off and I'm alone again.

That evening I call Pippa and fill her in on the move and the house. I don't say anything about the neighbours. I want a break from thinking about them. We discuss possible dates for her and Dermot to come and stay, and agree on a weekend in a few weeks' time. For the duration of the call, I feel much happier, joking and laughing and being more myself. But when the call ends I feel just like I do after my call with Nick – even more alone.

I can't get to sleep for ages. I try to read, then go downstairs to watch TV, hoping a late-night rerun of some mindless comedy panel show will drown the thoughts out, but flashes of the dog attack keep popping into my head. When I finally fall asleep, I have an unsettling dream, a confusing jumble of images, where the obese Ron and the huge dog are

somehow mixed up as one animal, a dangerous, feral crea-
ture, lumbering across the lawn, its hair a cross between the
dark coat of the dog and the stubble of Ron's head, Ron
snarling and barking his commands with blood smeared
around his mouth.

I wake up more tired than I was when I went to bed. I
write the dog dream down in my notebook, knowing full well
it won't help to banish the thoughts.

When Nick gets back we quickly decide it would be best
to avoid Ron and Jackie Evans altogether. I open up about
how lonely I've been feeling, and again, Nick is brilliant.
Even though we don't resolve much, just being with him
makes me feel more secure. I remember the mess I was when
I met him, grieving, angry and sad and chaotic, fighting with
Niall even though none of it was his fault. Nick made me
feel like I was the most important thing in the world, the only
thing in the room. He blocked out the noise of everything
else and pulled me out of the nosedive I was in. He was
beautiful, and shining with life, and I lost myself in him. He
saved me.

He pulls me into a hug, and I stop trying to be strong and
release all the tension and sadness I've been bottling up. He
apologises for being away all this time and says he'll stay in
Anglesey as much as possible from now on. We kiss, and race
up the stairs and make love like we did on the afternoon we
arrived here. I press my body into the warmth of him under
the duvet and feel what I haven't felt for weeks now: safe.

We lie in the afterglow, and catch up on gossip, and
laugh about stupid things. I tell him about my miserable
lighthouse trip, which sounds tragically funny now I tell it
back. We conclude this has all been a thoroughly bad start,
but it was a blip, and we are over it. We've only been here for

less than a month, so it's no surprise we're still settling in. We won't let it spoil our new life here. We won't think about those people next door any more.

But the Evanses aren't that easy to ignore. The building work continues five days a week, starting early, like a warped dawn chorus of drilling, hammering and sawing. Nick, who isn't a morning person at the best of times, shifts and fidgets in bed, tutting and huffing, then gets up and stomps about the house, muttering and swearing under his breath. Having him here is a comfort to me, but after a few days his good humour begins to fade and his irritation makes my own anxieties worse. So now I have Nick to contend with as well as the disturbance of the builders.

I try to settle into a rhythm, going to my workshop to answer emails and come up with new jewellery designs or complete items to fulfil orders. I complete the *Vogue* commission, and even though I'm not really happy with it, I tell myself that I must get on with things and send it off. The workroom is at the top of the house, and oppressively hot when the sun is out, but I can't open the window because the building noise is too distracting. Downstairs I can hear Nick talking heatedly on the phone, his frustration with the situation bleeding into everything. I get an email from the *Vogue* stylist saying they're changing elements of the feature and need me to make changes too. I wonder if they don't like what I've sent them and are finding a tactful way to deal with it. I realise I wouldn't normally be this lacking in confidence. I try to email back, but whatever I write, it sounds flat. I go through the motions of doing my work, but I feel constantly distracted. My heart is no longer in it.

Most days in the late afternoon, the building noise stops, and we go out onto the deck and reclaim the place as our own, look at the sea and chat. For a brief moment it almost feels like the idyllic place we imagined it would be.

But the illusion doesn't last long. All too soon other noises begin to drift over from the neighbours' side, their loud shitty music, or the cackling and screeching laughter of their horrible friends, or the soundtrack from the banal films they screen on their home cinema, all subwoofer rumble of car chases and shootouts.

And the dogs. At any time of day or night I can hear the piercing bark, yelp, snarl or whimper of a dog. This doesn't seem to get to Nick like the building noise does, but for me, since that incident on the lawn, the sound of dogs cuts to the very heart of me and won't let me relax. Even when there are long gaps between the dog sounds, I find myself anticipating them, like being in a room with a leaky tap, waiting for the next drip.

It all hangs over us as an unspoken threat. I hardly dare admit it to myself, but the truth is that Ron Evans is like a maggot in an apple, spoiling things, ruining everything.

Nick suggests occasional trips out elsewhere, for coffee or to dinner. We dress up, make an effort like we used to on our first dates. I watch Nick moving about the bedroom in a towel, buttoning a shirt, raking product through his lovely mop of hair. I enjoy picking out underwear, slipping into a silky dress, having an excuse to wear heels. We sip wine and hold hands across the table. I marvel and laugh at Nick's witty, interesting stories. These outings are lovely, but I can't help wondering whether Nick is taking us out just so he can escape the house. He'd be too proud to admit it, and I don't ask.

Returning from one of our coffee outings, we come over the crest of the rise in the path to our house and find Ron's big four-by-four coming the other way. Both cars slow to a halt. The track is narrow and the thick tufted grass rises steeply in rough clumps on either side. There is only room for one car and no place to pull off to the side. Someone will have to reverse.

Nick sighs and slips the car into neutral. The engine ticks over. He looks straight ahead at the tinted windows of the car facing him.

I sense trouble.

"Nick, let's just reverse."

"No," says Nick, firmly. "I'm not reversing. I'm further up the road than he is."

"Come on," I say, in as soft a tone as I can, hoping to dilute the tension. "We'll reverse, let him pass, and go inside."

"I'm not reversing," says Nick.

His voice is cold and brittle. I've never seen him like this. I can see his knuckles going white from how hard he is gripping the steering wheel. His whole body is tense.

"*He's* got less far to go. *He* should reverse to the fork and let us past."

Now he tries to make his tone calm and logical, as if he is just outlining a fact. But I can hear the waver in his voice. He is furious. I don't know what to do. I look out of my side window and wait. This has the feeling of something that isn't going to end well.

Nick tuts and flashes his lights a couple of times. The car in front doesn't do anything. It is obviously not going to reverse.

Maybe Nick is right, and it is only reasonable for Ron to move his car the short stretch back to the fork. But Nick didn't see what I saw. Ron *isn't* reasonable. This isn't a fight Nick can win.

I put a hand gently on his arm as a gesture of solidarity and support.

"Look, Nick –"

"Fine," he snaps. He rams the car into reverse and drives backwards far too fast, both of us swaying side to side and bouncing uncomfortably on the uneven track. He swings the car round the hedge and backs onto the road without looking. He screeches to a halt. After a moment the black four-by-four emerges sedately from behind the hedge and drives off up the road.

Nick crunches the car into gear and drives at speed up the track, bouncing us around again. He parks and goes into the house without speaking. I know he is angry with me now, as if being reasonable with him makes me somehow to blame. He needs to blame someone and he's chosen me. He's had to back down and decided it is my fault.

It's a silly misunderstanding. It feels bad at the time, like my awful trip to the lighthouse. But it's the sort of thing we'll laugh about later. Or I hope we will. But just as I am opening the front door, I hear a strange animalistic shout come from inside the house. I come in and walk to the kitchen. I can see Nick through the patio doors, out at the bottom of the garden, staring out to the sea. To the side of the window there is a patch of wall with a dent in it, where he must have punched the plasterboard on his way out.

I look at the flaking paint and plaster dust on the floor.

Everything is unravelling.

13

STAKES

Another week has passed. The grazing to Nick's knuckles is almost entirely healed and just some very faint marks remain. I look at where the wall in the kitchen was damaged. Nick has filled it, and skimmed plaster over the dent, and repainted it. If you didn't know it was there, you'd be none the wiser that anything had happened. But I do know. My eye is magnetically drawn to it. The paint is a slightly colder shade of white, and the light reflects off it differently somehow. I feel like I'll never not notice it.

We've been in the house exactly a month. How has it got out of hand so quickly? This is supposed to be our dream start together.

I recall Tiffany's mantra from yoga. *What's the point of fighting stuff you can't change? You have to accept things as they really are.* I have to believe that's true, or I'll be stuck – stuck by Mum's hospital bed, stuck giving her eulogy, stuck yelling and crying with Naill. We have to accept things as they really are and move on. Things change. Nothing is forever. Ron and Jackie will finish their new patio at some point in our lives and then we'll get back to some kind of peace and quiet. Until then, we just have to suck it up and get on with it.

I'm thinking about how I can pitch that to Nick, when my eye is drawn to something in the garden. I go to the window to take a closer look.

On the left-hand side of the lawn is a wooden stake, hammered into the ground. Actually, now I look, there are several stakes, forming a line that runs to the end of the garden and stops just by our gate to the beach. They look like the sort of thing you see in films when farmers or oil prospectors stake out their land. This must be Ron's work. But he can't be intending to put a fence here surely? It's through most of our garden!

Nick comes into the kitchen behind me. He slips his arms around my waist and kisses my neck. But after a few seconds he stops and his body goes rigid. I know he is looking over my shoulder at the posts on the lawn.

"What the fuck?"

He switches instantly into anger. He lets go of me, slides the patio door open hard, and stomps out across the grass. He grabs the first fence post and begins tugging away at it, straining hard, wiggling it back and forth with all his strength to loosen it, then wrenching it out of the ground. He throws it down and moves on to the next.

It looks like hard work. I watch him for a while and don't know what I'm supposed to do. There are a lot of posts and I guess it's going to take him some time. I figure now isn't the time to discuss accepting things as they are, so I go upstairs to shower, wondering what this escalation in hostilities will mean. Is this a border war now, on top of everything else?

As I'm dressing, I detect a faint smell of smoke. I hurry

downstairs. Nick's back in the kitchen. Out in the garden, there is a small fire burning on the lawn where Nick must have built a pyre with the fence posts.

"Those bastards are trying to steal our garden."

He is sitting at the breakfast bar, which is littered with crumpled balls of blood-stained kitchen roll. He has my nail bag open and is using a pair of tweezers to pick wood splinters out of his lacerated hands.

"They can't just do that, can they?" I ask.

"Of course they can't." He is angry. "We won't bloody let them."

Nick looks out to the lawn where his fire is still smouldering away. The smoke drifts across towards Ron's house, and he smiles smugly to himself as if it is some kind of signal communicating his resistance. I'm significantly less convinced that this small gesture of defiance will solve the underlying problem.

We are now in a turf war with the neighbours.

THE FOLLOWING morning we're just heading out to do some shopping when I almost trip over a bottle of wine on the doorstep with a note attached.

Dear Megan and Nick. Sorry, there appears to be some confusion about the boundary line. There hasn't been a fence there in the past, so Ron thought if we marked one out it would make things clearer. Hope that helps. You must come for drinks or film night soon. Jackie and Ron x

Nick reads the note in silence, then screws it up and puts

it in the bin. He goes back inside and I follow him. He takes the corkscrew out of the kitchen drawer, opens the wine and pours it down the sink.

We drive to the nice supermarket in Menai Bridge. I figure I'll cook us something nice tonight and kickstart my new plan of trying to put the crappy start behind us. *New start, new start,* I say over and over in my head on the drive back, trying to manifest it into being.

When we get home from shopping and go to unload the bags in the kitchen, we notice a new row of stakes on the lawn, on the same line as the last ones. But these are much thicker wood, and deeper in the ground. The tops look squashed, as if they've been hammered in with a pile driver.

I feel myself tense up. I'm not just worrying about Ron now, but how Nick will react to Ron. He dumps his shopping bags on the floor and walks over to the patio doors. As I watch him walk purposefully across the lawn, I feel suddenly sad thinking how hopeless his struggle will be, trying to get the posts out by hand.

But before he even gets to the first one, a cacophony of barking starts up, much louder than normal, and Nick leaps backwards, away from the posts. I hurry outside to see what he is staring at.

It is a dog, the thin athletic one that attacked the boy. It's on the end of a long chain that lets it reach almost to where the fence posts run. The other length of the chain must be somewhere on Ron's lawn, hammered in tightly, because the dog is up on its hind legs, straining at the chain, pulling it tight, baying and whining, trying to get free.

If it could only get loose, it wants more than anything to rip Nick apart.

This time the fence posts are staying put.

14

COOKING OIL

The line of fence posts marks a terrible new low. The building work gets a whole lot noisier now it is so much closer to the house. The sound of it lodges in my head like a dentist's drill. And it's all on *our* land. The outrageousness of what Ron is up to, and the feeling of powerlessness, is all-consuming. I feel physically sick.

I've let work slip. I read an email from the *Vogue* stylist and my heart sinks. Their deadline means they can't wait for my necklace and are using another designer. I realise I have to kickstart my work again, and begin to make some earrings I sketched a few weeks back, but I struggle to finish them how I want them and feel more frustrated than I did before I started.

I take a break and stare out at the sea from my workroom window. A wall of breeze blocks has started to go up a few feet back from the new fence posts, the same ugly ones that the dog kennel is constructed from. I keep drifting away from my bench to watch its progress. I can't bear to go out into the garden, convinced that the raucous builders, with their loud radio and their incessant banter, are laughing at me.

I return to my workbench and try to look past it, to just focus on the view. But I begin to feel like that weird dream I had: that I am on the very edge of the world, staring out into a great vast nothing, and my grip on the land is a precarious illusion, and at any moment I could slip over the edge and crash down on the rocks below.

Nick and I move through the house without much conversation. We can't seem to find anything to talk about other than the house – and not wanting to talk about that, we don't talk at all. I'm suddenly sad when I realise I can't remember the last time I heard Nick laugh.

I lie in bed at night and listen to the continuous sound of the sea. I thought it was so beautiful on that first evening. But now it keeps me awake with its incessant back and forth, like the persistent tick of some massive clock. I am uneasy. I can't help feeling it is the relentless plod, plod, plod of something bad coming this way.

Late in the afternoon, once the builders have gone, I go outside to get a closer look at what they've done. The breeze block wall now blocks my lovely view of the lighthouse. I notice to my horror that a gorgeous tree has been cut down to make way for the new structure. I didn't know it until now, but this was screening the view from our garden to Ron and Jackie's house. Our beautiful view of beach and sea and lighthouse has been replaced with breeze blocks and Ron's revolting castle.

I walk closer to the fence line, where I'm able to see into Ron and Jackie's garden. The plot of land is now vast in comparison to the scrap Nick and I are left with. Ron and Jackie are in the middle of the lawn, both on deckchairs.

Jackie wears a long dress and a straw hat over her face. She's on her back with her arms crossed on her chest, as if she has died and Ron has laid her out to rest in the sun. Ron's vast bulk is wedged into a pair of obscenely small speedos. He is sitting up in his chair, leaning forward and pouring vegetable oil from a huge plastic bottle into his hand, then rubbing it generously into the folds of his flesh, as if he is basting a turkey.

Behind them is the thin dog. It must have been excused guard duty and is lying asleep on the grass. Its collar is on, still attached to a long chain that snakes across the lawn, where it finishes at a large metal ring bolted to a flagpole. This is a thick, white-painted wooden column, about thirty feet tall, with a flag at the top. The flag flaps in the breeze and I can't quite make out what it says until it unfolds enough for me to read it: *Ron & Jackie's Place*. I feel like we are now the peasants on the edge of Ron's fiefdom.

THE WEEK DRAGS ON. Nick alternates his time between arguing down the phone with his boss, berating the estate agents about his house sale, and surfing the internet researching planning laws and neighbourhood disputes. The building work continues next door. Cars seem to come and go at all hours of the day and night.

My way hasn't ever been to rant and rave. Maybe that would be better, to vent my feelings instead of carrying them around with me like a hard ball in my chest. Some days I can hardly breathe. My heart races. I can't relax. I can't concentrate on work. What are we going to do? I feel trapped, and angry, fenced into my own home.

Nick probably thinks he is helping, trying to do something practical about it, and of course, he *is* helping in some ways. But he isn't helping *me*. I feel so sad, and he is too tied up in his own anger to be what I need – just someone to hug me and love me and tell me that it will be okay. Instead, I sometimes feel as lonely with him in the house as I did when he was away. I've been counting the days until this Friday and the end of Nick's three-month notice period from his work, so my heart sinks when he tells me he's been forced to agree to do an extra month.

"I don't understand," I protest.

"They're just being difficult about it," is all he says in reply. He doesn't say any more and so I'm forced to leave it.

And I have one huge, awful thought. I try to push it to one side until I can't ignore it any longer. Once I admit it to myself it is a belief I can't get rid of: If only we hadn't moved. I wish we had never left Manchester.

After a couple of days, it swells up inside me like a growth in my body. Eventually, it bursts.

"Why don't we just leave?" I ask.

"What?"

Nick has his head buried in his laptop on one of the civil law chat rooms he's joined.

"Why don't we just leave?" I ask again. "We could just leave."

He looks up at me and stares for a moment, as if he doesn't understand what I am saying. Eventually, he frowns.

"We've only just moved in. We can't just *leave*."

He says the word 'leave' so contemptuously his entire face creases up as he speaks.

"Where would we go?" he continues. "We were living in my house, which I've got an offer on from cash buyers. And we have all our money tied up in this place. What are we going to do – just abandon it? Put all our things in storage and go and live in a tent?"

"We could stay with Pippa and Dermot until we sort things out," I say. I've been going over the options in my head and think I have a plan.

Nick sighs. "Look, Megan, we're not just running away. Those bastards next door can't get away with this. It's not legal. If we go, they've won, haven't they? They can't just drive us out of our own property. They just... They can't. We won't let them."

He squeezes my arm, smiles, then goes back to scrolling through his website.

He says 'we' but as I look at him absorbed in his task again, I don't feel like 'we' are much of a team right now. We used to share everything, but something has shifted. I get a sudden horrible sense that there is a wall beginning to grow between us, as if someone has put a line of fence posts down the middle of our relationship.

15

TRAPPED

It is about 4 p.m. when I hear the first explosion.

At first, I think it must be something out in the harbour across the bay. I go to the window of my workroom and look out towards the beach, but there is no obvious source of the sound. All I can hear now is the dogs, barking and howling next door.

Again, a booming explosion rings out. I realise with a sinking feeling of inevitability that it is coming from Ron and Jackie's.

The breeze block wall means it's hard to see into next door's garden from my workroom window. But in the past few days I've figured out that if I move my work chair from my bench to the window and stand on tiptoes on it, I can see a little of what's going on. As expected, Ron is out there, up to something. But I can't see exactly what. Another explosion booms across the lawn. I have to find out what this is – building work is one thing, but this is something else entirely. This could be dangerous.

I climb down carefully from the chair and go downstairs.

Nick has gone into town for some free consultation he's set up with a solicitor, so I have to investigate alone. I slide open the patio doors, cross the garden and peer around the side of the breeze block structure, trying to get a good view of Ron without being seen.

"Hello, luv."

Jackie appears around the side of the wall. She's seen me before I have a chance to retreat. She waves a plastic carrier bag in my face.

"I'm just clearing up after the builders. Bloody crisp bags and burger cartons everywhere. They're nice boys but they wouldn't recognise a rubbish bin if it kicked them in the goolies."

We haven't seen each other since all this fence stuff started. I don't want a confrontation. I wonder how long I'll have to stand here making nicey-nicey with my fixed smile before I can go back in the house.

"How are you getting on, dear?" asks Jackie in a friendly tone.

"I'm okay, thanks."

"Would you like to come in for a drink?"

She's smiling at me as if there isn't this massive problem between us. I try not to lose it.

"I can't. I have some work to do," I say.

Jackie takes hold of my arm.

"Oh come on, sweetheart. Let's forget all this nonsense with the fence and you come over and have a drink. The men can argue all that out, but there's no reason you and I can't be friends."

She's still smiling at me. She hasn't let go of my arm and she clearly isn't going to take no for an answer.

What's the point of fighting stuff you can't change? You have to accept things as they really are.

Maybe Jackie is partially right. Ron seems to be the one behind all this. Jackie is loud, but essentially harmless. Plus, I reason, if I go into the garden I can get a better look at what Ron is up to.

"Okay, thanks," I say.

I follow Jackie across the large garden, having a careful scan around as I do. The dog has gone from its chain on the flagpole. Ron is safely right down the far end, by the cliff edge. The painfully thin boy who was attacked by the dog is with him, his arm in a sling. I'll keep my distance and slip away if he comes anywhere near us.

Jackie goes inside to get drinks. I keep my eye on Ron. He is in his usual tatty shorts and t-shirt, leaning on a shovel where he has dug a hole in the lawn. He has a cigarette lighter in one hand and is holding the flame to something in the other; I can't see what it is at this distance. He tosses the object into the hole. After a few seconds, another explosion booms out across the garden, and the dogs start howling again.

Firecrackers. He is throwing fireworks into the hole.

Jackie appears with a couple of drinks.

"Don't mind him, luv. Boys and their toys. He's trying to sort the rabbits. He says the bloody things are ruining his lawn. I enjoy the little fellers hopping about in the sunshine, but Ron says they dig holes and there's shit everywhere. To be fair, this morning it was like someone had thrown a box of raisins all over the place."

Oh God. The rabbits. I remember the first time we visited this house, how happy I felt when I saw the little rabbit jump out of the hedge, watched it innocently grazing on the lawn. First Ron has driven them underground with his incessant building noise and now he's trying to drive them out altogether – just like he is with me and Nick.

At that moment Ron gives out a massive roar of laughter and begins galumphing across the grass as fast as he is able, the thin boy scampering after. I look where he's heading and see a Perspex box, upside down, which has a rabbit in it. He must have rigged up some contraption over the exit from the burrow, and a startled rabbit has emerged and been trapped.

Ron is leaping about like an excited schoolboy. He gets to the box and slides a board underneath it, then turns the box over. The rabbit hops about a bit, exploring the walls of its prison. At least he's drilled a few air holes in the board. I'm relieved, as it means he must be planning to keep the rabbits alive and not just wring their necks. Presumably he'll move them somewhere up the coast away from the garden.

He looks across the grass with a stupid grin on his face and shouts.

"Ron one, Bugs Bunny nil."

I watch him push the box to one side. The thin boy picks up another empty box and starts to rig up a second home-made trap as best he can with one arm. I notice the injured arm in the sling is supported by a few off-cuts of timber strapped round with gaffer tape. It's obviously something Ron has bodged together himself, rather than take the boy to the hospital. He probably doesn't want anyone asking questions about his savage dogs.

Ron saunters back to the big hole he's dug and proceeds to throw another lit firework in.

Jackie watches him adoringly.

"I told him that'd never work, but it has. Look at him,"

she chuckles, "he's so pleased with himself. He'll never bloody shut up about it now."

I figure I've stayed long enough for it to not look weird. I down what remains of my drink.

"Thanks. I need to get back to things," I say.

Jackie gets up and walks towards my garden with me. We are facing the half-finished breeze block structure. From this side I can see it's not just a wall, but some kind of outhouse.

"This'll be lovely when it's done," says Jackie. "We're going to have a hot tub and some changing rooms with showers, and a fridge for the champers. Plus a sauna and a steam room for Ron. I can't stand the heat, but Ron likes a good sweat."

I don't know what to say. They are building all of this in the middle of *my* garden. I think of Nick, talking to a solicitor that moment, trying to find a way to knock it all down again. God, that will be wonderful.

"When it's finished you must come over," coos Jackie. "You're always welcome here, luv. You know that."

"I do. Thanks."

I go back into the house, feeling about as welcome as one of Ron's rabbits.

16

IT'S COMPLICATED

I'm upstairs when Nick gets back from the solicitor's. He usually calls up to me, lets me know he's back, but this time I hear the front door close and then him moving about downstairs.

I find him in the kitchen, back on his laptop, scrolling through emails and tutting. I stand in the doorway waiting for him to look up, but he doesn't. It feels like he knows I'm here but is pretending not to have noticed me. Why?

"Hello," I say.

"Oh hi," he says cheerily, pretending he's only just realised I'm there. He half looks up, smiling, but keeps one eye on the laptop, as if he is too busy to talk to me.

"How did it go?" I ask.

He keeps scrolling through web pages.

"Yeah, good. It was really useful. We went through all the stuff, and we're in the right, obviously, but these sort of disputes take a while to unpick. I've got to get on to the Land Registry, and the Planning Office and stuff like that. It's complicated."

He finishes and kind of drifts to a stop. He isn't properly looking at me now, or at the computer. He looks vaguely across the room, not really focused on anything, lost in his own thoughts. I wonder if this is what stress looks like. I cross the kitchen and sit down next to him. I take hold of his hand.

"Nick. *Nick.*"

I feel like a relative talking to a patient in a coma. I draw him back into consciousness and he looks at me properly for the first time.

"You can't do this all on your own," I tell him. "I'm here. It's my life too. I can help. Let me help. What's going on?"

He drops his guard and a huge sigh comes out of him, relief and exhaustion and sadness.

"Oh, Meg. It's a mess."

He sinks his head onto my chest. I stroke his hair, like I'm comforting a child.

"It's okay. We'll be okay," I tell him softly. In a weird way, I feel better now he's letting more of his worry show. If we can support each other like this, we can get through it.

"We need a solicitor on it. We've got to do it right," he continues.

"Let's get one then," I say.

He doesn't reply. Is there something else?

"What? What's the problem?"

He still doesn't look at me. Or *can't* look at me. Finally, he says one word, quietly.

"Money."

"What do you mean?" I say. "We've got money."

He lifts his head and looks at me. His face has changed completely. He looks pained. It is like he's aged ten years in ten seconds.

"No, Megan. No, we haven't."

17

PROMISE

It is too much to take in all at once. We don't have any money. How is that possible? Meanwhile, Nick is talking, fast now.

"All the money is tied up in the house. I didn't want to tell you. I didn't want you to worry. We couldn't get a mortgage as such while I sold my place, so I had to take a bridging loan. I thought it would only be a few weeks. But the buyers have fallen through and the interest rate is crippling. They're being completely bloody unreasonable. They're insisting we make the next payment in full. It's ridiculous."

Now I get why Nick had been so distracted – he's been bottling this secret up. But how can this be? *We don't have any money?* Nick deals with finances for a living.

I can feel myself getting angry. But Tiffany says *anger clouds judgement and disrupts inner peace and harmony*. I've spent too long getting angry – at doctors, at fate, at myself. It got me nowhere. I need to keep a clear head and hold my temper. I take a cleansing breath.

Then a thought hits me. "How did you get the loan?"

He's silent.

"The loan," I say pedantically. "If you haven't sold your house, and we haven't got a proper mortgage, how did you get the loan? What did you use as collateral?"

Again, Nick doesn't say anything. He just looks at me.

"This house?" I ask, incredulously.

"We do it at work all the time, " he says, "to finance deals. It isn't even money really. It's just moving figures about on a screen."

"You put our house at risk? All my money? Without telling me?" I can hear the anger rising up in me. Nick hears it too. We've never argued like this.

"I'm sorry." He mumbles it so quietly I can barely hear him.

"So what?" I say loudly. "We could lose everything?"

"I'm sorry, Meg. I really am. I thought it would just be a few weeks." He hangs his head, unable to look at me. He looks broken.

I'm too furious to speak. I find the strength to step away, and go out into the garden. It's a beautiful day, the first day of August and gloriously warm. For once, there's no noise coming from next door. I need to work out what to do. I can't afford to have my judgment clouded by anger. I close my eyes, focus on my breathing and locate my inner peace. I visualise my anger as a dark cloud blowing across a sky, moving away and revealing the sun. I open my eyes and focus on the horizon. The sea is bright and cool and calming.

Nick and I have never discussed money before. When I left Niall, it just seemed obvious I'd move in with Nick while the divorce went through. By the time Niall and I sold our house, I was pretty much a fixture at Nick's and there was no point looking for anywhere else. I simply kept the money in a savings account. Then when we found the Anglesey house, I transferred all my money into a joint account with Nick and we bought this place. One signature on a form and my entire life changed. Now I'm wondering whether I've signed everything away for nothing.

But Nick can't have messed up in the way he's saying, surely? I know a bit about what he does for a living, dealing with people's investments, buying and selling shares. He doesn't talk about it much and claims it's boring. But he must be good at it, because he paid off his mortgage and owned his massive house before he turned thirty.

Things change. Nothing is forever.

I reason it all through. Nick's house will sell eventually. It's a beautiful old Victorian property on three floors, full of original features. People will be falling over themselves to buy it. Plus I have my jewellery business. I must put all the stuff with Ron and Jackie to one side and throw myself back into that. Nick will finish working out his notice, so he's owed money from that. Plus, when he leaves he's due a big chunk of shares. We have credit cards. We might run up some debts, but we'll manage.

I go back into the kitchen. I take hold of Nick's hand again.

"We don't have *no money*," I say. "We have a cash flow problem. We'll work it out."

Nick grabs hold of me with the desperation of a drowning man.

"Oh God, Meg, I don't deserve you. You're too good for me."

"That's not true," I tell him. "But all this stuff – the money, next door... We're in this together. No more secrets, okay?"

"Yes, definitely," he says, hugging me. "I promise. I promise."

AND OVER THE next few days, this does feel like our real new start. Nick's loving and attentive. He works hard at his computer looking through planning law and trying to understand our position before spending money on a solicitor. He encourages me in my work and I start making jewellery again, pieces that I'm really pleased with. He brings me tea and enthuses about what I've made, inspiring me to do more, be brave and take risks. I start to feel that being in this crisis together is helping us act as one, and making us stronger as a couple.

But deep down I am not entirely at ease. I continue to have a series of troubling dreams. I am in a shop, going on a mad spending spree. I am making an awful visit to the dentist where all my teeth are removed. We are sitting together in my car, which is getting washed away by the sea.

It is exhausting. By the end of the week it has taken its toll. I go to bed desperate for refreshing sleep, but awake so anxious from these dreams that I am physically sick. I look these dreams up in my book, but it always tells me the same thing about money worries and powerlessness. I write them all down, but that doesn't stop the uneasy feelings, or the next night's bad dreams from coming.

If I want the nightmares to end I am going to have to do more than just write them down in my notebook.

18

SICK

Life is hard enough without trying to park in central Manchester, so I leave the car a couple of miles out of town and get the tram into Piccadilly. As I step out onto the platform, he's there to greet me.

"Hello, Megan."

"Hi, Niall."

I'm not sure what the correct protocol is for greeting your ex-husband. We hug awkwardly.

"Nice to see you," he says. "How was the journey? Shall we get a coffee?"

The cafes are pretty horrible around the station, but I don't want to walk too far and get caught in a lot of small talk. We find a Starbucks nearby and go in. There's one table free, littered with dirty cups and plates with cake crumbs. Niall goes to order drinks while I clear the crockery to a tray and clean the table as best I can with a few napkins. It's not a very pleasant start to the meeting, and I know it has every possibility of getting worse.

Niall comes back with the drinks. He's barely sat down before I jump in.

"I'm really sorry about this, Niall," I say, "but that pension I told you we didn't have to cash in, I'm going to need some of the money now."

He thinks for a moment.

"I see. How much of it do you need?"

"All of it. Sorry."

"It's fine," he says lightly. "When do you need it?"

"Well... as soon as possible. If that's okay?" I try to sound casual but I'm not sure I'm pulling it off. I watch Niall sip his coffee thoughtfully.

"That's fine, Megan," he says in a reassuringly light tone. "I'll get onto it this afternoon."

It's typical of him to not make a fuss and make things easy for me. But he hasn't quite finished yet.

"Can I ask, why do you need the money?"

One of the drawbacks of marrying an investigative journalist is that he doesn't let things go without a bit of digging. I guess it's understandable he's curious. But I really don't want to get into the details with him. It's hard enough that I left him for Nick. I don't want to start adding to the awkwardness by intimating life for Nick and me isn't so great right now.

"It's nothing really," I say, forcing a smile. "Just some stuff that's come up with the house we hadn't anticipated."

He looks at me directly.

"But what I mean is, are you alright?"

I feel like someone he's interviewing for a story he's about to blow the lid off. He knows me too well and he's seen right through my poker face. I drop my guard.

"I don't know," I say at last. "I mean, not really, if I'm

honest. Nick thinks I'm delivering an order. He doesn't know I'm here. He'd be mortified if he did. I don't really want to go into it, but if we can just get some money in the short term, we'll be fine. I can probably pay most of it back to you soon anyway."

"Don't worry about that," he says kindly. "It's your money as much as it is mine."

"Thanks." I smile, hoping I've said enough. But of course he isn't going to leave it there, with only half a story.

"Is Nick in trouble?"

"No. No, it's his house here in Manchester. His buyers dropped out and we've got a bit of a cashflow problem is all. As soon as his house is sold, we'll be absolutely fine."

I can feel emotion welling up in me. I haven't spoken to anyone about how worried I am. Jesus, please don't let me start crying here, in bloody Starbucks.

Niall smiles at me kindly. When you split up with people most times, there's a period you go through where you hate them. But that never happened with Niall. Sitting here with him now, I remember all the things I loved about him. He's a good man to have in your corner.

Just by being who he is, Niall draws the story out of me. I tell him about the building work and Nick's loan. I tell him about Ron and Jackie. I feel better just talking about it.

Niall sighs. "Look," he says finally, "I know you'll tell me I shouldn't be, but I'm worried about you."

"That's sweet," I say, "but you don't need to be. Just talking has made me feel much better. I'm fine."

"I'm sure you are," he says. "But there's a lot going on. Looking after your mum. Her not getting better. Our divorce. Moving house. These neighbours. It's a lot of change."

"I know," I say. "You're right."

"And I know you won't like this..." he adds, a little cautiously, "...but Nick... You haven't known him very long. Be careful."

I laugh.

"Oh, Niall. I get why you'd think that, but your job gets the better of you sometimes. You're trying to sniff out a story that isn't there."

"Maybe," he says. He sips his coffee. I can tell he isn't convinced.

"It's an illusion," I continue, trying to reassure him. "It's like these dreams I keep having. They're so vivid and awful, I wake up sometimes and have to run to the bathroom, I'm so sick with the anxiety. But they're just dreams. They're not real."

He's really looking at me now. He's so sure he's on to something. He's like a dog with a bone he won't let go.

"What?" I ask, laughing.

"Vivid dreams," he says. "And you feel so sick you have to run to the bathroom. Megan, are you pregnant?"

19

POSITIVE

I look at two pink lines in the window of a plastic strip. It's the second test I've done. There's no doubt about it: I'm pregnant.

When I go downstairs, Nick's at the breakfast bar, on his laptop, typing so hard I can hear the clacking of the keys from the other side of the living room. I go over behind him and snuggle my face in against his. His rough cheek prickles against mine where he hasn't shaved.

"Good morning," I say, kissing him. "What are you up to today?"

"The usual," he says. "An appointment with another solicitor. More research into sorting He Who Must Not Be Named." He gestures his thumb towards Ron and Jackie's house. "What about you?"

"Oh, not much," I say, as casually as I can, as I slide the pregnancy test onto the keyboard of his laptop. "I thought I might head out and do some essential shopping."

Nick looks down at the keyboard. I feel his body tense a little. What is he thinking? I haven't processed how I feel about being pregnant myself. I guess I'm waiting to see what Nick says. Right now, he isn't saying anything.

He turns to look at me. "Are you sure?" he asks.

"Yes," I say, "I'm sure."

He takes hold of me and looks serious. "How do you feel? Do you feel okay?"

"Yes," I say, "I feel fine. I've been feeling a bit sick, but otherwise, I'm good."

I wait.

Finally, I speak. "How do *you* feel?"

"Well," says Nick, "it's a bit of a surprise if I'm honest. I mean, it isn't something we've even discussed. But... good. I feel good about it."

"Yeah?" I ask. I can't work out if he's warming to the idea or saying what he thinks he needs to say.

"Yes, really. It's great news. I'm sorry if I reacted a bit weirdly. You just caught me off guard is all..."

"And?" I say. "There's something else?"

"It's just..." he starts, then pauses. "I guess it's this stuff with the house. My head is a bit in that and it's hard to just be completely happy in an uncomplicated way. If that makes sense."

It does. It makes complete sense. I feel it too, the fact that this good news is somehow tainted by the situation we find ourselves in. By Ron. Nick must see that thought flash across my face because he gets up and sweeps me up in a hug.

"It's brilliant news, Meg," says, and kisses me. "I'm seeing the solicitor in Holyhead later. We should go shopping for a few things, make it all feel a bit more real. We can go for a celebratory pint. You're on lemonade, obviously."

· · ·

I FEEL MUCH MORE positive about things as I walk around Bump & Bundle. Nick is at the solicitor's office, hopefully getting things sorted out with this boundary dispute, and I'm remembering everything Tiffany told us about embracing change. *Pay attention to the present moment with openness and curiosity, rather than being caught up in past regrets or future worries.* I put my hand lightly on my stomach and think about this very moment. I feel another flutter of butterflies, a mix of nervousness and excitement. But it's more than that now. I have Nick's baby growing inside me.

I scan the shelves and realise I am completely out of my depth. There's so much stuff. What do I need, in what order? I look at the prams and cribs and changing tables. How do I choose the right one? Maybe it's like picking wine in a restaurant. You resign yourself to the fact that you can't possibly know everything and then go by price. I'm sure we'll be fine if we pick something in the middle.

Everything is more expensive than I thought. You could probably get a second-hand car for the price of some of the prams. I recall the conversation I had with Nick, about money. We need every penny we have to pay the interest on the loan, so we can't go spending hundreds of pounds on baby equipment just yet. I try not to let the thought take the shine off the moment. We have until next spring to get everything, so waiting a few months won't matter.

I go to the book section and get a couple of books for expectant couples. I also pick up a book for Nick called *Don't Panic: the Survival Guide for New Fathers*, which has a cartoon drawing of a worried-looking sperm on the cover. I also get a couple of pairs of the smallest socks I've ever seen.

The lady on the till bags them up for me and smiles as she

rings in the amount. I wonder if she can tell I'm pregnant just looking at me. Then I remember I'm standing in Bump & Bundle buying baby socks – of course she knows I'm pregnant.

I laugh at myself for being such an idiot as I walk out of the shop.

"Oh hello, luv."

Shit. It's Ron and Jackie. The only thing worse than hearing them next door is seeing them in person. Ron is loaded down with shopping from Primark and Marks & Spencer.

"Oh, Megan luv," coos Jackie, "have you got some exciting news?"

She's looking at the bag I'm holding and the shop I've just come out of. There's no point denying it.

"Yes," I stutter. "It's very early days so we're not supposed to say anything to anyone. But, yes, we're having a baby."

Jackie screams with excitement, making a few passing shoppers turn their heads.

"Oh that's so exciting! Congratulations." She leans in and kisses me on the cheek. "Isn't it, Ron? We must have you over, for a celebration drink."

"Right enough," says Ron. "We're not really baby people. The only patter of tiny feet I like is taking the dogs for a walk."

"Oh shut up, Ron," says Jackie, slapping his arm. "Don't mess with the poor girl."

"I guess they shit about as much as the dogs," Ron continues, "so we'll have that in common."

Ron roars with laughter at his own joke. Jackie wallops him again.

"Pay him no heed, luv," she says. "He's just a silly bugger."

Ron stops laughing and looks serious.

"I hope it'll be one of them quiet ones," he says. "I can't abide hearing a baby cry."

Jackie rolls her eyes at me and tuts. "Men!" she says with a chuckle, as if Ron is some kind of amusing eccentric. "Have you been to the hospital yet?"

"No," I say. "It's very early days."

"Oh, how funny," says Jackie. "You'll be coming in here for it, into Holyhead. They've got a maternity bit here. I come in myself sometimes, for my veins."

She leans her weight against Ron and pivots round, hoicking her dress up to reveal a calf criss-crossed with ugly, purple, angry-looking varicose veins.

"They itch like a bastard. But I've got a very good man who injects them with something to make them fade away. And I'm on my diet, of course, when I can stick to it."

She makes a mock-guilty face and holds open a shopping bag to show me the contents, piled high with a variety of biscuits and Mr Kipling's cakes.

"Let me know if you have a check-up or anything, Megan luv. I'll be happy to run you in."

"Right, come on, you," interrupts Ron sternly. "Dogs'll want feeding."

He starts to stride off up the road at a surprisingly fast pace, not looking back.

"I'd better go, luv," says Jackie, "before His Majesty has a fucking aneurysm. See you soon."

Jackie hurries off after Ron, her flesh jiggling about as she skips to catch him up.

·   ·   ·

BY THE TIME I get to the pub where we've arranged to meet, Nick is halfway through a pint of beer.

"I got you a glass of wine," he says. "I thought a small one would be okay, this early. They didn't have champagne. When I asked for prosecco, the girl just looked confused." He smiles to himself.

"Thanks." I sip the wine. It's too sweet, and not cold enough. I'm not sure if that's the pub's fault, or the fact that it's been sitting on the table for some time. Maybe Nick's been here for a while and that's his second pint.

"How did it go?" I ask about the solicitor.

"Fine," he says. I wait, but he's clearly not going to say any more. We sip our drinks. I don't tell him about my encounter with Ron and Jackie. Silence descends. The pub is practically empty, just us and a man who sits on his own, reading a paper. Dull light bleeds in through the small dirty windows. It doesn't feel like much of a place for a celebration.

"Well, cheers!" Nick says at last. We chink glasses. "Here's to the future."

20

JOINT OF BEEF

"Who doesn't know what a cervix is?" says Nick in an outraged tone.

We're propped up in bed. It's Sunday morning, so we haven't been woken at an ungodly hour by the noise of building work. We're both reading our baby books.

"This assumes men know absolutely zero about women's bodies," Nick continues. He waves a page of his book under my nose. "Do you think they've deliberately drawn this embryo so it looks like E.T.?"

I look at the drawing. He's not wrong. "It's so you'll think having a baby is cute and not terrifying," I say.

"Right," says Nick. "You're playing host to an alien. Not remotely terrifying." He touches a rigid index finger against my belly and puts on a stupid voice. "Phooone hooome!"

He relaxes his hand and lays the palm of it tenderly on my stomach. He rests it there.

"Hello, little E.T.," he says gently.

"I've been doing the maths," I say. "I thought I was just off rhythm because of the stress and disruption of the move and next door. But I think I must be about eight weeks gone already."

"What does that make our due date?" Nick asks. "January or February sometime?"

"Sounds about right," I say. "I think they can tell us more when I have my twelve-week scan."

Nick looks thoughtful. "Could it have been that lovely shag we had the day we moved in here?"

"I don't know. But maybe, yeah."

This is nice. We are more like our old selves. And Nick seems to have taken to the idea. He doesn't seem as tense about it as he was when I first told him. I feel something I haven't felt for a while: happy.

"Hey," Nick says, "I was reading this."

He puts his book to one side and leans over to get his laptop. As he opens it I just notice he has yet another email from a solicitor open on his screen. He clicks off his mail program and Googles something.

"According to the NHS website," he reads, "'Your baby is now around 16mm long, which is about the size of a raspberry'."

"Why are they comparing babies to food?" I laugh.

"I know," he says incredulously. "It's all like that. "Next week he'll be the size of a strawberry. The week after he's like a small apricot."

Nick called our baby 'he'. There's already another person in our lives. It feels odd, but I like it.

"I like Week 31," he says. "By then, we're having a cabbage. In case you don't know what that is, they've helpfully included a photo of a cabbage."

Nick shows me the photo, with someone holding a cabbage in their arms like a baby.

"He's got your eyes," I say.

"And wait for this," says Nick, scrolling through pages. "This is my favourite. At 35 weeks he's the size of a joint of beef!"

"What?" I laugh. "It's meaningless. Beef isn't even one size!"

"I know. Look at that meal we had on Boxing Day. It fed twelve people." Nick raises his eyebrows. "Good luck giving birth to that."

I can't remember the last time we laughed like this.

Then we're interrupted by an almighty howling.

It's the dogs.

I'm used to the background noise of barking, yelping and whining, which comes mainly from the black dog they have chained out on the lawn. But this is different. It seems like something has set the entire pack off. The mood of our conversation is broken and it's not funny anymore. We're dragged back to the reality of our situation.

Nick closes the lid of his laptop a little too forcefully. He kisses me on the forehead.

"I'm going for a shower," he says gruffly.

He gets out of bed and I watch him walk to the bathroom. I understand his irritation. I feel it too. I try to go back to my book for a bit, but the dogs are just too loud. Something unusual is going on.

I get up and pull on my dressing gown, then head to my workroom. I move my chair to the window and stand on it, pulling myself up onto my tiptoes so I can see into next door's garden.

Ron is there, and he has all the dogs out. He must have hammered something into the lawn that he's attached their leads to, like tent hooks or something. They're all lined up at the beach end of the garden. They are very excitable.

"PLATZ!" Ron shouts, so loud that I can hear it at this distance through the window, and the dogs suddenly go quiet and lie down on their fronts. They are twitchy, tense and alert. They don't take their eyes off Ron. He walks round behind them. I can see him lean his massive bulk down awkwardly to each dog in turn, feeling around its neck. I realise he's fiddling with the collars, unclipping the leads. He seems to be talking to the dogs constantly while he's doing this. Even when unclipped, none of the dogs move. Eventually, all four are lying there, off the leads, waiting.

Ron walks back towards the house. He doesn't look back at the dogs, like a bullfighter turning his back on the bull. I have to raise myself even higher and press my face against the glass to see him down this end of the garden. He goes into the house.

Silence. I can't work out what's going on, but I look back at the dogs. They are on high alert. They know something is about to happen. I stand here, tense, on tiptoes, waiting for what comes next. It's a horrible, frozen moment. All I can hear is the faint sound of Nick's shower running. My breath is leaving condensation on the window where my lips are pressed against it.

Ron comes out carrying something boxlike under a blanket. He puts it down on the edge of the decking, then steps down onto the grass. He turns around and starts fiddling with the box. Ron's body now obscures my line of sight, so I don't know what he has there. I can see he's pulled the blanket off and tossed it to one side, but I can't see the box itself.

I have a terrible feeling I know where this is heading, but

I'm unable to come away from the window. I haven't blinked.
I can't move. The dogs are still lying down but they're getting
increasingly anxious and fidgety.

Ron spins round and thrusts both arms aloft. He's
holding an object in each hand. I see with horror what
he has.

Rabbits.

When I first saw him catch them, I was happy he was
keeping them alive. Now I hope with every fibre of my being
that they are dead. The dogs must be one hundred feet away,
but they have spotted what he's holding and are clearly
agitated. They keep their positions, but I can see they are like
coiled springs waiting to be released.

Ron swings his arms round and lobs the rabbits ten feet
or so in the air. As they fall to the ground he bellows a
command.

"FASS!"

The dogs explode across the lawn towards him. The
second the rabbits hit the grass I can see they are very much
alive. A fall from that height isn't an issue for them, and they
spring instantly off in different directions, breaking for cover
at the side of the garden. The dogs are motoring now, and
have to use all their strength and agility to change direction,
anticipating the path of the rabbits before they disappear.
The rabbits zigzag, but there are only two of them and four
dogs, and escape is impossible. The dogs somehow act as a
team, cutting the rabbits off, circling them, and rapidly
close in.

I shut my eyes just as the yelping starts. Eyes closed, I
climb down from my chair, trying to zone out the baying and
snarling I can hear from outside. I hurry downstairs, switch
the radio on and turn the music up until it drowns out the

dogs and all I can hear is the radio. I sit on the sofa and stare at the wall and try not to picture rabbits, try not to think about rabbits.

It's only when Nick touches me on the shoulder that I realise the music is so loud I haven't heard him come in. I look up at him, draped in a towel, concern on his face as shower water drips on the floor. He looks at me as tears are now streaming down my face.

PART 3

21

TANK

"What's that smell?"

As usual, the noise of the building work has woken me up, but there's something else in the mix now, a nasty, sewagey smell.

"Is it coming from in here?" Nick gets up and goes into the bathroom. I hear him open the shower door, then flush the toilet. "I can't tell," he says as he comes back into the bedroom.

We get dressed and go downstairs. It smells down here too. Nick goes around sniffing the kitchen sink and the downstairs bathroom.

"I can't work out where it's coming from," he says. "Maybe it's the drains."

He unlocks the patio door and goes outside. I watch as he heads round the side of the house, presumably to inspect all the drainage pipes from the bathrooms and the kitchen. After a couple of minutes, he comes back into view and starts wandering around the garden, looking down at the ground. He's out there for five minutes or so before he comes back in.

"It smells worse out there," he says. "I dunno what's going on. I've looked for a manhole cover but I can't find one."

"It's revolting," I say, practically gagging. I wonder if being pregnant has heightened my senses or if it genuinely is this horrible.

"Maybe it's something next door are doing," offers Nick. "Didn't you say they're putting in a hot tub? Maybe they're doing something to their drains..."

We sit in silence for a while. We both know that neither of us is going to strike up a conversation with the Evanses to ask them about their building work.

"I'll see if I can get some drain people to come and take a look," he says wearily.

I know what he's thinking, and I feel the same. More disruption. More money.

Later, I can hear Nick on the phone making calls to plumbers as I leave the house. I drive into Holyhead where I have an appointment with the antenatal clinic. I want to talk through the options regarding birthing centres or hospitals. I wouldn't want a home birth. The whole thing is scary enough, but doing it in a house that already makes me feel stressed is inconceivable. I meet a nice midwife who is matter of fact but reassuring, and who gives me lots of leaflets and makes it clear that this is something they do a lot, and I'm in safe hands.

I get to the car park and imagine what it will be like leaving a building like this carrying a tiny baby, clicking in his car seat, taking him home, lying in bed listening to the breathing in the crib at the end of the room. I remember those tiny socks I bought the other day and imagine putting them onto our little E.T.

When I get home, there's a van in the driveway – *Morris & Sons Drainage and Plumbing Services*. As I get out of the car, the sewage smell hits me. Whatever the issue is, it hasn't been fixed yet. I head inside and find Nick in the kitchen. A middle-aged man in blue overalls and a baseball cap comes in through the patio door. He has the name of the company embroidered on the overalls and 'Graham' sewn underneath.

"Ah," says the man, seeing me cross from the hallway, "perfect timing. I can fill you both in."

He proceeds to explain our drainage problems in the way some tradesmen have a habit of doing, addressing everything to Nick and not looking at me once.

"You've got a sewage issue. The smell's coming back into the house through your sinks and bath and toilets. If you were on the main drain we'd rod it or put a camera down if that didn't shift it, but you're on a septic system, with a tank, so rodding won't make any difference. It might need draining but it shouldn't just start smelling like this overnight, so you've maybe got a blockage in your soakaway or there's a rupture of your tank, which is bad news. I've looked for an inspection pipe and I can't see one. My gut, given how small your garden is and how big theirs is next door, is that your septic tank and inspection pipe are on their land."

Our land, I think, *which they've stolen*. But I don't say anything.

"I've knocked on next door," Graham continues, "but the owners are out and the builders don't want me over there without the owners' say-so. So I can't be certain, but that's my guess. If I was you, I'd pop round and have a word, see if they'll let you take a look around for manhole covers. Should be easy enough to spot – two or three covers within ten or fifteen feet of each other – unless they've turfed over them."

"Thanks," says Nick. "We'll do that."

Of course, we won't.

Graham picks his tool bag up and heads towards the front door.

"You need a specialist firm," he says. "Find your inspection pipe first, see what's what. As I say, it may need draining. When was it last drained?"

"We don't know," I say. "We only moved in a couple of months ago." I don't tell him we're just up from the city and so naïve that we didn't even know we had a septic tank until he told us two minutes ago.

"Right," he says. "Well, it might just need draining. Tank could be ruptured. Tree root damage possibly." He pauses and listens to the sound of drilling from next door. "Has that building work been going on long?"

"It's quite recent," I say.

"Hmmm," says Graham. He doesn't add any more, but we all know how to put two and two together. Eventually, he continues. "As I say, find your inspection pipe. Take it from there."

Once he's driven away and we're alone, Nick slumps down onto the sofa and stares morosely at the wall. "It's just one bloody thing after another."

"So," I say, "what now?"

"I don't know," says Nick. He keeps staring at the wall, as if some answer is miraculously going to appear there. But of course, we both know we've already been given the answer.

We have to go and see Ron and Jackie.

22

RABBIT

The longer I wait, the more anxious I feel. This is like being in the dentist's waiting room, dreading the moment they call your name. I know what's coming next and I just want it to be over.

I've been standing at the landing window for a couple of hours now. It's getting dark. Finally I see headlights and then the black four-by-four in the distance as it turns into the path from the road. It bounces up the lane for a bit before veering off and disappearing behind the hedge. Ron and Jackie are home.

I leave it five minutes then go downstairs. I'm at the front door slipping my boots on when Nick comes over from the kitchen.

"I've changed my mind," he says. "I'm coming with you."

"Are you sure?" I ask. On one hand, I'm anxious about being anywhere near Ron. But on the other, we need to keep things civil with him so we can sort this issue with the septic tank. Ever since that standoff between the cars, Nick has approached it as all-out war. It's not going to make our lives any easier if he starts kicking off. As if he can read my mind, Nick puts his hand gently on my shoulder.

"I'll keep a lid on it," he says reassuringly. "I hate the bastard, but I won't tell him that. I just don't want you going round there on your own. Okay?"

"Yeah," I say, giving him a smile. "Okay."

We leave the house and turn off towards the Evanses. As we crunch up the gravel drive, I can't help thinking about that first evening we came here, Ron grabbing me and whispering into my ear, "If you need anything, you come to your Uncle Ron." Well, now we *do* need something. It makes me feel ill that we have to come and beg for the favour of being allowed onto our own land, but there's no other way of getting this sewage problem fixed.

"OOOH, HOW LOVELY." Jackie stands in the open doorway and greets us like long-lost relatives. She's dressed in an ankle-length flowing silky dress and a thin shiny coat of some sort. "Come in, come in." She steps back to let us enter the house.

"We can't stay," I say as cheerfully as possible, but not moving. "We've just come to ask a favour."

"Oh don't be silly, you must have a drink. Ron! Ron!" She retreats into the hallway, bellowing for her husband and leaving the door wide open for us. Nick looks at me and raises his eyebrows. He sighs. Clearly, if we want to talk to them we have no option but to go in. Nick steps inside and I follow, closing the door behind me.

"Ron!" Jackie foghorns the name through the house. "Get your arse down here. We've got guests." She turns to us. "Now, luvs, what will you have?"

Now I can see better in the light of the kitchen I realise Jackie is actually in a long nightdress and a silk dressing gown. She's not wearing a bra and her ample bosom sags down and sways about in the deep V of her nightie. I do my best not to stare.

"I'm sorry if we're disturbing you," I say.

"Don't worry about that. Drink?"

"Nothing for me," I say, instinctively placing my hand on my belly. "Maybe a glass of water."

"Right you are, darling," says Jackie. "Nick?"

"Water's good for me too," says Nick.

"Oooh," sings Jackie, "you are cheap dates."

She swings herself round and trots over to the fridge, clattering handfuls of ice into glasses and hacking away with a knife to carve thick slices of lemon. She comes back to us holding three drinks.

"I may have put a bit of gin in it," she says with a naughty giggle, "but gin is mainly water, and you've got to wet the baby's head, haven't you?"

She hands us our glasses and then chinks hers heavily against ours.

"Up yer bum!" she toasts, and swills a massive gulp.

At that point, I see Ron coming down the stairs. I catch sight of his legs first, fatty and blotched, his swollen calves and thighs curiously hairless, like they belong to an enormous baby. My first appalling thought is that he's naked. But as he descends further I see he's wearing a towelling dressing gown which is too short and too tight for him. His stomach strains at the knot in the thin belt which barely holds him in. He takes each step awkwardly, his gown riding up disturbingly high as he bends his leg for each lumbering step.

It occurs to me what incredible energy it must take him to move around, or even just stand up.

"Oh it's you, is it?" he says as he enters the kitchen. He crosses to the fridge and emerges with a beer. "I'm not very happy with you two." He cracks open the can. "When you knocked I was just about to give the missus a good seeing to," he says and winks at me salaciously. Everything about him fills me with disgust.

"Ron Evans!" screeches Jackie, outraged, pulling her nightgown around her bulk as if to protect her modesty. "They don't want to know about that."

"Oh, it's nothing they don't do themselves," bellows Ron, "what with Megan here up the pole an' all. In fact, reach us down that bowl and we'll chuck our car keys in, make a night of it."

"Jesus, Ron, you filthy bugger." Jackie hoots with laughter and slaps him on his arm. Ron laughs hard at his joke. At least, I hope it's a joke. Something about the way he catches my eye again makes me look away fast.

"Anyway," says Nick brusquely, changing the tone of the conversation, "we've come to ask you something about the drains."

"Right," says Ron. "That stench, that's you, is it? I thought a whale had crapped on the beach."

Nick presses on. "We may have an issue with our septic tank, and we need to access the inspection pipe, but we think maybe it's where you're doing your building work."

Ron and Nick look at each other. I'm impressed Nick is keeping his cool. Neither says any more.

"Would we be able to come into your garden to take a look?" I say, hoping to interrupt the staring contest.

"Oh that should be fine, luv. Shouldn't it, Ron?" says

Jackie, heading to the counter to refill the glass she's already emptied.

Ron hasn't taken his eyes off Nick.

"So, what you're getting at," Ron finally says, "is that you'd like to come onto my land to have a look at your broken septic tank?"

"Well," says Nick in a voice that's beginning to show the strain, "whoever's land it is, we do need to get access to the tank so we can see what's going on."

"Alright," says Ron brightly. "No problem at all."

I feel a wave of relief wash over me. I can't believe he's agreed so easily and we haven't had a scene.

But then he adds, "Say please."

Nick is turned slightly away from me, facing Ron directly. I can see the stiffness in his shoulders as Ron smiles at him. Nick takes a breath.

"Please," he says quietly. The tension in the room is unbearable. Only Jackie seems oblivious, glugging several measures of gin into her glass.

"Then sure," says Ron lightly.

He starts to move away, but turns back.

"Oh," he adds, "and while you're at it, you should probably say sorry for making our garden stink of shit."

"*Our* garden you mean," says Nick coldly.

Oh Christ. This is what I thought might happen. He's lost it. He doesn't quite square up to Ron, but I can see the tension in his body. His arms are by his sides, but his fists are clenched, in frustration as much as anger. I'm scared of what might come next.

"You what?" says Ron, slowly and deliberately. He's got the confident authority of someone who knows for certain he's going to win any fight he gets into.

Nick goes off on one. "You know full fucking well that's our garden. A few wooden posts shoved in the ground don't mean shit compared to the deeds."

"You ponce in from the city," bellows Ron, "you haven't the first clue how to look after your house and you come round here making out it's something to do with us. And as for that fence, I had all that out with the pansy boys who were here before."

I wince at his description of Gavin and Peter. But what does he mean, he had all this out with them?

Ron blusters on aggressively. "That's my bloody land until someone tells me different."

"We're going to have you off there," barks Nick, "and sue you for trespass, *and* our legal costs, and then we'll look at the tank, and if your building work is what's damaged it, we'll sue you for that as well."

Ron looks murderously at Nick. But just when I think he's about to swing for him, he softens and his face breaks out in a smile.

"Chopsy little fucker, aren't you?"

I look at Nick. He's shaking. I've never seen him like this.

Ron turns to Jackie. "Princess," he says, "see our guests out before the evening turns nasty."

Nick is seething with anger. I walk over to him and take his hand and pull him towards the front door, drag him out of the kitchen before something bad happens. He seems almost dazed as I lead him off.

"And stay out of my garden," Ron calls as we go, "or your kid'll end up a fucking orphan."

There's real menace in the threat. I have no doubts whatsoever he'd turn to violence at the drop of a hat. He doesn't sound like someone who's just talking in anger. He means it.

Jackie follows us to the door. "Sorry about that, luvs," she says lightly. "He does get in a tizzy sometimes. I'm sure it will all blow over."

I open the front door and lead Nick quickly onto the drive. It's properly dark now and the sky is inky black. The moon is behind a cloud and the way in front of us is rough and hard to make out. We start to walk away from the house. But then Jackie's voice stops us.

"Megan," she says urgently. "Wait a moment. Wait here."

She sounds deadly serious. I watch her disappear back into the house. What does she have to say that's so important? Maybe now she has us outside and away from Ron there's something she needs to tell us.

I wait nervously for a minute or so and then she comes back out, carrying something. I can't properly see what it is in this gloom. It looks like some kind of bag. She comes over and hugs me, presses the bag into my hand and whispers gravely into my ear.

"This is for you. It's the most important thing you'll ever do in your life."

She steps away from me and scampers back into the house, closing the door behind her. I can't imagine what it is she's given me, or what she's trying to tell me.

Nick is muttering and cursing under his breath as we hurry back to our house. We open the front door and go inside, switching the hall light on as we do so.

Now I can see, I take out what's inside the bag.

It's a child's stuffed toy rabbit.

23

DRIFTWOOD

The blatant confrontation with Ron has changed something in Nick. He tries to hide it, but the ghost of his sour mood bleeds into our everyday life together, the hints of his surliness at dinner, the way he closes the door too hard and heavily, his background score of sighs and tuts and grumbles. His beautiful face has clouded over. His eyes look heavy and tired. The twinkle has given way to an expressionless murky flatness.

I feel bad for him. None of this is his fault, and I don't say anything... but a little bit of me can't help resenting him, pushing for this move to Wales. I know I agreed to it, I know I'm being unfair, but I can't shake the feeling somehow that we wouldn't be here, in this mess, if it wasn't for Nick.

I spend some time researching septic tanks, hoping I can find a solution. This isn't the romantic life I imagined for myself when I moved here. I learn all about them, what they're made of, how long they last, and whether you can repair them. I learn how they work, using natural bacteria to break down organic matter into liquid and a kind of sludge that gets emptied every few years. I'm wondering if we can just seal off the old tank, install a new one and not have to deal with Ron and Jackie at all. I sign up for websites and order brochures. After a morning of this, I'm an expert. But I've done as much as I can right now.

I try to throw myself into my work, but as I sit at my bench I can't pull my focus back from what I know is outside. I feel compelled to move my chair to the window and climb up to see if I can catch a glimpse of what is going on next door. Sometimes I see Ron in the garden, stripped down and wedged into a deckchair, baking his gargantuan body in the sun. At other times the garden is empty, and I stand for hours waiting to see him, as if knowing where he is will eradicate my unease. I don't know what I hope to achieve from any of this – seeing him or not seeing him. Days pass. Nothing changes. Nothing is resolved.

The noise and the smell and the stress, the presence or absence of Ron, make it impossible for me to work here. I leave Nick on the phone with the solicitor and stay away from the house as much as I can during the day. I drive into some of the small towns and villages, taking my laptop into quaint little cafes to catch up on admin. But I find I can't concentrate here either, and being on my own around strangers just makes me feel lonely. Even so, I begin to dread going home.

I try going down to the beach to clear my head, desperate to meditate, to cleanse myself. I struggle to remember what Tiffany said about harmony with nature, and interconnectedness, and being at one with the universe. I can't seem to join it all up now and my rehashed version of it just seems like a jumble of naive, meaningless nonsense. Instead, I'm overwhelmed by angst, and the immense expanse of the sea makes me feel small and insignificant, and my life feels like a tiny, transient speck against its vastness.

I feel like King Canute, trying to stop something that won't stop coming.

At night my sleep is increasingly broken and unrefreshing, and when I do sleep, I'm troubled by awful dreams. I wake up early, waiting for the noise to start. I feel drained and jet-lagged.

I'M SITTING IN A CAFE, writing one of my nightmares down in my dream journal, when I have a thought. What am I doing? Why am I just leaving things to Nick? Why am I letting the misery of my dreams seep into my daily life?

Jesus, Megan, who have you become? I faced the illness and the death of both my parents and I didn't give up. I got on with things. I moved forward. What the hell am I doing wallowing in self-pity?

I open my laptop and search Tiffany's website, trying to find a thing I vaguely remember her telling us, a phrase she once used. After a bit of scrolling, I find it.

> *On one hand, Buddhism emphasises the importance of acceptance and letting go of attachment to outcomes, cultivating acceptance in the face of life's ups and downs. But Buddhism also recognises the importance of mindful action, which involves being fully present and aware in the moment while making conscious choices.*

I realise I've let myself become a bit of driftwood, thrown

about on the tide of what Ron is up to. But I can choose to do something about it. I've been asleep. I need to wake up.

I don't know how far Nick has got with his research, but he doesn't seem to be getting anywhere, and I recognise how powerless I've let myself become leaving it all to him. I log into the local council planning portal, intending to check for myself what Ron has officially applied to build. I'm hoping he doesn't have permission for what he's doing. But when I find the plans, it's all there – his steam room and sauna, his showers and his hot tub, drawings of his bloody ugly pergola. There's another drawing too, a larger one, which is marked as a gym, though Christ knows what he wants with one of those. If they're digging the foundations for that, they could easily have damaged our septic tank. I click to another page and see the side elevation. The gym is on two storeys and has a cinema room above it. It's vast.

The planning application shows a boundary line where the wooden stakes were put. But it doesn't make sense, their house having all that land and ours being squeezed into a corner. And if our lives are bad now, our view will be even worse when that gym and cinema go up.

I feel sick, seeing it all in black and white.

I search further back, for the plans for their actual house. After a bit of digging, I find them. Again, it's all officially signed off as they have it, their revoltingly tasteless mock castle. How can a council sign off on such a disgusting building? It would be funny if it wasn't so awful, and if it wasn't right next to us. The planning application for the house doesn't show the buildings in the garden, but it does have the boundary line. It's the same one again, where the wooden stakes went, boxing us in.

I check the name of the planning officer who signed off

on these drawings. It's a man by the name of Menzies. Then I go back and check the drawings for the sauna and stuff. Menzies again.

Finally, I look at the planning application for Peter and Gavin's house, now our house. That was built a few years before Ron's place. Once again, it's Mr Menzies who has signed off on all the drawings. Weirdly, these don't show a boundary line at all, but there certainly isn't one where Ron has put his fence in. But I don't know anything about planning, or what needs to be on these plans.

I write an email to the contact address, asking for a meeting with Mr Menzies. I'm not sure what will come of it, but whether Nick has already seen this or not, I want to know for certain whether what's going on is correct, and what our rights are if our septic tank is on their land.

I remember something Ron said the other night, about having all of this out with Gavin and Peter. I wonder what he meant. The easiest thing would be to ask them. I call Gavin's number and it rings for a while, then goes to voicemail. I leave a breezy message asking if he can call me back.

I drive home feeling better than I have for a while. Nothing has changed, but at least I'm getting on with stuff. I'm keen to see if all this tallies with what Nick has discussed with the solicitor. But Nick's car isn't on the drive, and when I go into the house he's not there. Looking out of the kitchen window I can see the sun is beginning to lower in the sky. I open the door and step onto the decking. The builders next door have stopped for the day and even the sewage smell doesn't seem so bad.

I go back inside, grab a rug, and write a note for Nick inviting him to join me on the beach. I walk across the garden and down our cliff path. I take my shoes off and feel the warm sand between my toes. The beach is utterly deserted. I find a smooth patch of sand, spread out the rug and sit down. It's the middle of August and exactly the sort of glorious summer evening we moved here for. I feel a connection to this place, and to Nick, and to our unborn baby. We have each other. We will be all right.

The sun gets lower. I've been here a while now, and it's beginning to get chilly. I check my phone to see if I have a signal. I do. But Nick hasn't called, and neither has Gavin. I try calling Gavin again, and once more the call goes to voice-mail. I leave another short message. Then I call Nick. He answers. He's at home. He didn't see my note. By now it's too cold on the beach, and getting dark, so I tell him I'm coming back. I ring off.

I pick up the rug and shake it free of sand, then wrap it around my shoulders. The sand has stuck to my feet, so I carry my shoes as I walk back towards the house. Approaching the cliff, I begin to get a whiff of the sewage. By the time I reach the path, it smells much stronger than I remember it. I begin to go up towards the house, but I've only taken a few steps when I see something glistening and wet in front of me. It's trickling and moving, running down the cliff like a tiny stream.

Only this isn't a stream.

Raw sewage is now coming down the path.

24

MR. MENZIES

We sit in a dull, grey, featureless waiting room.

Two days have passed since I spotted the trickle of sewage on the pathway to the beach. That has got steadily worse, and now it's too dangerous to walk on safely even if you did want to contend with the smell and the prospect of wading through a river of filth. We're hemmed in, squeezed on one side by the building work and prevented from accessing the beach at the end of the garden by overspill from the septic tank.

I've called Gavin's number again a couple more times, but he hasn't got back to me. It's increasingly apparent they're avoiding us.

Nick hasn't said much since I told him about this appointment, but I can tell he's grumpy about it. Maybe he sees me getting involved as some kind of criticism of his inability to fix things, like he's somehow failed.

A young woman comes into the waiting room and tells us that Mr. Menzies is free now. She leads us to his office. When we arrive, he's sitting behind a desk with an ancient-looking computer screen, which acts as a wall between us. He doesn't stand to greet us. We sit down in hard plastic chairs.

"I understand from your email you have some questions about the properties at Bae Breuddwyd?"

"Yes," I say, trying to adopt a friendly tone. "We recently bought one of the houses and we want to understand planning permission around some building work our neighbours are doing."

"I'm sure I can clarify," says Mr Menzies. "I have all the files here."

He pivots his screen round so we can all see it. He already has the relevant files open and clicks through them in quick succession.

"Your property was built first, approximately five years ago, based on these approved plans here. Subsequently, the remaining area of land above the cove was rezoned for additional housing and your neighbour's property was constructed last year based on these approved drawings. A subsequent application by your neighbours to construct additional outbuildings to the rear of their property was approved six months ago."

"So," I ask, "the boundary line on those later drawings, where the gardens meet... That's right, is it?"

"Yes," says Mr Menzies officiously, "the drawings are correct."

He turns his screen back round to face him.

"And can I just ask," I say hesitantly, "what do you mean by rezoned?"

"The land bordering your property wasn't originally zoned for building, but that was subsequently revised."

I'm trying to work out what this means as Mr Menzies throws a look at his wall clock.

"Is there anything else I can help with?" he asks. We've been in all of two minutes and it feels like the meeting is over. I look at Nick, who hasn't said anything. Is that it? Isn't there anything about this he wants to challenge?

Nick stands up. "Thanks for your time," he says, and looks at me.

So that's it. We're leaving.

"TALK TO ME, NICK."

We're in a sandwich bar not far from the planning office. It's mid-morning, and the place is quiet. Nick is poking at the froth in his coffee with a spoon, stirring a little white heart round and round until it becomes one dirty brown layer. He's been racing round trying to sort things out for days, but now he's ground to a halt. Maybe he's burnt out. All the fight seems to have gone out of him.

"Nick?" I say again, trying to call him back into the room. He looks up at me. "What do we do next?"

"I don't know." He sighs wearily. "What can we do? That's the boundary line."

"I won't accept that," I say, raising my voice a little too loudly. "What do the solicitors say?"

"They say *that!*" he says, exasperated. "They say that's the boundary line. There's nothing we can do about it."

I lean into Nick and talk in a hushed tone. "Look, obviously we wouldn't have bought the place if we'd known they'd be building all that crap right on top of us. If it's on the plans, Peter and Gavin must have known, surely."

"Maybe," says Nick morosely. "I don't know."

"Well," I say, "if they *did* know and they didn't say anything, isn't that misrepresentation or something? Surely they can't do that. No wonder they're avoiding us. Is that legal? We should find out. And what about the solicitor who did the sale? Shouldn't he have told us something? He must be responsible somehow. If he's missed it off the survey we should talk to someone, the Law Society or the Ombudsman or someone. People can't just fuck up without consequences."

"Maybe," says Nick again. "I don't know. Can we just leave it for now, go home?"

"Okay," I say reluctantly. "Sure."

AS WE DRIVE BACK, my concern for Nick grows. What has he been doing all this time? Maybe he just got stuck and didn't know how to tell me. He doesn't just seem burnt out, he seems defeated, maybe even depressed. Perhaps he feels what I felt, that he's responsible for this somehow. Maybe he thinks I blame him. Maybe he feels he's failed because he isn't able to fix it.

I guess he wants to be the strong one. But seeing him like this, sad and vulnerable, my heart fills with love for him. It's not his fault. He mustn't blame himself. I want to make him feel better. I want to take on some of the burden he's been carrying all this time. We're in this together. We're a partnership. When he said we're on this adventure together he was right, and I realise that has to be for the bad stuff as well as the good stuff. Now I need to be the hands that are waiting to catch *him*.

As we pull into the drive, our car bumps along the gravel until we reach the fork in the road. A new sign has been put into the ground, a tall timber post with a square of wood at the top with a single word daubed on it in aggressive red paint:

PRIVATE.

We can't see the other house hidden behind the curve of the hedge, but we both know it's there. It's a shadow that looms over everything. One thing I know for sure is that I don't need a sign to keep me out. Wild horses wouldn't drag me back there.

Once we're home, I tell Nick I have to deal with a few work emails. I kiss him and leave him sitting on the sofa. I head up to my workroom and close the door. Nick may have had the fight knocked out of him, but I haven't. I'm determined not to let Gavin and Peter just ignore my calls and get away with this. I dial Gavin's number and prepare myself to unload on him big time.

But instead of ringing and going to voicemail, the call connects directly to a synthetic voice with a message on loop:

This number is not in service. Please check your number again and redial. This number is not in service. Please check your number again and redial.

Gavin's phone has been cut off.

25

ORANGE JUICE

It's Sunday. Given how stressed Nick's been, I've encouraged him to take a trip out on the ferry to Dublin, to see an old uni friend of his. His mate Brian, who lives over there, will pick him up at the other end. They'll have lunch, an afternoon crawling through a few gloomy old pubs, and Nick will head back about 8 p.m. The ferry takes a couple of hours, so he'll be home around midnight.

He looks tired as he leaves the house early and I wave him off in his car. I give Nick two minutes to get clear of the house, then I rush around like crazy getting ready. Within twenty minutes I'm ready and on the road.

I spent a couple of days fuming about Gavin and Peter – and resolved to do something about it. I sent Pippa a text, casually asking if she had their new contact details. She pinged me back half an hour later with an address in Tideswell in the Peak District. It's going to take me just under three hours to get there. I don't even know what my plan today is for making this trip. I feel we've been duped, and I hate the sense that someone has wronged me and got away with it.

As I'm driving, I recall the dream I had last night. I was in Venice, on my Interrailing holiday, an early foggy morning with proper thick banks of fog. But in this dream, I'm with Nick, not Pippa. We've got up early and it's incredibly atmospheric. We're walking up narrow paths next to canals, and we can't see the end of the path because of the fog, like walking into a cloud, and if we look back, we can't see where we've come from. Our footsteps echo brightly off the walls. We come to the end of a passage and a figure emerges from the fog as we approach. It's Gavin. There's no one else about. It's completely quiet. We ask him directions and he tells us where we need to go. We go the way he sends us, and take turn after turn, round corners, across bridges, until we have no idea where we are, and haven't found what we're looking for, and can't find our way back. We're just lost in this maze of alleyways and canals, in this fog.

I turn to tell Nick I think we're lost, but see him vanishing into the fog bank. He's gone. I want to run after him, but I can't see where I'm going and I'm afraid that I'll run headlong into a canal. So I just stand there, the cold fog pressing in on all sides as if it's going to crush me.

I'll have to write it down in my journal when I get back home. Though I don't need the interpretation book to work it out; I've got the hang of it by now. Gavin, sending me and Nick off on some hopeless path where we'll end up lost and alone. And, if I'm honest with myself about it, me still blaming Nick for blithely leading the way and me foolishly following on behind.

Whether today will achieve anything real I have no idea, but I'm positive Gavin and Peter knew what they were drop-

THE WRONG NEIGHBOUR   133

ping us into, what path they were sending us down, and I refuse to let them off scot-free. If nothing else, I want them to look me in the eye and admit they lied to us and cheated us. At least the feeling of being made to look a fool won't keep eating me up like it is right now.

Because I'm both hyped up and pregnant, I have to stop several times to pee, which adds another three-quarters of an hour to the journey. Eventually, I arrive in Tideswell. The satnav takes me through a wide street with rows of monumental grey stone buildings, then off up some roads that rise steeply above the town and open out with fantastic views of the countryside. By the time I get to my destination, I can see that Peter and Gavin have moved to a fantastic old farmhouse on lots of ground. They haven't exactly suffered since leaving Anglesey.

Considering there aren't any other houses nearby, there are a lot of cars up here, all parked on one side of the road, on a grassy verge, as close to the wall as possible to allow traffic to pass. I find a space on the end of the row of vehicles and park.

I've no idea what I'm going to do now I'm here, but I don't let myself sit in the car stewing on it. I get out and walk towards the farmhouse. As I do, I can hear quite a bit of noise and music coming from the rear of the house. I hear voices too. That must be what all the parked cars are. They're having some kind of party.

I go round the side of the house and through an open gate. There's a young girl in a black dress, holding a tray of drinks. She smiles at me.

"Here for the housewarming?" she asks.

A housewarming. How appropriate. "Yes, thanks," I say, as I help myself to an orange juice.

I step around the side of the building and into the garden. It's enormous, and fantastically landscaped, with lots of low walls, paved areas and raised beds. It's a playful mix of archways, water features and interesting sculptures, but at the same time not so artificial that it clashes with the natural landscape beyond. It's amazing. It's everything that our garden in Anglesey could be but isn't. The moment I see how nicely they're living, it makes me resent Gavin and Peter ten times more.

I stand near the house looking at the groups of happy, laughing guests. Then I spot Peter wandering amongst them. He seems, from a distance, much more gregarious than I remember him. I barely recall him speaking at all. Maybe getting away from Ron has given him a new lease of life. He spots me, and stares for a moment, smiling, trying to work out who I am out of context. I guess he figures it out, as he stops smiling and breaks eye contact with me, then threads his way through the people in the garden. I watch him as he goes, disappearing and reappearing behind other guests, until he eventually arrives at Gavin. The two of them have a huddled chat while Gavin throws a glance in my direction. Then they both come my way. I still don't know what's going to happen, but whatever it is, it's about to start.

"Gosh, Megan, what a lovely surprise," beams Gavin, who I now realise is the star actor of the pair. Peter hangs back in the cautious way I recognise from the first day we met.

"Look, Gavin, let's not bullshit each other," I say. "You're not pleased to see me and I can't say I'm pleased to see you. But cancelling your phone contract wasn't going to stop me coming to find out what the fuck you're playing at and how you think you're going to get away with it."

I'm surprised at how angry I am. I'm angry and loud. A couple of the guests nearby turn their heads at the tone of my voice. Two months of pent-up frustration are coming out. I didn't know what to expect from today but I can feel I might start screaming and not stop.

"Shall we maybe take this inside?" asks Gavin, his smile now showing distinct signs of strain.

"What, away from your beautiful garden, you mean, and out of earshot of your lovely guests? I think not," I say. "You'd better start talking fast, or I'm gonna kick off so much that everyone here is going to know exactly how you've shafted us."

I feel my fingers clench around the heavy glass in my hand. I want to throw my orange juice into Gavin's face, and the glass with it. But I don't.

"You mean, tell you about Ron," says Peter.

"Yes," I say.

Gavin gives Peter some kind of look I can't read, but I assume it's to shut him up. But Peter ignores him. He steps towards me.

"What's happened since we left?" asks Peter in a tone that somehow calms me.

I spend the next five minutes giving him a potted history of the horrors we've endured, the building work, the threats of violence, the disputed boundary line and the meeting with Mr Menzies in the planning department, the damage to the septic tank and the huge fence.

"Look, Megan, I'm sorry," says Peter. "Truly, I am. I know what you're going through because we had it too, months of it, while he was building their house. Arguments turning into veiled threats and intimidation. Horrible, abusive, homophobic stuff. I thought Gavin was going to have a nervous breakdown."

Now Peter has started it's clear that Gavin is all mouth, but that Peter is the backbone of the couple. Peter carries on.

"The fact is, they just shouldn't be there at all. The land they are on was never cleared to build another house on, not when we bought our plot. We would never have built if it was. Evans must have pulled some strings at the council or something. The moment we saw it was going up we knew it had completely ruined the plot we were on. We tried to challenge the planning decision, but we got nowhere. We tried to talk to Evans, but you've met him. You know. There's no talking to him. We were just at the point of ditching everything for the sake of our mental health... and then you came along."

"If you knew what they were like," I say, "how could you possibly inflict them on someone else?"

Gavin jumps in. "It was you or us," he says stridently. "You've no idea what it got like. If I have to choose saving us from Ron or saving you, I'm throwing you under the bus every time. I'm sorry, but there it is."

I'm agog from the brazenness of it. "So you took us for suckers and rushed us into a sale while they were out of sight on that cruise?"

Gavin and Peter exchange a look.

"Listen," says Peter. "Be careful. *She* was on a cruise – Jackie – but Ron wasn't."

"What do you mean?" I ask. "Where was he?"

"Prison," says Peter. "He wasn't on a cruise – he was in prison doing time for assault."

Oh God. Assault. Ron really is as dangerous as he seems.

"So that's it, is it?" I say bitterly. "You're not going to do anything about it?"

"*Caveat emptor,*" says Gavin bullishly. "You bought it, so it's your problem."

I can see I'm going to get nowhere here.

"Thanks for absolutely nothing," I say, and start to walk out of the garden. But I stop and turn back. "Actually, I need to use your toilet."

I sit, peeing, frustrated that even my angry exit was defeated by my bloody pregnancy bladder. I look around the lovely bathroom and think how much I'd like to smash it up. Hurl my glass of orange juice through the glass shower door. Pick up the heavy marble soap dish and bring it crashing down on the sink. Shove toilet paper down the plug hole and turn the taps on full.

But I don't. I flush, wash my hands and leave the bathroom. An elderly lady is waiting outside the door. She smiles at me. She has a kind face.

"Sorry to keep you waiting," I say.

"Oh don't worry about that, dear," she says gently. "There are other bathrooms, but I'm too old and stubborn to go upstairs. Anyway, I'm sure you needed it more urgently than me."

She's looking at my stomach, then gives me a knowing look. She's the first person who can tell. My bump is only tiny, but somehow she's spotted it.

"Congratulations," she says and squeezes my hand in a motherly way. I get a warm feeling. "I'm Mary, Gavin's mum."

"Nice to meet you. I'm Megan."

Gavin's mum, the one who has cancer. She looks really happy and glowing, and I wonder if she's gone into remission again. Once my mum got ill, it was just a slow, steady decline to the end.

"I hope you don't mind me saying, but I'm glad to see you looking so well," I say. "I'm sure you'll kick it."

"'Kick it'?" she says, looking confused.

Oh no, maybe I've said more than I should. "I'm sorry. I didn't mean to upset you. Gavin mentioned you'd been ill."

"I think there's been a bit of a mix-up, dear," says Gavin's mum brightly. "I'm not ill. I'm as fit as a fiddle."

I hurry out of the house and to the car. I can't believe that I actually felt sorry for him. My poor mum's cancer. I get into the car and sit there, too angry to drive. I feel tricked, and stupid, and taken for an idiot.

I don't know what I'm going to do, but I'm not going to let them get away with it.

26

FUCK

"We thought we'd go to a few more places," says Nick, "but we had a steak sandwich in Doheny and Nesbitt's and got settled in a corner and couldn't be arsed to move all day."

It's about ten in the morning. Nick is slumped on the sofa, regaling me with tales of his Dublin exploits yesterday.

"I had a Guinness or three and Brian had too much to drive me, but it was only twenty minutes in a cab from the pub to the port. I was probably a bit over the limit when I got back here, but I made it from Holyhead okay."

He looks at me with a broad smile. He's happier than I've seen him for a while. He looks handsome, and he has his sparkle back, which makes a change from me looking at him and thinking he looks tired or stressed.

"I'm really glad you suggested I go," he says. "It did me a lot of good. And how was your day?"

"Well," I say, a little tentatively, "I went to the Peak District."

"The Peaks? Why?"

"I went to see Gavin and Peter."

"What the fuck, Megan!" Nick nearly explodes out of his chair. This is the reason I didn't tell him anything before I went. I knew he'd be disapproving.

I proceed to fill Nick in on my trip. I tell him everything – Ron's assault conviction, Gavin's smug suggestion it was our own fault if we'd bought the house, and his mum's fake cancer.

"I can't believe you did that without talking to me!" He sounds hurt and angry.

"You're joking, aren't you?" I say to him scornfully.

We're mid-argument when there's a knock at the door. I answer it to a man in an orange fluorescent jacket.

"Alright, luv? I'm from the council." He flashes an identity card at me. "We've had a call from one of your neighbours about a suspected leak on the cliff path. Okay if I take a look?"

What next? "Sure," I say. "Do you want to come through?"

"It's fine," he says. "I've got some gear, so I'll go round the side. Down the end, is it?"

Nick and I watch from the kitchen while the council man walks across the garden and disappears through our gate. *One of our neighbours!* Ron, of course. I can't imagine he's contacted the council to help us out.

"You've got a nerve having a go at me about doing something without telling you," I say. "After all the stuff you've done behind my back!"

Nick mutters something unintelligible under his breath, then goes quiet. We sit there in an awkward silence until the man emerges five minutes later and knocks on the patio door. I open it.

"Right," he says. "Did you know you've got raw sewage coming out down your path?"

"Really?" I say. It seems sensible to play dumb.

"Yes. I'm surprised you can't smell it. It's leaking down to the beach, onto a public area. That's a public health violation. I'm going to have to serve you with a Statutory Nuisance Notice requiring you to get that repaired. Provided you comply within fourteen days, there won't be any further action."

"Right," I say. "We'll get onto that." I don't mention our inability to access the tank, as I know it won't cut any ice.

"Looking at the amount of liquid that's seeping into the soil," he continues, "I'm not convinced that won't render the cliff face unstable. It's chalky here and susceptible to erosion. That's a public safety issue. I'm going to have to get an engineer down here to look at it. We may need to designate that area of the beach out of bounds for now, possibly put some support into the cliff face."

"Right..." I say. "That makes sense." It's one thing after another.

"I do need to let you know," he continues, "if we do that, we'd likely seek to recover the cost of the work from you. It's down to you to ensure private property doesn't damage public property. If I were you, I'd get someone on it as fast as possible before it does any more damage. And obviously, don't use that path."

We watch as the man trudges off.

"Fucking Ron," mutters Nick. But he seems more sad than angry. He sighs.

"So what do we do?" I ask.

"Wait for the engineer I guess."

"No, not about that. About Gavin and Peter."

"I guess they're right," says Nick. "We're stuck with it and now we'll have to get on with it."

I can't believe it. I don't want Nick to be upset, obviously, but I thought he'd be as furious as I am. But he seems so resigned to our fate. It's almost like he's more annoyed with me for stirring it up than he is with them for dropping us into this mess. All the fight has gone out of him.

I decide not to push it. I make us some tea and tell Nick I'm going upstairs to do some work.

But I'm not. I'm determined not to just play dead and roll over.

I search through my files until I come across what I'm after, an email from the solicitor who handled the purchase of this house. David Hughes Associates. I jot down a few notes of things I'm planning to ask about. I'm worried I'll get too angry about how David Hughes has totally messed up and dropped us in it. Having some notes will help me not lose it on the call. *Navigate conflicts with mindfulness, compassion, and wisdom,* as Tiffany would say.

I call the number.

"WHAT THE FUCK, NICK?"

I'm standing at the bottom of the stairs. Nick is still on the sofa, where I left him. His untouched tea sits cold in his cup on the side table.

"What?" He's looking at me. He looks genuinely worried, like someone who has been caught out.

"No more secrets, you said." I can hear the constriction in my throat, feel my face flush. I could cry at any moment – but more from anger than sorrow.

"What?" he says again, like he doesn't very well know what he's been hiding from me.

"I've just been talking to the solicitor who handled us buying this house," I say. "Anything you want to tell me?"

He just stares at me. If I was him, I'm not sure what I'd say at this moment either.

"You knew, Nick. He told you the land had been rezoned, he told you there were boundary issues, and he told you to get more searches done."

"Jesus, Megan, what do you want me to say?" He's jumped up from the sofa and is staring at me.

"He's forwarded me the email he sent you," I yell, waving my phone in front of him. "It's all here. The stuff about the garden, the fact that the septic tank was on the unzoned land, which is now part of next door's garden. He even says *if we proceed with the purchase, it will be against his advice.* You knew all this, Nick, but you told him we were happy to buy anyway."

"We had to make a decision, fast, or we were going to lose the house," he shouts at me, like I'm an idiot who doesn't understand. "We didn't have time to fanny about. We *talked* about this when we first came here."

He's angry. *He* is angry with *me*.

"We *didn't* talk about this," I protest. "If you'd told me what the solicitor said then –"

"Not about *that!*" he barks, interrupting me. "Not that. We talked about not playing safe, taking chances, taking risks. Do you think I'd have got my house in Manchester if I hadn't taken risks? For fuck's sake. We said we were going to go for it!"

He sounds so contemptuous, like I'm the one who has got it wrong, like I'm being stupid. I stand there, open-mouthed, in shock. I can see the sofa has moved as he's jumped up and knocked into the side table. His mug has fallen over and cold tea is running down onto the cream cotton of the sofa.

"Listen," Nick says, his tone softer, "Meg... This house is amazing, we both know that. We've got a bargain. Gavin was being pushy with the timetable and if we hadn't said yes, then and there, we'd have lost it. Yeah, the solicitor said there might be a couple of flies in the ointment, but I figured we should take a chance and go for it."

He comes over and puts his hands on my shoulders, and looks me straight in the eyes.

"It was a calculated risk. I knew that. But that's what I do for a living."

He smiles at me, like the issue is somehow resolved. What does he think I am? He's treating me like Graham the plumber, who never once looked at me, just explained it all to the man in the room. He's acting like it's somehow too complicated for me to fully comprehend.

I get a sudden flashback to that first day in this garden, him holding me by the shoulders just like this, asking me to trust him. Only I don't feel like I'm jumping into an adventure now. I've jumped for the hands waiting to catch me, and he's dropped me, dropped me into this world of shit.

"No more secrets," I say to him again. "You promised me."

"Oh, fuck this!" he exclaims. He storms across the room and out through the front door, slamming it hard as he goes. After a few seconds, I hear his car door shut and the engine rev. There's a spray of gravel as he speeds off the drive, and I listen to the engine note fade until it gets lost in the sound of power tools from next door.

I mop up the puddle of spilt tea and do my best to sponge the rest of it out of the sofa before it stains. I do a few essential work emails. I'm too wound up to eat lunch. Still no sign of Nick. The afternoon gives way to the evening. I'm not hungry, but think I should eat. I cook myself some pasta. I don't call Nick and he doesn't call me. I attempt some yoga, but my head is too full to do it. I take a bath, hoping it might help me to relax. It doesn't. I load the water with bubble bath, preferring the dense perfumed smell to the vague stench of sewage that clings to the air. All the while, my mind keeps replaying our argument over and over. How did our adventure turn so rapidly into this nightmare? I dress for bed, listening to the music that drifts over from next door, some awful film again, with a bass-heavy eighties synth soundtrack and noisy car chases. I read my baby book for a while but it only makes me sadder, then turn off the light and lie in bed, alone.

I MUST HAVE FALLEN asleep because I wake up feeling someone hugging me while I'm curled up on my side. It's dark and I'm confused at first, and I'm not sure whether this is real or another of my dreams, but then I hear Nick's voice and know he's really here.

"I'm sorry, Meg."

I can smell the beer on his breath. I'm not sure what time it is.

"I know I fucked up. I'm sorry. Forgive me, please. I'm sorry."

He's kissing me, pressing himself into my back. I can feel through my nightdress that he is naked.

"Let's talk about things in the morning," I say. I still have my back to him.

"I love you, Meg. I can't believe I have you. I'm so lucky. You're too good for me. I saw how much you loved the house and I just wanted to get it for you. I wanted you to have it. I'm sorry."

He's mumbling a jumble of thoughts. He sounds so sad and fragile. I want to forgive him. All the while he's pressing into me in the dark, cupping my breasts, running his hands along my thighs, hitching my nightdress up.

"I couldn't bear it if I lost you. I'm sorry I messed up. I love you. I promise..."

His words drift into a muddle of incoherent thoughts, and his kissing and stroking becomes more urgent, more sexual. I don't turn over to face him, but I don't push him away either, and I soften slightly and allow his need to be with me drive the moment as we drift into having sex. He is urgent and intense. The room is pitch black, and I feel lost in a void, passive and adrift, like a small boat on a rough sea.

It doesn't last long. He comes to rest, his face buried in the nape of my neck, mumbling something I can't properly hear before the rhythm of his breathing changes and I know he has fallen asleep. His arm is draped over me, his hand resting on my stomach.

I lie there, thinking about our relationship, and our baby just under his hand. I know he is sorry. I know he means it. But I still feel what I've felt all day – a weight, like a lump I'm carrying around inside me. Not the baby. Something else. I want to forgive him. I want to. But I can't.

Everything has changed.

27

FLAGPOLE

It's Saturday. I'm in the kitchen eating a sandwich when I hear a car on the drive. Then there's a knock at the door. I assume it must be some kind of delivery I have to sign for, so I go to answer it.

Pippa and Dermot are standing on the doorstep with a couple of overnight bags.

Shit. With everything that's going on, I've completely forgotten *this* is the weekend we invited them to stay.

"Hello!" I sing out a greeting, hoping they haven't seen the surprise on my face. We all hug on the driveway, and then I lead them inside.

"We weren't sure this was the place," says Pippa. "You can't see anything from the road. Dermot drove up and down the same lane about twenty times before we turned in."

"It's not my fault," says Dermot. "I'm a city boy. I don't understand the countryside. I'm used to the basics, you know, like road signs, road names, that sort of thing."

"Oh shut up, Dermot." Pippa laughs. "Christ, this place is amazing!"

They've dumped their bags by the door and are wandering through the lounge and kitchen, peering up at the gallery above, striding over to the garden doors.

"Oh my God, you're so close to the sea! Dermot, look."

"You guys take a look outside," I say. "I'll make us a drink in a minute. Nick's upstairs. I'll just let him know you're here."

"Right-o," says Dermot, sliding the patio door open.

"Oh, and don't go down the path to the beach," I call to them, not wanting them to start wading through a river of shit in their first five minutes.

Upstairs, I nudge Nick, who rolls over slowly towards me in the bed, still half asleep.

"It's midday. Pippa and Dermot are here," I say urgently. "It's this weekend. We forgot."

"Oh Christ," he mumbles and rolls back over with a pained groan. I can tell from the noise he's still nursing his hangover.

"SORRY ABOUT THE TAKEAWAY," I say.

It's about 8 p.m. We're shovelling down platefuls of surprisingly good Indian food from a place that's just a couple of miles up the road. By now we've explained to our guests the terrible faux pas of forgetting that they were coming. But I've known Pippa long enough for her to find it funny rather than insulting.

"Forget it," says Dermot. "This is delicious. Anyway, what does it matter you forgot to go shopping if you've got a good stash of booze in?"

And we have, cases of the really good stuff from Nick's old cellar. We've been drinking since mid-afternoon. Or rather, these three have. They're all quite drunk. I'm on the soft drinks, of course, and as a result, I've had to tell them that we're pregnant. They're the only people who know, other than Ron and Jackie.

"Don't curries help induce labour?" asks Dermot.

"Yeah, but not in the first ten weeks, you pillock!" Pippa shoves him playfully.

We've been looking at my dream interpretation book. Pippa and Dermot take turns to remember things they've dreamt about and then look the interpretations up. Dermot invents bizarre, ridiculous dreams that always end in blatantly obvious sexual metaphors – huge chimneys, trains thundering through tunnels, the Eiffel Tower, sausages – then acts the simpleton like he has no idea what they could be about as he looks them up, pretending to read the interpretations.

"Your dream can only mean one thing. You're a pervert whose wife should definitely give you more blowjobs."

Pippa screeches with laughter.

"Well, you can't argue with that, Pip," he says, waving the book in the air. "That's not just me saying it. That's science."

It's enormous fun, and for the first time in I don't know how long I feel genuinely relaxed.

I'm on the sofa. Nick is sitting on the floor in front of me, leaning against my legs. He turns and smiles at me, places a hand on my knee. We haven't had a chance to discuss yesterday's argument, and now he's being exceedingly lovely. It could be the drink, which seems to have worked the miracle of curing his hangover. Or maybe he's feeling guilty and making an extra effort. Either way, it's nice to have Pippa and Dermot here, and to have a bit of fun instead of digging away at each other about the neighbours.

We've also told them all about Ron and Jackie. Compressing the whole two-month saga into half an hour of anecdotes makes it sound hilarious to the drunk Pippa and Dermot, who haven't experienced the grinding daily misery of it all. Nick plays up to this, making the Evanses sound like larger-than-life, comic characters. But I can't see it that way. Going over all our encounters again doesn't seem funny to me. I just find it upsetting. I try not to let anyone see it's unsettled me.

"At least your house stinks of curry now instead of shit," laughs Dermot.

"Yeah, sorry about that," says Nick. "Believe it or not, you kind of get used to it."

"You don't," I say.

"What about that party at ours," says Pippa, "where the drains had all gone wrong and we had to hire a Portaloo for the garden?"

That's the party where we first met Gavin and Peter, where this whole house nightmare started.

"Christ, yes," laughs Nick. "Queuing in the freezing cold in your garden waiting for a piss. Remind me why we were doing that."

"We were having work done on the utility room," says Dermot. "We got a bloke in who turned out to be a right cowboy. He fixed a tiny bit of wall for us and then washed a ton of cement down our kitchen sink. Everything hardened up and nothing would drain away. We had all this stuff coming back up the loo and the shower. They had to dig half the garden up in the end and replace the pipework."

The others are laughing, but I'm finding it hard to laugh,

given that we probably have to dig up our entire garden to fix our own sewage problems.

"I think that was when we first met Gavin and Peter," I say casually. "How are they doing? Have you heard from them?"

"I think they're okay," says Dermot. He doesn't say any more.

"Have you got their new number again? I need to ask them about something and I can't seem to get through," I say.

"Oh?" says Dermot. He gets up and wanders to the kitchen window. "I'm sure I have it. I'll dig it out later."

I suddenly worry that Pippa and Dermot know Peter and Gavin are avoiding us and aren't letting on. Is Dermot ducking the conversation?

"It's a shame we can't get down to the beach," says Dermot. "We could have a fire."

"Yeah, shame," says Pippa, raising her eyebrows at me. "A bonfire started by a drunk. Sounds like a great idea."

"D'you think it's too dark to see into next door's garden?" Dermot continues, his face pressed against the blackness of the glass. "Maybe I could go and have a poo in his new shower block, see how he likes it."

"Yeah," laughs Nick. "Or lay a log on his sauna."

They're all giggling at this idea.

"Come on," says Dermot, sliding open the patio door, "let's take a look."

"Really?" asks Nick, half laughing.

"Yeah," says Dermot, stepping outside. "I want to have a look at his flagpole. Look that up in your dream book."

"Okay," says Nick, leaping up and following Dermot. They're both tittering like kids.

"Nick..." I say in a serious tone, trying to call him back.

I'm sober, and the sensible one. This feels like a bad idea. I look at Pippa, hoping for backup.

"They're like bloody schoolboys," she says, but she's laughing, and she gets up and trails after the men to the garden.

I follow Pippa and step outside onto the decking. The sun set an hour ago, but it's been muggy all day and it's a warm evening. Clouds scud across a half moon, casting a shadowy gloom across the garden. The hedges and grass look black in this light, and I can just make out the building work on the edge of our property, like a high, featureless prison wall. The sea is a mass of black somewhere in the distance where the garden disappears into nothing.

I can vaguely see Nick and Dermot moving about on the lawn, their chatter and giggling merging with the soundtrack of the action film Ron must be screening next door.

"What are they doing?" laughs Pippa, as the men shush each other loudly, and I watch their silhouettes move towards next door. "Didn't you say there was a dog?"

"The dog!" I call out to Nick as a warning.

"Here, doggie!" calls Dermot in a half-whisper. Nick and Pippa are laughing. "Woof, woof! Come here, doggie. I've got a nice bone for you..."

We all listen, but all I can hear is the music from the film and the tittering of the men on the lawn.

"No dog," says Dermot. "I'm going in."

"Dermot!" Pippa rasps in a loud schoolmistress-y whisper. "You cannot take a dump in their neighbours' garden."

More tittering.

"Alright, alright," slurs Dermot. "Spoilsport."

I'm relieved, as I hope this means they'll be coming back inside. But I'm out of luck.

"I know!" says Dermot brightly. I can just about make him out, stumbling about on the lawn. He falls over. "Ow."

"What are you doing?" laughs Pippa.

"I'm taking my trousers off, of course. I'm going to put my pants up his flagpole."

"Jesus, Dermot, no!" says Pippa. But from her tone, it's obvious she thinks it's a funny idea, however outrageous. Nick is laughing too and encouraging Dermot. It's only me who has the feeling that this is incredibly foolish.

"Success!" says Dermot. I think I see him get to his feet. He starts to wave something round his head. "Pants at the ready. Tally-ho!"

Dermot's shape moves towards the edge of the garden. Nick's follows. The two of them are lost against the dark of the breeze block wall.

We listen in silence for a moment.

"What are they doing?" asks Pippa. She's half laughing, but I can tell even she is having second thoughts about this. Now we can't see or hear them this doesn't feel remotely funny.

"Nick?" I call. "Nick?"

There's no reply.

Suddenly, a noisy barking goes up from the dogs. I don't think they're on the lawn. It sounds more like they're still in their kennel, but the way the sound drifts around at night it's hard to tell. Then a light goes on in Ron's garden. It's low, hard and bright, like car headlights on full beam. It must be some kind of security light on the back of the house. It all happens very quickly.

I feel horribly powerless not knowing what's happening. I jog from the decking to the edge of the garden, hoping I'll be able to see Nick and Dermot between the patches of building work. As I get there, another noise booms in. It's the soundtrack from the film, louder now Ron has opened his back door and come out onto his deck.

"Hey!" he shouts angrily.

I catch a glimpse of him as he steps down onto his lawn and disappears from view. I only see a flash, but I think he is holding something. A glint of something metal.

I can't see anything now, but I can hear shouting – three voices: Nick, Dermot and Ron – but I can't make out what's being said under the noise of the barking dogs and the movie soundtrack. The security light must be on some kind of motion sensor because it goes out, and everything is dark. The dogs are frantic with agitated whining and howling, and the driving bass of the music is joined by screeching tyres and a gunshot and Pippa screaming out Dermot's name.

I have a sudden horrible feeling when I realise I'm not sure if the gun shot was part of the film or has actually come from the garden.

It's chaos. I stare into the darkness, willing my eyes to pick up some kind of movement.

But I can't see anything.

28

THE WRONG NEIGHBOUR

"He tried to knock my head off with a fucking shovel. He nearly bloody killed me."

Nick is back in our garden, protesting to two police officers. I'm in the kitchen. The patio doors are still open, so I can hear their conversation, particularly Nick, who is speaking at volume. He is extremely agitated. He doesn't seem remotely drunk anymore.

"I never laid a bloody finger on him!" shouts Ron, who is a few feet away, with another two policemen. "Though if I had it would be his own pissing fault. I was defending my property. Bastard hooligans!"

Pippa is on the sofa, agitated. A WPC is sitting next to her.

"Why aren't you looking for Dermot? Why aren't you looking for my husband?"

"We're taking everyone's statements right now," the officer says. "Once we've got things clear, we'll be able to understand what's happened. My colleague is outside looking around now."

"Do you know anything about these, sir?" asks one of the officers with Nick. When I look, I can see he's holding a pair of underpants. Nick laughs.

"They're not mine," he says. "I think they're Dermot's."

"Yes?" says the officer. Unlike Nick, he isn't amused.

The curtains at the front of the house are drawn closed, but through the glass in the front door I can see the flashing blue lights of the police car. Four officers in the garden, another one in here, and another one looking for Dermot. They've sent three cars. The sirens were on when they arrived. I don't think Nick should be laughing.

"Look," says Nick, in the sort of patronising tone that implies he's going to clear everything up and this will all be over, "we were just mucking about. We'd had a bit too much to drink and Dermot... well... he thought it would be funny to put those pants up next door's flagpole. They have a flag-pole in their back garden."

Nick smiles, hoping the police will see the funny side of the prank, which they absolutely don't.

"So," says the other officer, "you admit you were tres-passing in this gentleman's garden?"

"I wouldn't call it that exactly," says Nick. "We were just having a lark."

"Tell that to my wife!" shouts Ron. "She's upstairs, shit-ting herself. Last week he was in our house, threatening me with all sorts, and now he's trying to break into my garden. Christ knows what he's after."

Ron sounds agitated. Is he putting on a show for the police, or have Nick and Dermot genuinely spooked him? Who did he think was coming for him? You don't have guard dogs like that for no reason.

"It's not like that at all," protests Nick. "If anyone was threatening anyone, he was threatening me and Dermot."

"And where is your friend Dermot now?" asks the first officer.

"I don't know," says Nick. "We were in the garden and it was dark. We were just getting to the flagpole when the dogs started barking, and then there were lights and shouting and Evans was waving a shovel about, screaming his head off. It was terrifying. We ran for it. I went for a hedge and managed to keep my head down, then I scarpered back over here. Maybe Dermot lost his bearings or something. I didn't see him after that. Maybe he's hiding in the bushes. He's probably terrified he's gonna get murdered if he comes out."

"Right," says the first officer, looking around the garden. "You and you, have a look around. See if we can find where he's gone to ground."

The other policeman with Nick and one of the ones with Ron head off into Ron's garden. I can see torchlight moving across the lawn intermittently. They call Dermot's name occasionally, like they're trying to call a missing cat in for dinner. The whole thing is surreal. I take a breath and think about how much worse things might have been. Yes, Nick may be in trouble now – but what could have happened if those dogs had been let out? It's too terrifying to think about.

"Right. Mr Evans, in a moment, if you'd like to go with this officer back to your house, we can get a formal statement. And sir..." the policeman who's clearly in charge turns to Nick.

"Nick Greenacre, Officer," says Nick, in a friendly way. He's still trying to take the heat out of the situation.

"Mr Greenacre, I am arresting you on suspicion of trespass with intent to commit a criminal offence."

"What?" Nick's clearly thrown by the way this has ramped up.

Oh, Jesus, I knew going into that garden was a terrible idea. He may not have been savaged by one of Ron's dogs, but Ron has got him another way.

"You do not have to say anything," the policeman continues, "but it may harm your defence if you do not mention when questioned something which you later rely on in court. Anything you do say may be given in evidence. Do you understand?"

"No," says Nick, "I don't bloody understand. He nearly brained me with a pissing shovel."

At that moment a shouting goes up from the end of the garden. I can't make out what's being said. It's one of the policemen, I assume. I see torchlight moving on the lawn. After a moment, there's a crackle on the radio of the officer who just arrested Nick.

"Alpha, this is Delta. Do you copy?"

He reaches for his radio. "Delta, this is Alpha. Copy. Over."

"Alpha, I'm at the end of the garden. I think we've found the other suspect. It looks like he's fallen over the edge of the cliff."

All hell breaks loose. Pippa screams and tries to run into the garden, but she's restrained by the WPC. I go to the open door of the patio, but from the look I get from the police it's clear I shouldn't go outside. The dogs all start howling and barking next door. The other officers are busy radioing their control room for an ambulance and consulting about what to do next, attending to Dermot and dealing with Nick, all in the confusing dark of the garden.

In the middle of all the commotion, I see Ron. He

doesn't look panicked anymore. He's smiling. He looks at the distracted police and then, out of earshot, he leans forward with a smirk. I can just make out the words he mouths to Nick.

"You've fucked with the wrong neighbour."

PART 4

29

MANTRA

The evening unfolds like a nightmare.

Nick is handcuffed and taken away in a police car. An ambulance arrives, and a specialist team get Dermot off the cliff. An air ambulance lands on a nearby stretch of land, so Dermot can be hurried to the mainland. It's clearly very serious. I watch as a team of medics wheel him across the garden strapped to a stretcher. They think he has broken his back.

Pippa is understandably distraught. I try to comfort her, but she is inconsolable, and desperate to know how she can travel with Dermot. I get the feeling she doesn't want to talk to me and suspect that she blames us for drawing them into this terrible mess. Dermot was mucking about, but it's our fault he came into contact with Ron.

They decide to fly Dermot to a trauma unit in Bangor. Pippa can't go in the air ambulance, but two of the police are sent to the hospital in case he regains consciousness and can give a statement. They say Pippa can travel in the car with them. She goes upstairs to get her bags from the spare room. As she hurries out with the police, she barely looks at me. I'm told someone will return to take a statement from me later. Then everyone leaves.

I rattle around, tidying some things on autopilot in a kind of daze. I go to bed and turn out the light. I reach my hand out in the dark and touch the empty side of the bed where Nick would normally be lying, and then I imagine where he must be, on his own, in a cell, waiting to be interviewed. I don't know if that thing in TV dramas is true, that he gets a single phone call, but he hasn't called me. What happens next? Am I supposed to pay bail? Can I take him clothes and a toothbrush? I realise I don't even know where he is.

Then I imagine where Dermot must be lying, in a hospital bed somewhere. Will he have regained consciousness? Or maybe he's in an operating theatre right now? Christ. He fell off a cliff. Is he even alive?

There's no way I can sleep. I have a sudden thought about something, the day after I first saw Ron and Jackie on their drive, the day everything bad began to happen. I turn on the light again and take out my dream journal from the bedside table. I find the entry for that night.

> *Nick and I are driving from Manchester to Anglesey, and when we arrive the house isn't here. Everything else is the same. The garden is here, but no house. I am really upset, but Nick is fine about it. I go to the edge of the cliff and look down and the house is all smashed on the rocks. "The house has fallen off the edge of the cliff," I say. And Nick says, "Don't you remember, that's what it's supposed to be like." Then I wake up.*

I have the awful feeling I am living in that dream.

Dermot has fallen off the edge of the cliff and is smashed on the rocks. And somehow, Nick doesn't share my concern about things. We aren't together on this. I'm upset, and he doesn't help me. I am fenced in by a wall, and I can't escape to the sea, and Nick isn't here when I need him.

The same thought loops in my head. *We shouldn't have come here. We have to get away. We shouldn't have come here. We have to get away.* It merges with the sound of the waves, coming in and going out, and becomes a mantra playing in my mind, over and over, until it's the one thought I have and I fall asleep.

30

SERENITY

The following morning my anxiety ratchets up even further when I get a call from the police asking if they can come and take a statement from me.

An officer shows up and I tell him about the day, the drinking, the silly idea to go into the neighbouring garden to play a prank. I try to be clear about how harmless and ridiculous it all was. Then I find myself drifting back to earlier incidents, the argument in Ron and Jackie's kitchen, the cars meeting face to face on the path. I try to explain how terrible Ron has been in all of this, but as I describe each encounter, I can see how Nick looks like someone who fuelled the fire of this dispute. Once the policeman goes, I don't feel I've helped Nick's case. But hearing myself say it out loud, I'm aware Nick hasn't helped himself in all this either.

I haven't heard or seen anything of Ron and Jackie today. Even the building work and the dogs have gone quiet. I find the silence more disturbing than the usual noise. It's the same horrible feeling I get when I see a spider run across the carpet and disappear under the sofa. Where are they? What are they up to?

I spend an agitated couple of hours wondering what the hell we're going to do next. We absolutely, unquestionably cannot stay in this house, that much is certain. I try to make a plan, but in my unsettled state, I can't get the thoughts straight in my head.

I REMEMBER a time when I was splitting up with Niall, feeling so sad as I looked at two lonely piles of belongings we'd separated. I recall reading something that helped, and search through a couple of books Tiffany recommended until I find the passage in a paperback called *Serenity*:

> *Cultivating contentment with what one has, rather than constantly seeking more, can lead to greater inner peace and fulfilment. Living a simple and frugal lifestyle can reduce the burden of material desires and promote mental well-being.*

I realise we're letting money govern our choices. Maybe if we just get away from this house we can find our way onto some kind of clear path. Sure, this whole Anglesey episode has been bad, it's been an ungodly shitshow of a mess. But it's only three months of our lives. If we get away, it'll be like none of this ever happened, like we dreamt it.

Maybe it's a blessing in disguise that Nick's house sale has been held up. We can go back there and sell this place. Even if we take a loss, we'll be out of here and safely away from Ron – me and Nick and our baby. What's money compared to our mental well-being?

I put a bookmark in the book and decide I'll show it to Nick later when I suggest going back to the house in Manchester.

As I'm reflecting I get a call from Nick. He tells me he's fine. He tries to be upbeat on the call, but I can hear the strain in his voice. He's been bailed and released and is going to be home later. He's just having a meeting with a solicitor.

I figure I'll make us something nice for dinner. I carry on as normal, do some food prep, then I call Pippa to find out how Dermot is getting on. She hasn't replied to the text I sent yesterday, though I can see that she's read it. Her phone goes to voicemail.

I see an email has come in from a company I contacted about septic tank repairs. Depending on the damage, they say work might range from draining and patching the tank internally to digging out and replacing the entire thing. It could cost us thousands – and that's before we factor in digging up and restoring all of Ron and Jackie's building work. This could ruin us. Again, I tell myself it's only money. The priority now is to get away from here.

It's about 4 p.m. when I hear the cab. I hug Nick on the drive. Once I have hold of him, I don't want to let go. He's rigid at first, but then I feel him relax and he leans into me. I don't know how long we stand there.

When we go inside I look at him properly. He looks grey and exhausted, unshaven and with messy hair, his eyes dark and puffy. He can't have got much sleep, and he must be hung over as well.

"I know we need to talk," he says, "but would you be okay if I get a shower and lie down for half an hour?"

I hear the shower running upstairs. I can't imagine how Nick must be feeling about his ordeal, the confusion of emotions he must have on top of being shattered. I make a cup of tea, just in case he wants one, but when I go up, the shower is off and he is already collapsed on the bed. I pull a throw over him and close the curtains, where the late afternoon sun is beginning to dip into the room and hit the bed. I leave him to sleep.

I do a little more cooking and lay out the table nicely. I try to read more of the *Serenity* book, but I have to keep going over the same couple of pages because my brain won't retain the information. I put the book on the table to show Nick later. It gets to 7.30 p.m. and the meal is ready, but I don't have the heart to wake him. I serve food onto a couple of plates and cover them with foil so I can reheat them later.

I'M WATCHING the news on a low volume when Nick finally appears at just after 9 p.m.

"Jesus," he says. "Sorry about that. I'm utterly shattered. I feel like that bastard *did* hit me with a shovel."

He looks across the room, sees the table I've set out nicely, and spots the pans in the kitchen.

"Did you cook?"

"Yeah," I say softly. "Would you like something?"

"Please. I'm absolutely starving."

I go into the kitchen and put both plates on top of saucepans of simmering water to heat up. We sit at the table. I peel back the foil from the plates and Nick shovels the steaming food into his mouth like he hasn't eaten for a week.

"Oh, that's good. I need this," he says. "I feel a bit more human now."

I watch him eat for a while, as I pick at my own food. It's late, and hunger has passed me by. There's so much I want to ask Nick, and tell him about my Manchester plan, but I wait for him to finish eating before I talk. Eventually, he puts his fork down and pushes the plate away.

"Thanks," he says. Then he stares at his plate for a long time. I can feel he's building up to saying something, working out where to start.

"It was such a stupid thing to do," he says quietly, still looking down. "I feel I've messed everything up. With the house, with you, with Dermot. How is he doing? The police said he was in surgery, but they wouldn't tell me much."

"I don't know," I say. "Pippa isn't answering my texts."

"Shit." Nick finally looks up at me with a pained expression. "I'm so sorry."

"Just tell me what happened," I say.

"It was horrible, Meg. I know I was arrested, but they really do treat you like a bloody criminal. The cells are miserable and depressing, and I just kept thinking about you. They left me in there for ages, I don't know why. Finding me a solicitor maybe. Anyway, they interviewed me in the middle of the night, and I explained again how it was all some stupid drunken prank that went wrong. But they kept asking me about next door, suggesting all this stuff about me being threatening with Ron and intimidating him in his own home. It was ridiculous, but they wouldn't let it go. They've decided I'm the bad guy."

This feels so weird, talking about Nick being arrested. How can they possibly think he is the aggressive one?

"What did your solicitor say?" I ask.

"Not much," says Nick. "He looked knackered. They must have woken him up from somewhere, poor sod. I told him about everything and he said it was better to just tell them honestly what happened. I think he was as surprised as

I was when all this crap came up making Ron out to be a real victim."

Nick goes quiet and pokes the last few bits of food around his plate with his fork.

"And?" I say. "What does he think?"

Nick breathes out deeply. "He thinks I don't have much of a defence. If it goes to court, I was trespassing. I've admitted it. I'm technically guilty, he says. It's just about mitigation and whether anyone believes it's serious. We were just putting some pants up a flagpole, for fuck's sake. Hopefully they'll just give me a caution."

"Is that what he thinks? That at the very least you'll get a caution?"

"Yeah," says Nick ruefully. "I think so."

I mull this over.

"Does that mean you'll have a police record?" I ask.

"It does, yeah."

Nick shakes his head. I can see he's kicking himself. How can a stupid, drunken prank get so out of hand? I look at the cover of the *Serenity* book. A young woman is cross-legged with her back to us, sitting under a beautiful willow tree in a tranquil Japanese garden with meticulously arranged stones and a still pond.

Nick sighs again. "There's something else," he says, tentatively.

"What?" I can tell from his tone something bad is coming. What could be worse than this?

"I spoke to work," says Nick. "I had to tell them about the arrest. They're not happy."

I'm confused. "Why did you tell work? You don't know what's going to happen yet."

"I missed a meeting I was supposed to be in today," says

Nick. "Plus, there's a clause in my contract about not bringing the firm into disrepute, or something."

"But you haven't, have you," I say. "At least not until something comes of it."

"Anyway," Nick continues, "I've told them and they're not happy. Well, more than that. I have to leave immediately, or they'll sack me. So I've left."

"Okay," I say. "I guess you were going anyway. And they've been making you do stupid hours while you work out your notice. So maybe it's no bad thing."

"Right," says Nick, "exactly. Only downside is, I'm not getting that share package I'm due."

"What?" I sit there trying to take this all in.

"If I didn't agree, they'd sack me for gross misconduct. I'd never get a reference. So I had to suck it up."

This doesn't sound fair at all. The rug has been pulled out from under everything. "That can't be right," I say.

"Whatever," says Nick, rather sharply, as he gets up. "Right or not right, it's done. It's over. We'll be fine. I'll get something down here like we planned. We'll be fine."

He wanders towards the kitchen with our plates, obviously wanting to end the conversation. Then he pauses and turns back.

"Oh," he says, "and a bit of good news. My house sale went through. So that's Manchester dealt with."

I watch him turn and scrape the remnants of the dinner into the bin. My *Serenity* book lies unopened on the table.

31

INVOICE

I'm woken by voices. This isn't the usual buzz and thud of power tools. This is something different – a chorus of men's voices which appear to be coming from our garden. Nick is asleep and seems dead to the world. My guess is he's still exhausted by his arrest and interview, and so I get up and leave him crashed out. I go quietly downstairs and into the kitchen.

Looking through the back window I can see exactly what is going on. A team of men are erecting a fence along Ron's boundary line. But this isn't the normal sort of fence you'd see in a domestic garden. This is a dense, thick wire mesh, the kind you'd put around a tennis court in a park. Lengths of heavy wire netting are being unrolled from a huge tube and stretched between thick metal supports, several of which have already been dug into the ground. The tops of the supports bend over at an angle, to make it difficult for anyone who tries to climb the fence. The only thing missing is barbed wire.

All I can think is that our garden looks like a tiny, feeble prison yard.

Ron is directing the action, pacing out the line for the fence, barking at the workmen, spurring them on. It's not yet 8 a.m. and the sun hasn't got that hot, but he is beetroot red and sweating copiously from all his marching about, his moist t-shirt clinging to the thick ripples of his body. He grabs one of the men by the collar with his sausage fingers and indicates the location of a pillar. As he does so, he catches sight of me looking out from my kitchen. He beams a broad smile at me and gives a cheery wave.

I step back from the window. There's something even more upsetting about his apparent friendliness than his hostility, acting as if Nick's arrest and Dermot's injury are some trivial spat that can be brushed under the carpet. He's gloating, of course, trying to provoke a reaction, enjoying the chaos and hurt he's caused.

By the time Nick gets up it's nearly lunchtime and the fence is practically finished. He just stands in the kitchen, staring at it. I'm trying to work out what he's thinking. He knows the reason we are trapped here is down to him. Maybe he doesn't want to draw attention to the situation because it will reflect badly on him.

When I realise he's not going to say anything, I head upstairs to my workroom. I need to throw myself into my work. We need the money. Some orders have come in on my website, and I check the stock I have, parcel a few packages up, and set about making some more earrings. It feels good to be doing something constructive.

Early in the afternoon I head downstairs, planning to go out and post my orders. Nick isn't around. I guess he must have headed off to see his solicitor or something. Is this going to be our relationship now, two people going about their tasks, occasionally crossing over at bedtime or breakfast? Whatever the honeymoon period was, I fear it's well and truly over.

Nick's car is gone from the drive, but Pippa's is still out there. I get into my car and drive into the nearest village that has a post office and send my neatly wrapped packages.

As I'm coming back up the drive to the house, Jackie appears next to her *PRIVATE* sign and waves at my car frantically. She's on the drive and I have no option but to stop. I wind my window down but stay in the car with the engine running.

"Hello, luv. How are you doing?" Jackie is all smiles and jolliness, as if there's nothing remotely wrong between us all.

"I'm fine, thanks."

She's wearing another of her long, brightly coloured dresses, like something transplanted from the 1970s. She has a straw hat with an absurdly large brim clamped onto her head with one hand. I wonder if she has some kind of issue with the sun, as she never seems to expose an inch of her body to it.

"And how's the baby doing?" she asks. "Is it kicking yet? I have absolutely no idea about babies. I've never been around the little buggers."

"It won't be kicking for a few weeks yet," I say.

"It must be very odd having something inside you wriggling about," she says. "I only have that with Ron, and that's bad enough!"

She roars with laughter.

"Sorry, luv," she says. "I've got a bloody filthy mind, I'm afraid, and a mouth to go with it."

"Anyway..." I say, making it clear I'm keen to head off.

"I'm sorry about all that nastiness the other day," says Jackie. "It was a shock getting woken up in the middle of the night and all those flashing lights and wotnot. Ron was quite upset about it. He told me to stay in the house. What a to-do, all those police everywhere."

"Yes." I'm not sure what she's expecting me to say.

"Anyway, I'm glad you're okay, sweetheart. And whatever's going on between those boys, it doesn't mean we can't be friends, does it?"

It's the second time she's suggested this. It's bizarre, under the circumstances. Perhaps she's incredibly lonely. I can't imagine what it must be like, living with Ron, but I guess she needs all the friends she can get.

"I really must get back. I'm actually dying for the loo," I lie, trying to escape.

"I won't keep you," says Jackie. "I'm glad I saw you. I wanted to give you this. I was just headed up to yours to post it now."

She hands me an envelope.

"I thought I'd run it up to you, but I'm out of breath just coming this far, and my pissing hat's blown off twice between here and the house."

I look at the envelope and assume it's another invitation for drinks. Why they think we'd ever set foot in their house again is beyond me.

"Thanks for this," I say, waving the envelope. I begin to move the car slowly forwards.

"Bye, luv. See you soon, I hope." Jackie waves at me as I drive off. I wind the window up. I look in my rearview mirror as I head up our fork of the lane, and watch her still waving enthusiastically.

Nick's car is in the driveway. When I go inside he's in

the kitchen. He looks forlorn, and despite everything going on between us, I feel a wave of sympathy. The arrest, and all the stuff with his job... it all feels so unfair. I go over and hug him. He turns and kisses me, and I realise that even in these small moments we can build bridges between us and stay connected. It's us against the world.

"I ran into Jackie on the way back," I say.

"Shame you didn't run *over* Jackie on the way back," quips Nick.

"I think they've invited us for drinks again. Can you believe it?" I drop the envelope down next to Nick and go to the fridge to get myself some water.

"What the –"

He's holding the opened envelope and is staring at the piece of paper he's taken out. He sounds more stunned than angry.

"What the fuck? Look at this!"

I go over and take the paper from him. It's a note from Ron with an invoice attached. It's a bill for half the cost of the garden fence.

"He can't honestly expect we'll pay this, can he?" I ask, dumbfounded.

"He's deliberately trying to wind me up," says Nick. "It won't work!"

But he *is* wound up. He snatches the note from me and thunders across the room to the front door.

"Nick – where are you going?"

"Back in a minute," he says in a steady, determined voice, opening the door.

"Please," I call, "don't do anything stupid."

Slam. The door is shut. He's gone. I sit anxiously for a moment, wondering what to do next. Should I follow him, intervene, drag him back to the house? I don't think I can bear it if something else happens.

After a couple of minutes, I'm relieved when Nick returns unscathed.

"I ripped it up and shoved it through their door," says Nick smugly. He paces around the kitchen, too wired to sit down. "I shouted through the letterbox that he'll have a long fucking wait before they see a penny from us."

Nick's grinning from ear to ear as if this little moment of defiance has allowed him to score a victory. But of course it hasn't. We're at war.

I have the horrible feeling that like all wars, it will get much worse before it gets better.

32

BE CAREFUL

It's been three days now and Pippa hasn't responded to any of my messages.

Because she had to hurry off, she's left a few things here in the house – wash bags and phone chargers and stuff – as well as her car keys and car. I check my insurance and it allows me to drive someone else's vehicle. I decide I need to force the issue, so I send her a text.

Hey, Pippa. Hope things are okay. I have to be in Manchester tomorrow, so I'm going to drive your car over. I'll get to your house about 2 p.m. It would be great to see you, but if you're not there, I'll put the keys through the door. Xxx

After a couple of minutes I can see she's read the message, but she doesn't reply.

. . .

IT'S with some anxiety that I walk up the steps and ring the doorbell of Pippa and Dermot's house. I wait for a moment and it seems like no one is in. But then there's movement behind the stained-glass panel in the door, and finally the door opens and there's Pippa.

"Hi," I say, leaning forward to hug her. I can feel a stiffness in her body, a reluctance to hug me in return. I step back. She looks sad and tired.

"You'd better come in," she says flatly, then turns and wanders up the hallway. I follow her through the house and into the kitchen.

"Tea?" she asks.

"Please," I reply.

She sets about making us tea. The atmosphere is frosty. I can see the kitchen needs a good clean, and the sink has dishes that look like they've been there for a few days.

"How's Dermot?" I ask, while she clatters the cups, opens a cupboard for teabags.

"Not good. I don't know. He's awake now, at least."

She pauses for a long time.

"He's broken his back."

She stops by the kettle. It has boiled and clicked off, but she doesn't pour water into the cups. She just stares at the worktop. "They think the operation went well, but they won't know for a while. They don't know if he'll be able to walk again."

"Oh God, Pippa, I'm so sorry," I say. "I feel so bad about it."

"I wish we hadn't come." She gives me a hard look. "I wish we hadn't visited you. I wish we'd never come anywhere near those people."

"I know," I say. "Me too."

Pippa sighs and pours the water into the mugs.

"How's Dermot doing?" I ask. "You know, in himself?"

"You know Dermot." Pippa laughs humourlessly. "He's being upbeat about stuff. He's always making a joke of it. It's his way. He's amazing. I know he's scared. That night must have been horrible, though he says he can't remember much. It must be terrifying, not knowing what's going to happen in the future."

Pippa passes me my tea.

"Thanks for bringing the car over. It's been a nightmare getting to the hospital without it, to be honest."

She sits down opposite me at the table.

"I know it's not your fault," she says at last. "I'm just so bloody angry about it. They shouldn't have been pissing about like that, the bloody idiots. But even so, it's a big price to pay for one silly mistake."

"Will you send him my love? Tell him we're both thinking of him."

"Sure," says Pippa.

It's strained, but I'm glad we are talking again. I love Pippa. I want to be here for her, and I can't bear the idea she's cut off from me. I hope she'll feel more like my friend again and be able to use me as someone to talk to. I get up, go over and get a biscuit from the jar on the worktop, but only as an excuse to get to the sink. Pippa must be worried sick, too busy and distracted to do anything around the house. I casually fill the sink with hot water, begin to do a bit of washing up.

"Thanks," she says, allowing me to carry on.

"Nick won't say much. All he says is that he was the one getting chased about by a violent psychopath swinging a shovel, but *he* is the one getting painted as the aggressor."

I scrub at a pan irritably with a brush.

"They were both bloody fools to go over there, but it seems so unfair what's happened as a result. Particularly to Dermot, of course."

"I know," says Pippa. We are both silent for a while. How can one tiny moment change the course of your life forever?

"I wondered if Dermot could remember anything," I say, slightly hesitantly. "I mean, anything to support Nick's claim he and Dermot weren't the aggressive ones..."

"I'm not sure," says Pippa tentatively. I can tell she doesn't want to talk about it. "I'll see if he's up to it next time I go in. If it feels right, I'll ask him."

"Thanks," I say. I decide not to push it.

"And what's happening with you and Nick, with the neighbours and stuff?" asks Pippa.

I want to tell her... about the fence; how Nick didn't tell me about the stuff with the house purchase, and how he's now lost his job. I want to tell her we are short of money, and trapped in a house we have fallen out of love with, with neighbours we hate. I want to tell her how my relationship seems to be going from bad to worse. I want to talk to my best and oldest friend about my constant background anxiety. But she already has enough on her plate, so I don't say anything.

"Be careful," says Pippa, out of nowhere.

"What do you mean?" It seems like such an odd thing to say.

"Dermot can't properly remember what happened that night. The police came to interview him. I was in the room with him. He told them what he could – getting pissed, taking his bloody trousers and pants off and going into the garden to look for the flagpole, then the lights and the noise and running..." She trails off.

"What?" I say, sensing something wrong.

"He was joking about it with them, you know, running around in a stranger's garden bollock-naked. It's funny, isn't it?" She laughs fondly. "And that's Dermot's way, to make a joke of it. Probably wanting to put the police at ease, lying in that horrible room with those machines bleeping and tubes coming out of him. But he went quiet at the end, stopped joking. He said he couldn't remember anything, but I could tell something was off with him. Once the police left, I asked him what was going on."

She's suddenly still and serious.

"And?" I ask. "What was it?"

"He said he didn't know how he'd run through that fence and off the cliff. He wasn't sure. It was all very chaotic... But he thought it's possible he didn't fall."

I'm confused. "What do you mean?"

Pippa looks straight at me.

"He thinks maybe he was *thrown* off the cliff."

33

RECKLESS

Pippa runs me into town and drops me at the station. I haven't booked a specific train back. I've just missed one, and there isn't another one for an hour and twenty minutes. I think of going for a coffee, but I don't really want one. Besides, I remember how Niall and I struggled to find anything half decent round this way.

I hang about looking in the shops at the station, trying to kill time – but my thoughts keep going back to Pippa and Dermot, and the shitty world of pain they're in. I do feel better, having seen Pippa, but something has changed. The seriousness of what she's going through casts a shadow over our friendship. Whatever happens to them now, it will always be tainted because of visiting me.

Is it possible that Ron deliberately threw Dermot off the cliff? I've seen Ron in action, but the idea that he might be capable of that sort of violence shifts everything up about a million gears. How can Nick be the one who's been arrested if it's Ron who attempted to murder someone? His arrest makes no sense, and getting thrown out of work because of it seems so unfair. He's been cheated out of that share package we so desperately need to sort the septic tank.

I'm angry now. There's still over an hour before my train. Nick's office is only a minute's walk from here. Before I have second thoughts and back out, I leave the station and walk briskly across Piccadilly Gardens, past the Arndale and into the side streets.

"Paul Overman, please," I say as I get into reception.

I've known Paul for some time. Nick's firm were big on socialising, so we went to several events together. I give my name. I wait while the receptionist calls up to the offices. Then there are questions over whether I have an appointment. The receptionist has a disapproving tone, which only riles me further. I have to wait a while, but eventually, she sends me up in the lift.

"Megan, hello. This is a nice surprise," Paul says as he shows me into his office. I'm sure it *is* a surprise, but I doubt it's a nice one. "How can I help?"

"Look, I'll come straight to the point, Paul. This thing with Nick and our neighbour, it's a bloody terrible situation, but if you knew the guy in question you wouldn't for a moment put the blame on Nick. Plus, we don't even know if it will go to court yet, so I think it's a bit rich you getting rid of him just so you can save yourself a few quid. That money is nothing to you and everything to us, so I hope you'll have the decency to reconsider."

I stop my rant. Paul's been frowning at me silently for most of it.

"I'm not sure what you mean," he says.

"Oh, come on," I scoff, "of course you do. It's a shitty way to behave, and you know it."

"No, Megan," Paul says, quite firmly. "I mean I've no

idea what you're talking about – this incident with a neighbour and Nick being arrested."

"But that's why you've pushed him out," I exclaim.

"No. I know nothing about any of that."

I'm confused.

"We were forced to let Nick go because he made a series of exceptionally bad trades completely outside the scope of how this firm operates and lost a significant amount of money. He was reckless, and he wasn't honest about his dealings. He hid things and he lied to me. The firm had to cover his losses to the tune of... well, let's just say a *lot* of money. *That's* why we let Nick go."

While I'm trying to get my head around what's going on, Paul continues.

"Nick agreed to leave immediately rather than be fired on condition he go without shares. He's lucky he got off so lightly, to be frank. His behaviour was tantamount to gross misconduct. I don't know anything about this other stuff you're talking about. I haven't seen or spoken to Nick for three months."

I'M ON THE TRAIN, heading back home. It's a slow route, stopping every ten minutes or so on its way to Chester.

Three months?

There's a relentlessness to the starting and stopping, speeding up and slowing down, and the churn of passengers getting on and getting off in waves at each halt. It reminds me of the sea, the endless back and forth, and that thought makes the journey feel interminable.

Then we get off at Chester, and I have a twenty-minute

wait in the cold. The station waiting room is locked, and the cafe is long closed.

I'm happy to get on the Wales train for the warmth, but that's about it. Again the train stops practically everywhere. I've got two hours of this.

Three months?

I think about the other stuff Paul said. The lies and deception. The covering up. That's what Nick's done with me, lying to me, keeping information from me, sucking me into this terrible situation I'm struggling to escape.

How else have I been fooled? Is everything about Nick's relationship with me all smoke and mirrors? Nick arriving on the scene and pursuing me so relentlessly, and me falling so profoundly and distractingly in love that it was impossible not to act on my feelings? Nick dazzling me into taking a chance, like he did with those investors before frittering away all their money on bad choices?

I think about Niall again. Was I reckless, leaving him?

On an impulse, I call Niall's mobile. To my surprise, a woman answers. I tell her my name, though it must have come up on his phone, and she tells me he's just on his way. Eventually, he comes on the line.

"Sorry about that," he says. "We've ordered a takeaway and I thought that might be the driver calling. I was just getting out of the shower."

I can tell he's embarrassed. We have a slightly stilted conversation where he explains that the woman who answered is Maya, and they've been dating for a while. I tell him I wasn't calling about anything important, I'll catch him another time, I'll let him go.

"Are you sure?" he asks. I can hear the concern in his

voice, wanting to be certain that he's not somehow leaving me in the lurch.

"No, really, it's fine. Speak soon," I say, and we ring off.

I don't even know why I called him. I'm an idiot. Whatever stupid, unformed, pie-in-the-sky thought I might have had, Niall's clearly moved on. And that's good. I'm happy he has. I really am. Though something about it makes me feel less connected to anything.

The train trundles on. We've crossed into Anglesey now and I'm about fifteen minutes away from Holyhead, where Nick said he'll pick me up. I texted him to say when I was arriving, but I didn't mention anything about visiting his office. I keep going over what I've learnt today, what it all means – and what I'm going to say to Nick when I see him.

Reckless.

Paul's word, that keeps echoing around my brain. Nick was reckless at work and got fired. But that's how he's been with everything to do with Wales. Reckless in the way he agreed to buy the property against the solicitor's advice. Reckless in the loan he took out. Reckless going into Ron's garden and provoking him.

As I exit the train station I can see Nick parked up in his car. When I get in, he leans across and kisses me.

"That's a long day. You must be knackered," he says. "How are you feeling? Okay? How's Pippa?"

I update him on how the conversation went. I don't say anything about Dermot's suspicion that Ron threw him off the cliff. There's other stuff Nick and I need to talk about first. Somehow I manage to bite my tongue until we get home.

The second we get through the door it spills out of me.

"I saw Paul today."

"Paul?" asks Nick casually. I can't tell whether he genuinely hasn't made the connection, or if he's just playing dumb to buy some time.

"Paul Overman," I say. "Your ex-boss."

"Oh, *Paul*." He's taking off his coat and shoes. I notice he doesn't look at me. "Where did you see him? Walking through town or something?"

"No," I say quite lightly. "I went to the office."

"What?" Now I've got his full attention. He's staring at me. "Why? Why would you do that?"

Nick's tone is sharp. He's got that aggressive, chippy tone people adopt when they know they're in the wrong and go defensive.

"I went there standing up for you. Don't I feel the idiot!"

Nick shuffles. "Aren't you going to take your coat off?"

"I don't know," I say, still standing by the front door in my coat and shoes. "I don't know if I'm staying yet or not."

Nick pauses for a moment. Is he planning his next move? Working out how little of the story he can get away with telling me? I can see now he's drip-fed me titbits of information, keeping me in the dark as much as possible. Does he realise I'm finally on to him?

"What did he tell you?" he asks.

"Oh, I'd say pretty much everything." I smile humourlessly.

"About firing me, you mean? He's a bloody hypocrite!" Nick is surprisingly strident. "People give us their money and they want us to make more money with it. They know what they're doing. He knows playing the markets is informed gambling. I was doing my job. Buying and selling shares. It's what we do. Trying to win big is risky, but people know that. It's the first thing we tell them, by law. *The value of your investments may go down as well as up.* We make them sign a piece of paper with that on, for Christ's sake. Yeah, I had a bit of a bad run, but it would have all worked out fine if Paul hadn't waded in and stopped me playing the long game. So it wasn't my fault, Meg. No way. Not at all."

I don't know what I was expecting, but I thought there might be a bit of humility in it, or an apology. Not this angry rant.

"Whatever the reason you left work, you lied to me," I practically shout.

"I wanted to tell you," he says, more softly. "I really did. But we had all the stuff going on here and I didn't want to worry you, what with the house, and then the baby. I didn't want you to have the stress."

He moves towards me, but I step backwards.

"No! I refuse to let you twist it, as if lying to me is somehow doing me a favour. And where were you, for weeks and weeks, when you pretended you were going to work?"

"I was out, following up leads for other jobs. And I had meetings with a solicitor about unfair dismissal, but technically I agreed to leave, so..." He trails off. "The house sale was delayed, so I slept there."

"But we took all the furniture!"

"I got a sleeping bag and a blow-up mattress," says Nick feebly. I picture him lying on the floor of our uncurtained rooms in Manchester on his inflatable mattress. It seems so pathetically sad.

"That's why I was keen for us to come to Anglesey," he says. "To get away from all the shit and have a clean start."

I laugh. "Oh yeah, look how well that's worked." I hear the bitterness in my voice.

"Please, Meg," he says plaintively, "take your coat off."

"Is that why we moved so fast?" It's all falling into place. "You wanted to get away from Manchester as quickly as possible because you'd already been fired? You ignored the solicitor because you wanted to move at any cost."

"It was for us, for you and the baby, and I could see how much you loved this house –"

"Stop it!" I shout. "Don't you dare make it my fault. The record's a bit scratched, don't you think? And I wasn't even pregnant then. Don't make out this isn't all because of you."

"Meg –"

"No," I interrupt him. "I don't want to hear any more, not tonight. Go away. Just leave me alone, please."

"Okay. Okay. I'm sorry."

Nick heads upstairs.

I feel like my eyes have been opened. First, all the stuff with the house, and then that stupid loan – and now this. Nick *is* reckless. He's a gambler. All the things I was drawn to with Nick – his charm, his sense of adventure, the way he pursued me with such relentless intensity... He made me feel I could take risks, take chances, embrace the unknown and leap into an adventure. I found that unbelievably exciting when I first met him, but now it just seems foolhardy and dangerous. Of course, you get an adrenaline rush if you're leaping from one secure hold to another on the trapeze. But if you're performing without a safety net and you start to fall, exhilaration just turns into panic. I feel that movement in my stomach again, that butterfly-sick-anxiety feeling.

I'm still standing here, in the doorway, with my coat and shoes still on.

Wearily, I begin to remove my coat.

Even if I wanted to, there isn't anywhere else for me to go.

34

UNNEIGHBOURLY

It's a baking hot day, the final week of August, the very height of summer. As it's the weekend, I have my workroom window open, confident I'm not going to be deafened by the noise of power tools. It's nice for once to be in here and not feel I'm going to suffocate in the dead, airless heat. However, not long after lunch, the noise of people talking and laughing begins to drift into the house, followed by the thud of music.

I move my chair round the bench and have a look into the neighbours' garden – of course, it's going to be Ron and Jackie making the noise. It looks like they're having some kind of party. The garden is full of thuggish-looking, pasty men and sunburnt women in swimwear, like a grotesque parody of the party Gavin and Peter were having. I watch a few of them wander towards the fence and out of sight and assume the gathering must be to celebrate the completion of their hot tub – though from this side the building still looks like crudely assembled breeze blocks. It must be like going for a dip on a building site.

I can see Ron – enormous, topless and glistening with

sweat – over by a barbecue, onto which he's loading fat hand-fuls of raw sausages, to the consternation of the baying dogs. He's talking volubly to a couple of men next to him. One of them looks familiar and I have a horrible feeling he might be one of the policemen who came here the night Nick was arrested. It would make complete, depressing sense if Ron was best buddies with the police. I can hear snatches of his barking voice over the volume of the music, but can't make out what he's saying. Then I realise the reason I can't piece it together is because he's speaking Welsh. Evans. Of course. Of course he's in with the locals. I've always felt Ron and Jackie were the interlopers, intruding on our lives. But they're the locals and *we're* the unwelcome outsiders.

I climb down carefully and go to my desk, then start to Google on my computer. Eventually, I find what I'm looking for – a news report about Ron Evans' conviction for assault. Aggravated bodily harm, some ugly fight in a pub car park with a chap by the name of Russell Povey. The fact that Ron is a brick shithouse of a man and this lad was only nineteen is mentioned as a significant factor in the attack, as is the fact that the boy was nearly blinded in one eye. Ron pleaded not guilty and claimed self-defence, alleging Povey had hit him first. Povey said he'd never seen Ron before, and the first he knew of his existence was when he was violently attacked as he was leaving the pub. One witness said it looked like Ron would have killed the bloke if his mates hadn't dragged him off. Ron was given six months, but got out in three.

Some other music kicks in, much louder than before. It's deafening. It can't be pleasant for them over in their garden if it's this ear-splittingly loud over here.

I head downstairs to see what Nick makes of it all – but as I come into the kitchen I realise this new music isn't coming from Ron and Jackie's place, but from our house. The patio doors are open, and Nick has dragged our Hi-Fi speakers out onto the decking. The amplifier is halfway across the room, and he has a tangle of extension cables rigged up to get everything as far as it can into the garden.

I turn the amplifier down. Within seconds, Nick thunders inside.

"Leave it!" he snaps and turns the music back up. He spins on his heels and walks back outside. I follow him.

He has both speakers stretched to the extreme of their cables, off the decking and onto the lawn, both pointing directly at Ron and Jackie's house. Some terrible, thundering noise-rock is blaring out, full of machine gun drumming and guttural shouted vocals. It's not like anything I've ever heard Nick listen to before. It must have been chosen for its unpleasantness.

"What's going on?" I shout at Nick over the racket.

"Just playing them at their own game," yells Nick with a grin.

At this point Ron appears at the fencing and starts shouting something our way, but it's impossible to hear him over the music. His face is red and angry. His fingers are clasped tightly on the fence. The mesh presses into the flesh of his bare stomach, and little squares of fat poke through the gaps. When he steps back, white lines criss-cross his body momentarily before they turn red again.

Nick gives Ron a friendly wave and yells in his direction. "How do you like it?" He sits down on a lawn chair he's laid out, leans back in his shorts and t-shirt and cracks open a beer. It's the most relaxed I've seen Nick in weeks.

"What's going on, Nick?" I shout again.

"Thought we could have a party," hollers Nick.

"I don't understand."

Nick doesn't try to explain. He reaches down by the side of his chair and hands me an envelope. It's open, and I take out the folded paper inside. It's dated at the end of last week and must have come in today's post. It's a letter from Ron's solicitor, outlining the stress and anxiety that's been caused to his client, and the fear that he and his wife are living under. I glance up at Ron, who is still ranting away at the fence and looks whatever the polar opposite of fear is.

"I'm on my own property, mate. I can do what I like!" yells Nick glibly, grinning and waving his beer about.

There's a second piece of paper inside the envelope. It's a restraining order, stating that Nick isn't to approach, contact or go within fifty metres of Ron or Jackie on his own property, or one hundred metres elsewhere. He isn't to molest, harass or intimidate either of them. I'm not sure what Nick thinks he's doing with this loud music if not harassing them, but I guess he thinks it lets him score some petty victory within the bounds of the injunction.

I can't cope with this.

I go back upstairs and into my workroom, closing the door behind me. I shut the window. Even so, the sound of Nick's music is almost deafening. I imagine this is how those prisoners in Guantanamo Bay must have felt when soldiers played pop music non-stop at full volume into their cells. I honestly think if this continues I'll go mad.

Slipping on my shoes, I go downstairs again and out of the front door. I don't bother letting Nick know I'm going out. He's so fixated on Ron that I don't think he'd care anyway. I walk down the drive and plan to go up the road a bit, cut across, and find another way down to the beach. If I go far enough and out towards the tide I'm sure I can find a spot where I can't hear music from either house.

I only get as far as the fork in the road when I hear a voice.

"Alright, luv! Oi!"

A brutish little man in swimming trunks, flip flops and a towelling robe is thundering down the gravel towards me. He has a squashed, broken nose and cauliflower ears, and looks like a retired boxer. He must be one of Ron's hot tub posse. I wait for him to catch me up.

"Can you turn that music down?" barks the man, more an order than a question. "Some of us are trying to enjoy a bit of peace and quiet. It's bloody unneighbourly."

Unneighbourly! After everything that's happened, the thought hits me as absurd. I start to laugh. And the more I laugh, the more ridiculous the whole thing feels, this furious man in his little trunks, complaining to me that *I'm* being unneighbourly in the face of the worst case of unneighbourliness I've ever experienced in my life. Hilarious. I laugh and laugh, increasingly hysterically, unable to catch my breath, the absurdity of the situation releasing all the emotional stress like a tap. I fall to my knees, rocking with laughter, no longer able to regulate my feelings now the lid has blown off, some kind of animalistic howl coming out of me as the tears stream down my cheeks.

35

AN IDEA

Nick found me kneeling on the drive, brought me home and took me upstairs. He gently undressed me and picked a few small pieces of gravel out of my knees, where they had pressed into my flesh. I sat placidly on the edge of the bed, staring down at my legs and marvelling that they left distinct white indentations but didn't break the skin.

Maybe that's what a breakdown looks like. I don't know. Anyway, by this point I had stopped laughing or crying and become very still. Nick put me to bed and I was convinced I wouldn't sleep, but I must have drifted off almost immediately, a heavy, dense, thick sleep that smothered me into unconsciousness.

I wake up in my bedroom. Things are quiet. The sun bleeds in at the shaded window, and a small, thin beam of light finds its way through a gap between the curtain and the wall, drawing a brilliant dazzling line that cuts across the floor and up the wall at a crisp angle, ending in a sharp point. Everything is peaceful and relaxed and I feel warm and content.

I lie here for a moment and feel more rested than I have for a long time. I smile when I realise that for once I've had a night uninterrupted by a dream.

"OH, HI," says Nick, standing up to greet me as I come down the stairs. "Are you okay? Can I get you anything? Water or something?"

"No, I'm fine, thanks." I wander to the sofa and sit down near where I can see Nick has been, reading the paper.

"I'm glad you're feeling better," says Nick, settling again. "I was worried about you. Christ, I'm sorry about that music stuff. It was stupid of me."

"Don't worry about it," I say. I still feel incredibly calm. The sun is blazing through the kitchen windows, reflecting off the white walls. It's shimmering and beautiful.

"I've had an idea," I say.

"Oh yes?" Nick gives me his full attention.

"Well, it's more of a decision really," I say. "We're going to sell this house."

Nick sighs. He looks at the ground. I can see he's trying to think carefully about how to reply to me. Eventually, he speaks.

"Meg, sweetheart, you've had a shock and I can understand why you might not be thinking completely straight." He's using the sort of tone you'd use with a confused old person. "Do you remember, we discussed selling the house before? The problem is, all our money is tied up in it, and if we sell now, under the current circumstances, we'll lose a small fortune."

I hold his gaze. I can feel a small smile on my lips. I have the confidence of absolute crystal clarity.

"I don't think you understand," I say, very calmly. "We have to sell this house."

"No, Meg –" Nick starts, but I interrupt him.

"No, Nick. You don't get it. I don't care how much we lose. I don't care how much it makes you feel like you've lost face, or if it means Ron wins. We can't stay here. We can't."

"Megan..."

"We can't. We absolutely can't." I'm still looking directly at him. He tries to stare me down, but I don't look away. I've never been more certain of anything in my life. "If you don't agree, right now, I'm going to go upstairs and get my bag and leave. I either go with you, as soon as we can, or I go on my own, this morning. Either way, I'm going."

Nick looks at me intently. Then he slumps.

"Alright," he says quietly. "We'll go. I'll call some estate agents."

"No need," I say. "I called some when I woke up. They're coming tomorrow afternoon."

I SPEND the rest of the day clearing up around the house. I realise that since all this stuff has happened with Ron and Jackie I've let the place go; I haven't cared what mess we live in and it's become a bit of a shambles. I look at it with fresh eyes and try to imagine myself as an estate agent. It makes me remember the first time I saw it. Regardless of whatever has happened since, I can still recall that awed feeling I got when I walked in here. I need to recreate that.

Nick throws himself into things too. I'd like to believe it's because he supports my decision, but I suspect it's because he's determined to lose as little money as possible on the sale. I guess that's fair enough.

Something about us doing this together – the simple act of hoovering the floor, wiping down the work surfaces – gives me a feeling that there might be a future for us. If we can make this work, get away, make a clean start, then there's a hope. Nick messed up for sure, but I think he's been a bit humbled by the experience.

My phone vibrates a couple of times through the afternoon, and annoyingly it's calls from estate agents cancelling their visits. After the first two messages I'm frustrated, but when another one rings to cancel the appointment I begin to feel this can't be just coincidence. For a moment I wonder if it's Nick who has secretly called them and made them stay away. But then I see his phone charging in the kitchen and realise it's been there the whole time, plugged in the wall for hours while he's been cleaning the bathrooms upstairs. The cancellations can't be down to Nick.

The following morning two more agents leave messages cancelling. I call one of them back to see if I can get to the bottom of it, but all they say is that they have someone off sick. How can I argue with that? It's completely credible. Maybe I'm just being paranoid because I'm so invested in us leaving.

We still have one appointment set up for 3 p.m., and I'm nervous as the time approaches that they simply won't show up. But at five past the hour a Mini pulls into the drive with a huge estate agent's logo painted on a board on the car roof. It's with relief that I let the driver in.

He introduces himself as Chris. He's only just in his twenties, wears a cheap shiny suit that looks a size too small, and has a razored haircut more appropriate for a fifteen-year-old schoolboy. He is loud, brash and cocky, a walking cliche. Maybe they teach them this stuff at estate agent school.

"Would you like a coffee, Chris?" asks Nick. "We're having one."

We've been brewing coffee all morning, hoping it will mask the sewage smell.

"I'm fine, thanks."

We offer to show him the house, but Chris says he'd rather wander around on his own if we're okay with that, so he can 'get the feel of the place'. He proceeds to pace about the space, taking measurements with his little laser machine and jotting down notes on a clipboard. He heads upstairs, then outside, while Nick and I sit on the sofa and act like everything's normal. The dogs next door start up a terrible unfriendly barking as he approaches the fencing. After twenty minutes of inspecting, he comes back inside.

"It's a lovely house," he says. "How long have you been here?"

"Oh I don't know... A bit," says Nick evasively. "We have to move for work reasons."

"Under normal circumstances, people would fall over themselves for a place like this," says Chris. "But there's a couple of issues. Excuse me mentioning it, but the sewage smell. Are you having work done on your drains?"

So much for the coffee.

"Yeah, a small bit of work. Nothing serious." Nick smiles.

"Well," continues Chris, "you need to get that finished off before you show anyone round. That'll kill you dead in the water before you even start."

"Right."

"Also," he continues, "your garden. It's on the small side. And that fence by your neighbour, that's new, is it?"

"Yes."

"Yeah, that's a bit of an eyesore. And their dogs are a bit lively, aren't they? Do they make much noise?"

"Not really, no. You don't notice it after a bit," I lie.

He stares at his notes and scratches his head. I watch a tiny cloud of dandruff sprinkle onto his shoulder, like dust in sunlight. Blow by blow, this terrifyingly young man is destroying any hopes we have of escape.

"Can I ask about that security tape at the end of the garden? And all that scaffolding on the edge of the cliff?"

"Yes," I say. "The council are doing some work to ensure the cliff face is stable. They've put in a bit of support." What I don't tell him is about the truckload of council employees who showed up the other day and proceeded to clad the face of the cliff like a tower block being repaired – or that we'll be footing the bill for that.

"Right," says Chris. "Well, I'll need to talk to my boss about this really, but I'd say that until the drains and the cliff are repaired, it's not worth putting this house on the market."

"Okay," I say, "but let's suppose we *did* put the house on the market as it is; what might we get for it?"

"I couldn't say," says Chris. "It just isn't marketable right now."

"But just for argument's sake," I say. "What would we get for it, in its current condition?"

Chris looks at his notes again. "I think I need to get my boss to give you a ring," he says. "We wouldn't sell the house in its current condition. It wouldn't sell. It wouldn't. Why don't you give us a ring once the drains and cliff are sorted?"

We watch him drive off.

So that's it. No amount of freshly brewed coffee is going to cover up the mess we're in. We're trapped.

36

EARRING

Nick gets a call from his solicitor to tell him they've set a court date. It's much sooner than we were expecting. As it's a bit of an open-and-shut case, with clear evidence and Nick pleading guilty, they can move it through fast. I'm not sure what this means, with everything else hanging over us, but I guess it will be one thing out of the way. Nick heads in to discuss barrister options.

I'm glad to have the place to myself. I have some serious thinking to do. I grab a notebook and jot some thoughts down, hoping things will be clearer if I see them on paper, but when I've finished it's like one of those logic puzzles with conflicting snippets of information that seems impossible to solve:

The septic tank has been leaking for three weeks.
We can't sell the house as it is.
We have to repair the septic tank.
We can't get access to the septic tank to repair it.
I can't stay here as things are.

I have no money to leave and nowhere to go.

It goes round and round in my head like a sudoku where I've filled in a number wrong somewhere and I'll never get it to add up.

I hold the pen hovering over the paper. Is one of the things to add to my list the possibility of leaving Nick? I can't think straight about that either, with all this other stuff going on. Our relationship has taken a battering, but maybe if we were free of this house, things wouldn't seem so bad. It's a massive step, especially with the baby coming. I put my hand on my stomach and feel the small bump.

There's a knock at the front door. I'm not expecting anyone, but with the seemingly endless visits from various engineers, council employees, police and so on, I'm not surprised there might be someone else to add to the catalogue of woes. But when I open the door, I'm shocked by who I see.

Ron.

"Alright, luv? I hope you don't mind me calling uninvited."

He's dressed as usual in shorts, these a ghastly green and orange check pattern. There's a drawstring belt that seems to be made of frayed rope like one of his dogs has chewed on it. It's pulled tight around his massive stomach, which is exposed under a ballooning short-sleeved shirt which he wears unbuttoned. His gut pokes out like a bowling ball. He's got one of those fat stomachs that seems solid, like a hard sphere.

"Okay if I come in?" He's leaning against the door jamb, breathing heavily.

"Actually, I'm busy," I say, still holding the door only half open. No way do I want him in here.

"You really should let me in," says Ron. "I think it'll be in your interest."

He steps forward and pushes against the door. I have a physical reaction to him being so close and step back instinctively. I can feel his huge weight keeping the door open and I know there's no way I could stop him if I wanted to. He's in the house before I can do anything about it. I think it best not to turn it into a confrontation, so I step backwards as if it was my idea to invite him in.

What the hell does he want?

"Don't worry about that restraining order," says Ron in a cheery tone. "I saw soppy bollocks drive off a while back. He's a bit more than one hundred metres away now, isn't he?"

He's been watching the house. He knows I'm on my own.

Ron comes into the hallway and closes the door. He walks into the living room space slowly, looking around and sizing it up, just like Chris the estate agent. Just like I did when I first came here.

"Big old gaff, isn't it?" he says. "First time I've been in here. The fairies who were here before never invited us over. Dunno why."

He looks at the huge stretches of white walls, the high galleried ceiling over the living room, and the minimalist kitchen. "Bit fucking empty, isn't it?" he says. "Looks like you haven't unpacked yet."

"What do you want?" I ask.

"Whoa, little pony, what's your hurry?" says Ron. "We can have a bit of friendly chitchat before business. Maybe we got off on the wrong foot, you and me. No reason we can't start again and make things nice and friendly."

I don't say anything. Not for the first time, it occurs to me I'd much rather he was plain horrible. There's something about him being friendly that's infinitely worse. I feel wrong-footed and uncomfortable.

"What are they, silver?" he asks. It takes me a moment to work out he's looking at my earrings.

"Yes."

"You make them, did you? I seen you're a fancy jewellery maker."

"I did, yes." How does he know about my work?

"Well," says Ron in a syrupy tone, "aren't you the clever little thing?"

He walks over towards me. I back up, but I'm pressed against the kitchen work surface. Ron holds his massive arm out and brushes the hair away from my ear with his thick fingers. He strokes my earlobe gently between his thumb and forefinger.

"Nice," he says, under his breath. I'm terrified of what he'll do next.

"I'd get some for the Princess," he says, "but she likes something a bit more blingy, if you catch my drift. Why put a stud in your lughole when you can wave a chandelier about? If you've got it, flaunt it, I say."

He's still stroking my ear. What has he done, Googled me, looked me up on the internet? I think of my website, photographs of me he must have looked at, my exposed neck, wearing earrings and necklaces. I don't want to show how uncomfortable I feel, so I step sideways and go over to the sink to get a glass of water.

"I'll have one of those while you're there."

I fill a second glass. Reluctantly, I walk back across the kitchen. Once again I'm closer to him than I'd like to be. I extend my arm for him to take it. But he doesn't reach out. I just stand there, holding the glass.

"What's a classy girl like you doing with a scrote like that?" he asks. "Market trader toerag like him? I know the sort. He's a barrow boy made good. A monkey in a suit. He's batting above his average with you, isn't he, luv? What's the appeal? Hung like a racehorse maybe?"

He laughs and takes the water. He gulps it down with a horrible guttural sound, like a gurgling drain. A bit of it runs down his chin but he doesn't wipe it away.

"A beaut like you deserves a proper man."

I back away. "If you don't want anything, I think you should go."

"Impatient little jill, aren't you?" He laughs. "Fair enough. Let's get down to what I come for."

Ron sinks himself into the sofa. It's low and soft, and he doesn't have anything firm to brace himself against. He sort of rolls into it. He isn't able to shift his weight once he's down so just lies there, at a slightly awkward angle. It would be comical if I didn't find everything about him so grotesque. It makes me feel sick having this brute of a man in my home.

"I seen you had one of them fellers round from Pelhams the other day."

Pelhams is the estate agent Chris came from. Nick's isn't the only car he's watched come and go.

"Thinking of selling, are you?" he asks, knowing full well what the answer is. "It's a shame that, you going when you've only just got here. We never even got you over for a barbecue. Your fella came round, of course, but that was under different circumstances."

He laughs, pleased with his joke.

"Still, if you've made your minds up I won't try to persuade you. Quote you a good price, did they?"

"They're working it out now," I lie.

"Yeah, thought not," says Ron. "Maybe you should get a couple of other firms round. I do know a few estate agents as it happens. I could put in a word."

His snide tone confirms it's Ron who is behind all the other estate agents cancelling their appointments. But if he's so hostile to us being here, why is he hellbent on getting in the way of us leaving?

"Or here's an idea," he says. "I might be interested in taking the place off your hands, for the right price."

Is *that* what this is about? Ron wants this house? It can't be that, surely. But maybe this could be a way out for us.

"Oh yes?" I say, as lightly as possible. "What sort of price were you thinking?"

Ron smiles.

Then he names a figure which is a quarter of what we paid. It's laughable. So much so that I actually laugh. Only it isn't remotely funny, because Ron means it.

"Are you laughing at me?" he asks. There's a steeliness in his voice, and I'm reminded just how dangerous he is. All his stupid banter made me forget for a moment what a dangerous, vicious animal I'm dealing with.

"That's a laughable price for this house," I say.

"Is it?" says Ron. "I wouldn't know about that. I don't want the house. I want the land. Try not to let what you think it's worth cloud your judgement, because I'll be knocking the house down."

Christ. He wants to wipe us and all traces of us off the land.

He grins at me repulsively. "You probably wanna take me seriously, because I think this is what's known as a buyer's market."

"No sale, I'm afraid," I say, as forcefully as I can.

Ron rolls over in the sofa and struggles to get up. He's massive and awkward, and it's awful to watch. He gets to his feet and finds his balance.

"You think about it," he says firmly. "You give it a long, hard think. Because you won't be getting offers from anywhere else any time soon. You're sunk in a world of shit. Even your bankrupt trader boyfriend can understand that. Maybe you should have a word with him."

Ron shuffles over to the doorway.

"Tell him your uncle Ron says good luck in court."

And he's gone.

I realise how much I'm shaking from the tension of it all. There's a hollow dent in the sofa where Ron was. I lock the front door and go upstairs, wanting to be out of the space he just occupied. I sit on the bed, unable to work out what to do.

At last, it makes sense. The hostility, the damage to our septic tank, the fencing us in. His plan all along has been to drive us away and have the land for himself.

And what makes it worse, he knows we don't have any other options.

37

CAKES

I'm in the kitchen cleaning when I look up and see him at the patio window.

Ron.

The shock of seeing his grinning red face pressed against the glass makes me leap back in horror. Nick's still out at his solicitor's meeting. Ron must know he's not back yet because he's been watching Nick's car. He knows I'm alone. I don't understand why he's returned, or how he's got round to the back of the house. Whatever he wants, it can't be good.

His hand is on the door handle and before I know it, he's sliding it open. I'm positive the door was locked. How can this be happening? Maybe he secretly unlocked it when he was in the kitchen earlier. He's opened the door completely and now he's stepped inside.

I'm frozen with fear. I should run, but I'm too terrified to do anything. Slowly, Ron walks towards me. He reaches out his hand, and I can see his fat fingers are greasy from sweat. They look grubby with something, and I realise it's traces of smeared blood, blood from the dead rabbits. He doesn't say anything. All I can hear is the sound of my own breathing, in and out, merging with the sound of the sea coming in and out on the beach outside – all of it underscored by the thin whine of the black dog on the lawn next door, baying plaintively for something.

Ron's hand stretches out and strokes a stray lock of hair away from my ear. His fingers begin to massage my earlobe, playing with the stud in my ear. He grasps the earring between thumb and forefinger and squeezes. I can feel the pressure.

Then suddenly, and with incredible force, he yanks his arm downwards and rips the earring through my ear.

I jolt awake. The patch of bed I'm lying on is drenched in sweat.

In the kitchen, I write the dream in my notebook. Having filled in as much detail as possible, I flick back through the other dreams I've recorded since we got here ten weeks ago, most of them bleak and miserable, upsetting nightmares or transparent metaphors for the awful situation I find myself in, out of my depth, trapped, powerless and anxious, mainly about Ron, but – terrible to admit it to myself – increasingly about Nick.

By now it's obvious that writing these dreams down doesn't stop them. If anything it's prolonging the experience, going over it the following morning, reliving all the details rather than putting it behind me and getting on with my day. But whenever I pick up the notebook I can't help thinking about Mum, that it was her idea to write the nightmares down. Somehow the process keeps a connection with her alive, and I can't just give it up.

Nick comes downstairs and kisses the back of my neck as

if things are fine between us. He spots the notebook as he does so.

"Another one?" he asks.

"Yeah," I say, closing the journal. I don't want to go over it with him. I've already told him about Ron's visit yesterday and his insulting offer for our house. I don't want Nick to know how much it rattled me, that Ron has invaded my dreams as well as my kitchen.

Nick suggests we should head out somewhere today for a walk and some lunch, get away from the house and try to make a concrete plan around our options. I feel guilty about my list, that one of my options is thinking about leaving Nick. We need to talk about it, but I don't have the energy until I'm clearer in my own mind. Nick sounds more upbeat than he has for a while and I get the idea he might have a plan of his own. I really hope he has. In any case, it will do us both good to have a change of scenery.

NICK DRIVES us out along the coastal paths to North Stack Lighthouse. This isn't the one we used to be able to see from our garden, but a much larger, more remote lighthouse at the northern tip of Anglesey.

It's the final week of summer holidays before kids go back to school, and I'm anticipating crowds or people, but when we arrive at the small car park, there's only one or two cars. There's no sign of a lighthouse. Nick gets out his phone and, after researching for a bit, discovers that the place he was thinking of was *South* Stack Lighthouse. Where he's brought us doesn't have a lighthouse at all, but a boring-looking building that houses a fog warning system. We've come all this way for nothing. Nick calculates the time it would take us to get to the other place as he'd intended, but that will leave us too late for a booking he's made for lunch.

All in all, it's a bit of a disaster. I tell Nick it doesn't matter, as we lean against the car and stare at the choppy sea, my hair whipping against my face and the vague taste of sea salt on my lips. But I can tell Nick is annoyed with himself. Yet another thing that hasn't gone to plan.

We give it five minutes before we're both getting cold, then we get back in the car.

"Actually, I'm pretty hungry," I say. "I could do with an early lunch."

He's chosen a cafe called The Cormorant, which we drove past once but have never visited before. An old shop bell chimes above the front door as we come in. It's quiet inside. It's an old building that's been knocked through, but it has an eccentric layout. People must have been tiny in the old days, because the size of the rooms and the low ceiling make it feel like a doll's house. But the oddness of it somehow adds to the charm. There only seems to be one lady working here. She's in her seventies I'd guess, and tiny like the cafe. She greets us warmly in a thick Welsh accent as we come in and directs us to a small table out of the way in a nook at the back. The walls are covered in shelves with a host of bric-a-brac, porcelain ornaments and glass animals, old chintzy dolls and such.

Because it seems like the place to do it, we order a high tea. Our pot of tea comes with mismatched cups and saucers, and we get plates of sandwiches with the crusts cut off and a cake stand with scones, fairy cakes and slices of Battenburg. It's unbelievably cute. The playfulness of it all works its way into us. I park my worries about Nick and we share excited smiles about cucumber sandwiches and Viennese whirls, and compare notes about our childhood favourite treats. We're more relaxed than we've been in ages, and it gives me a feeling of hope for our future. As if on cue, the baby kicks and starts doing somersaults. Nick shuffles his chair around the table and puts his hand on my belly.

"That's it, little E.T.," he says. "You give that Swiss roll a good old kicking."

The woman comes over to check on us. The plates and cake stand are still half full.

"How are we doing?" she asks.

"Absolutely delicious," I say, "but I think it's defeated us."

"Not to worry," she says, clearing the plates, "I can pop those in a box for you to take home."

"Thank you."

"Just across for your holidays, are you?" asks the woman.

"No," I say. "We live here. We just moved to Bae Breuddwyd – you know, Dreamer's Cove."

"Dreamer's Cove, is it?" she says. "The 'Bae' part is right enough. 'Breuddwyd' isn't quite the whole of it though. It *could* mean dream. I'd say maybe more a hope or a yearning. A vision even. It could be a whim, or a pipe dream. It's very beautiful on that coast, but those lighthouses are there for a reason. Many's the voyage that got crashed back onto the rocks. I guess one person's dream is another person's nightmare." She chuckles. "I'll get that cake box."

"Oh. 'Nightmare Bay'," I say once she's gone. "That sounds more accurate."

"That's her party trick, I bet," says Nick, "putting the frighteners up the tourists. The locals as well, if they're not born and bred."

"Talking of nightmares," I say, keeping it light, "did you

have any thoughts about what we do next about the house? About Ron?"

Nick pulls his chair closer to mine. His eyes flit briefly around the cafe. A couple of people have come in at the far end, but it's still very quiet.

"I have, as it happens. I've been thinking it over quite a bit, and I've had an idea." He looks at me steadily. "We could kill him."

I laugh. "Yeah, that would certainly solve all our problems."

But Nick isn't laughing. It takes me a moment to register that he's not joking.

"Think about it. If I lure him to the edge of the cliff, I reckon I can push him over. He's big, but that could work in my favour. You know, gravity, inertia, whatever it is. Once he topples, he won't be able to stop himself. It'll look like an accident."

I stare at him, bemused.

"I'd need you to back me up," he continues. "He likes you, doesn't he? Maybe we could use you to lure him over?"

I'm stunned. "Are you serious?"

Nick looks at me. I think he's trying to read my take on it all. I'm just about to react when the cafe woman comes back.

"Here you go. These'll keep you going for a while." She places a cake box on the table, stamped with an ink-block outline of a cormorant, and tied with a ribbon.

"Thanks," says Nick casually.

"I've taken the liberty of bringing the bill," she continues. "We are cash only, I'm afraid."

I'm desperate to ask Nick what the hell he's thinking, but we have to wait as the woman stands over us, smiling, while Nick rifles through his wallet. He takes out some notes and puts them on the small silver plate with the folded bill.

"I'll get your change," she says and wanders off.

"What the *fuck*, Nick?" I whisper under my breath.

"Shhhh," he whispers, tilting his head to indicate that the woman is still at the front of the shop, at an old till, possibly still within earshot. We wait in awkward silence for a few moments until our change is returned to us.

"What the hell are you thinking?" I exclaim through gritted teeth once we're alone again.

"Nothing," says Nick, forcing a smile. "Forget it. I was joking. A bad joke, that's all."

Problem is, I am absolutely certain that he wasn't joking. He's trying to back away from it as if it never really happened. Only, it did happen. Nick suggested we murder Ron.

The bell on the cafe door tinkles in the background.

"Nick, we need to talk about this, because –"

"Shhh!" whispers Nick sharply, interrupting me. I follow his gaze to the door to see who has just come in.

It's Jackie. She's with another couple of women. I can't hear what she's saying, but she speaks warmly to the cafe owner before being seated at a table off to one side from the entrance. They're out of sight, but I can hear Jackie's screeching laugh echoing around the cafe, spoiling the charm of the place with its vulgar brashness.

"The injunction," says Nick. "It covers her as well. I can't be this close to her."

"Nick –"

"If she sees me, I could be arrested. I'd breach my bail. I could go to prison."

As inconspicuously as possible, we put our coats on,

creeping about in silence like a couple of shame-faced criminals. As soon as Nick sees I'm ready he gives me a nod, then
turns his head to one side as he walks briskly across the cafe
towards the door. I follow him, flushing with embarrassment.
First I'm driven out of my own home, and now I have to
sneak around on the entire island like a bloody thief in the
night, head bowed like a leper.

We walk to the car in silence. Nick starts driving. He
puts the radio on and I can tell he's trying to act like everything is normal. Like he hasn't just suggested we murder
someone. I feel numb. Who is this person I'm sitting next to?
I thought Ron was our problem... but is Nick potentially
violent, like Ron? How have I ended up here?

"Damn!" says Nick, so forcefully that it makes me jump.

"What?" I say. I wonder if he's going to come clean about
what just happened. Is he going to talk to me honestly about
it? But all he says is:

"We forgot the cakes."

38

SUPPORT NETWORK

I rerun the conversation over and over in my head. Nick claims he made a bad joke that fell flat. He said it again in the car on the way home. But something about it amplifies all the doubts I've been having about him. *Reckless.* It seems so apposite. What could be more reckless a solution to our problems with Ron than killing him?

"Megan?

The midwife leads me from the waiting room into her office. It's a typical NHS set-up, all blue-grey and clinical. Everything looks like it's seen better days. She reminds me of her name, Sue. It's the same kind but efficient woman I saw last time. I'm here for my routine 12-week antenatal check-up. As we came through, I noticed Sue pause briefly in the waiting room doorway to see if anyone else was going to get up and join me. But I'm here on my own. I can't quite explain to myself why I didn't tell Nick about the appointment, even before his disturbing suggestion about Ron.

Sue doesn't question the fact that I'm here on my own. They must see people in all sorts of situations. But it does feel odd to me. I'm holding Nick at arm's length. There are question marks over our future. I'm withdrawing and trying to rely more on myself. I wonder if this is a maternal thing too, instinctively protecting my baby from anything that might harm it – including its father.

Sue bombards me with a mass of information sheets on nutrition and diet, exercises, and a timetable of various antenatal classes. There are workshops on breastfeeding and leaflets about maternity benefits I might be able to claim. It occurs to me that our financial situation with the house could be so dire I might need to claim these. She asks me about what support network I'll have through pregnancy, labour and beyond. I mention Nick but don't go into any detail. I don't want to think for now whether I do have him as a support. Sooner or later I'll have to work that out for myself.

"Have you drunk water?" she asks.

I have, as it told me to in my letter. "I could do with a pee."

"Right," says Sue. "Let's get you scanned first, then you can go for a wee and bring me a sample."

She leads me into another room and I meet someone called Amida who explains she is a sonographer and is going to give me an ultrasound to check the baby's development and confirm my due date. I assume I'll have to strip down to a gown, but she asks me to lie on a couch covered in blue crinkly paper, lower my trousers to my hips and pull my top up. She tucks more blue paper around the waist of my trousers and my top, then squeezes cold gel on my tummy and begins to rub the probe over me. It's quite hard pressure, but it doesn't hurt.

The screen she's looking at is angled towards her. She's quiet and concentrates on her work and the image. The room is silent. For the first time, I worry that she might find something wrong. She moves the probe again and I hear the digital whoosh of a heartbeat, in and out. It's fast, like a little bird, like the sea in fast-forward.

"That sounds good," says Amida, and I feel a little wave of relief.

"Thanks," I say. "I don't want to know the sex."

I didn't know I wanted to keep this secret until right now.

"Don't worry," says Amida, "I can't tell that for sure anyway until your next scan in six weeks."

"Ah, okay."

"I can tell you how many babies you're having though," says Amida.

Oh God. I hadn't for a moment considered I could be having more than one.

"Would you like to see?" she asks.

"Yes, please," I say.

She swings the screen round so I can see it. It takes me a moment to work out what I'm looking at, but Amida talks me through the image. A single, healthy baby. She moves the probe a little more and then clicks a button. A small printout of the image emerges from a slot. She hands me a roll of tissue and I wipe my tummy down and get dressed.

Back in Sue's room, she gives me a small plastic pot and sends me off to the toilets to have a pee and get a urine sample. I sit in the cubicle, relieved to be peeing and relieved that my baby is healthy. I feel the stress lift off me with the good news, and only at this moment do I realise how worried I've been. I return to Sue's office with a bit of a spring in my step.

Sue does some tests on me. She measures my height and

weight and takes a medical history. She asks about my
parents, and though it makes me a bit sad to think they're not
around to see their grandchild, she assures me that their
conditions are unlikely to be hereditary and aren't relevant
factors in the health of the baby. She takes my blood pressure. I feel the cuff tighten around my arm and then softly
deflate as the machine exhales. She stops talking as she
makes a note of the result.

"That's a little high," she says. "Let's take it again."

She repeats the procedure.

"Do you have a history of high blood pressure?" she asks.

"No," I say, "I don't."

She has been quite straightforward to this point, but now
she looks worried.

"Well, it's unusually high, to be honest. It may just be all
the excitement of today, but I think we need to keep an eye
on you. I want you to make an appointment with your GP
and I'll send him a note. We'll get the results of your urine
test back in a few days, but I'm going to take some bloods
now so we can check you out."

I turn my head away while she takes a blood sample.

"Are you under any unusual stress at the moment?"

Unusual stress? Where do I start? I live next door to a
psychopath, my garden smells like a sewer and is fenced in
like a prison yard. I've lost all my money, my boyfriend is
about to go on trial for trespassing and he's suggested we
murder someone.

"We've just moved house..." I say weakly.

"Let me give you these," says Sue. She reaches for
another pile of leaflets. These are all about well-being and
mental health, counselling services and so forth. There's one
on mindfulness and yoga, and I realise I haven't thought

about Tiffany and my spiritual well-being for days. It seems like rearranging deckchairs on the Titanic.

"Can we talk about your support network again?" asks Sue. "Is there a reason you've come on your own today?"

I realise without my parents, with Pippa so distant, and with Nick as he is, I *don't* have a support network. Christ, I can't even be honest with my midwife.

My breathing starts to get quicker. I feel lightheaded. I can't catch my breath and I begin to panic. My chest tightens. I reach out and grab the edge of the table to steady myself, to keep a grasp on something solid.

Sue puts her hand on my arm. "Breathe, breathe," she says, as if I'm going into labour.

I don't want her to know why I'm panicking, but my concern about that only makes me panic more. I'm clammy and sweaty. I feel like I could be sick, or pass out. I look at my hand, the knuckles white where I'm gripping the desk. Somehow, looking at my hand brings me back into the room. I focus on my hand, my arm, my chest. The room stops spinning. I'm aware of my breathing and I instinctively think of the exercises I learnt with Tiffany. I manage to slow my breathing down and feel some of the tension leave my body. I relax a little into the chair. The feeling I might faint passes.

"Tell me what's going on," says Sue.

I know I've had a panic attack, but I don't want to talk about it, about all the things that are making me panic.

"Asthma," I lie.

"Do you have your inhaler?" she asks.

"They don't work for me," I say. Another lie. Maybe I'm talking rubbish. They thought I might have asthma when I was about twelve, did some tests and gave me an inhaler for about a week. But it was just a chest infection and I never used an inhaler again.

Sue gives me a glass of water. She asks me to wait and tells me she wants me to talk to a doctor. Her tone makes it clear there's no point protesting – and in any case, I feel a bit wobbly still and couldn't go anywhere right now. After a while, I'm led into another room where a doctor runs through my medical history and looks at my notes. He asks me again about asthma and I say the same thing as before, that I have it occasionally and the inhalers don't work for me.

"There's no record of that in your adult history," he says. But he seems to accept it. He says there's an increased risk from it during pregnancy, which I don't worry about as I know I'm making stuff up and I don't have asthma. I have plenty of other stuff to worry about anyway.

He looks at my records again and writes me a prescription for a number of things – iron tablets, vitamin supplements, something for the blood pressure I think. By now I'm struggling to listen and just want to be out of here.

"Thanks," I say, forcing a smile which I hope will convince him to stop asking me any more awkward questions.

"Fill those prescriptions at the pharmacy downstairs. I'll call your doctor, and I want you to come back and see us in two weeks."

IN THE CAR PARK, I sit in the driver's seat of the car and cry uncontrollably. Though I've underplayed it in Sue's office, I feel overwhelmingly guilty. What Nick and I have done, where we've put ourselves, could be damaging me and my baby. A bag of tablets and the leaflets are piled up on the passenger seat next to me: gestational diabetes; preeclampsia; anaemia; depression and anxiety; postpartum psychosis; OCD; loss of identity. I feel like I'm barely holding it together. I clutch the tiny ultrasound printout and worry about what I'm going to do next.

I'm startled by a knock on my car window.

It's Jackie.

For a moment I panic, thinking she must have followed me here. But then I remember her telling me about her visits to this hospital for her veins. She makes an odd flapping gesture with her hand, and I realise she wants me to wind my window down.

"Megan, luv, are you okay? Open the door. I'm getting in."

Without further ado, Jackie waddles around to the passenger side of the car, opens the door and wedges herself in awkwardly, shoving the leaflets and pills to one side. Christ, I must look a wreck.

"Ow, you fucker!" she exclaims. I look down and see she has a large white dressing on the back of her leg. "Pardon my French, luv. I've just had my calf lasered and it stings like a bastard."

She sees the ultrasound picture I'm holding. She reaches out and takes it.

"Is this the little baban? Not much of a looker, is he?" She laughs.

I'm trying to get control of my tears. I really don't want to be crying in front of Jackie, of all people, but I can't seem to stop myself.

"Oh, don't mind me, luv," says Jackie. "I was just trying to lighten the mood, silly cow that I am. Why don't you tell me all about it?"

"I'm fine," I say. "I was just heading home."

"You're not fine," says Jackie forcefully. "You're a bloody state. Poor girl like you, in the middle of all this mess and muddle. All this stuff with your fella and my Ron, and you with a baby to worry about. It's no wonder you're having a little weepie on your ownsome."

There's something about how she talks to me, her bluff directness, that feels refreshing after all the creeping about and secrets. She reminds me of Mum.

"I've said it before, and I'll say it again," she continues, "whatever's going on between those two, it doesn't mean *we* can't be friends. Us girls have got to stick together. You need something, petal, you just ask me."

She puts her thick, heavy hand reassuringly on my arm.

"I love the bones of Ron, but he's no angel, let me tell you. He's left me to deal with shit on my own many a time. When he gets into his work, he's not all laughs and jokes, that's for sure. They like to be all big and macho, but they're like useless little children, aren't they? Men can be proper cunts sometimes, excuse the expression. It's women who hold it all together. We're the strong ones. So you dry your eyes, luv. Don't let the fuckers grind you down."

She reaches into her handbag and pulls out a clump of tissues.

"Blow your nose. Now, are you okay to drive?"

I'm not crying anymore. "Yes, I am."

"Good," she says, opening her door. "I'm off to get me nails done. Don't be a stranger." And with that, she's out and limping purposefully across the car park.

In the middle of everything, can *Jackie Evans* really be the best support network I have?

39

BREATHE

Nick pokes a bowl of muesli with a spoon, clearly with no appetite.

It's the day of his trial. He's wearing a smart suit, the one he'd been putting on every day when he headed off pretending to go to work. Now at least he has a real reason to wear it.

"Are you sure you don't want me to come?"

He looks up at me. "Really, I don't want you to. You know what the midwife said. If you can avoid any more stress, you should."

He scrapes the contents of his bowl into the food waste bin.

"Anyway," he says, "it's all going to be pretty quick. I was drunk in someone's garden. Nothing bad happened – well, not to Evans anyway. I'm pleading guilty. I'll be in and out. My barrister says I'll just get a slap on the wrist."

He smiles reassuringly. Since that horrible visit to the midwife, I've been doing everything I can to deal with my stress. The doctor can tell me about my blood pressure, but he doesn't know all the things I'm not telling him, what's been happening at home. That's the stuff I need to change.

I still feel guilty about the impact I might be having on the baby's health. There's a section in some of the books about yoga during pregnancy, and I've been trying some of those exercises. Taking my physical and mental health seriously seems to be having an effect. I feel better.

Searching for exercises, there's a phrase on Tiffany's website I come across that sticks in my mind, and I jot it down on a piece of paper:

> *All difficult experiences are impermanent. The mountain is in front of us, we climb the mountain, we come down the mountain and the mountain is behind us. Cultivate patience, resilience, and acceptance. Breathe and move forward.*

I hope I'll feel more positive about my future with Nick once the mountain of his trial is out of the way. He hasn't mentioned our conversation in the cafe again. The one about killing Ron. Maybe he *was* joking.

The other thing I've been thinking about since my midwife visit is Jackie. She seems to like me, in spite of everything that's been going on. Once the trial is over, things will hopefully cool down between Nick and Ron. Then I plan to go to Jackie and see if we can get access to their garden and our septic tank. Fix that, and we have a chance of selling the house. Maybe we won't get what we paid for it, but we'll certainly get more than Ron offered us. We'll be able to salvage something. We'll be able to leave. I should try to make things work with Nick if I can.

Breathe and move forward.

Nick leaves for court, and I rattle around the house trying to occupy myself. I do a bit of yoga. But it's impossible to focus. All I can think about is Nick's trial. It feels stressful not knowing what's happening. I quickly get dressed and make the drive to Llandudno.

I'VE NEVER BEEN in a court before. It's bland from the outside, the sort of anonymous 1970s redbrick civic building that could be a town hall, an arts centre or a school. There's a security point when I arrive, and a uniformed guard puts my bag through a scanner as if I'm at the airport. I walk through a metal detector and get my bag. He asks me to turn my phone off. Everyone speaks in hushed tones as if we're in a library or a church.

He directs me up some stairs to the public gallery. It's a narrow room with two rows of hard seats overlooking the main court space. A man and a woman in their forties sit at one end, looking miserable. I don't want Nick to know I'm here or be surprised if he sees me, so I pick a chair on the back row, figuring if I lean back I'll be out of sight.

A case is underway, about the extension of some pub hours around an upcoming bank holiday. It's something that sounds routine, and it's over quickly. One group of people process out and another group enter, including a young man in his late teens or early twenties. The couple near me in the gallery shift their attention visibly, and I figure they must be the lad's parents.

The case is announced, which concerns a driving offence. The boy has been caught speeding and driving without insurance. He's pleaded guilty and his barrister makes some kind of argument in mitigation about his occupation as a plumber's apprentice and how much he needs to be able to drive for work. The boy looks sick and his parents are holding hands. I feel sorry for them.

The magistrate listens carefully and then consults briefly with someone sitting near her. She addresses the room. The insurance thing is serious, but she recognises he needs to drive for work. She bans him for three months, gives him points on his licence and a small fine. The boy and his parents look relieved, and the whole process seems very considerate and fair. As the man and woman leave the gallery, I feel reassured that Nick's going to get a sensible hearing. Surely the injustice of him being here will be obvious for everyone to see.

Another group come in. I spot Nick brought in through a door and I lean back, making sure he can't see me. I'm nervous, and I feel my heart beating faster. There's some administrative business where charges are read. Nick confirms his name and address, swears an oath, and gives his guilty plea. I can't see anything because I'm leaning so far back, but I can hear the nervous catch in his voice.

Much like the case before, Nick's barrister starts making a plea in mitigation on Nick's behalf. He talks about the foolishness of the act, that Nick was drunk and silly, but is full of remorse. There was no damage caused and no criminal intent. It's everything we've been saying for weeks.

Then the magistrate says before sentencing she believes there is a victim impact statement. I hear movement in the room and then someone is asked to confirm their name.

"Ron Evans."

My heart nearly leaps out of my chest. Ron is here.

I dare to lean forward until I can peek over the railing to see him. Instead of his usual t-shirt and shorts, Ron is in a suit. He somehow doesn't look as massive in his dark, tailored outfit. He looks respectable. He takes a sheet of paper from his pocket and unfolds it.

"Madam Magistrate," reads Ron, in a sombre, courteous tone, "I am giving this witness impact statement on behalf of myself and my wife to explain the profound impact this incident has had on our lives. We experienced a harrowing invasion of our property, shattering the sanctity of our home and creating a sense of fear that stays with us to this day."

He's laying it on thick. He sounds genuinely worried. Has he got someone to write this for him?

"We felt utterly defenceless. I was personally threatened by the intruder, who was wielding a wooden beam and exhibited menacing behaviour."

"That's rubbish!" a voice shouts out. It's Nick. He's lost his cool. There's some shushing and Nick is warned to stay quiet during evidence. I have a sinking feeling that shouting out like this will be a black mark against his character. It makes him look hot-headed.

Ron continues. "His demeanour was hostile and aggressive. I felt as though I was staring into the eyes of pure malevolence."

This seems designed to sound as bad as possible. It's such a gothically odd way to describe something, but it makes an impression – especially as Nick has just shown himself so angry.

"The safety and security of our home has been shattered. We now feel a constant sense of unease and apprehension."

I think about Ron and Jackie's hot tub party the week after Nick was arrested. They didn't seem very uneasy then.

"Since that night, I am nervous and have trouble sleeping. The trauma of the event has taken a toll on my wife's mental well-being, and she has been forced to seek medication for her nerves."

Nick's right. It's all rubbish. But somehow it's highly convincing rubbish.

"Madam, the trespassing incident has left an indelible mark on our lives, and the lingering fear that he may return. We implore the court to consider the profound impact on us and to administer the most severe punishment to ensure that justice is served. Thank you for considering this statement."

"Thank you, Mr Evans."

I hear the scrape of a chair as Ron leaves the witness box.

I'm worried now. Nick's excuses for doing something drunk and stupid feel pathetic in the face of what Ron is suggesting he's going through. It's all lies – but if I was the magistrate, I'm sure it would have an effect on me.

Things only get worse when the magistrate starts the sentencing. She reveals that Nick has a prior conviction for criminal damage from years earlier, something he's never told me and which I knew nothing about. What the hell? In an instant I realise Nick didn't tell me to stay away to protect me from stress. He was protecting himself and yet another bloody secret.

The magistrate says that this indicates a pattern of behaviour, and that although this incident on its own is relatively trivial, in combination with Ron's statement and Nick's prior conviction, it makes things more serious.

Nick gets a 3-month prison sentence, suspended for two years.

Breathe and move on was the plan.

But how in God's name do we move on from this?

40

A SUDDEN SHIFT

I'm in the corner of a cafe trying to process what just happened.

Those words from Ron's statement in court echo around my head: *I felt as though I was staring into the eyes of pure malevolence.*

Is that really Nick? It was so dark that night I have no idea what really happened. Plus, Nick has previous convictions. He's done something like this before. And with the mood he was in that evening, maybe he really did threaten Ron. He even joked to me that we kill him. If that *was* a joke.

I search on my phone and find a local news story about Nick's earlier conviction. He was found guilty of 'violent affray' when he was in his early twenties. There was some kind of pub brawl and Nick ended up being fined and having to do community service.

Like the magistrate said, there's a pattern emerging around Nick's behaviour. From the start I found him exciting and adventurous, but now I stop and reconsider. It reminds me of the way he pursued me, hot-headed, determined, and impetuous. I got carried along in the moment. But what if I hadn't? What would he have done to me then? Nick's all charismatic energy when things are going his way. But now I see he's a liability when things go against him. Dangerous even.

WHEN I GET HOME I think about confronting Nick – but instead, I wait to see what he's going to tell me. A kind of test. The truth is, there's been a sudden shift in how I think of him. He's lost my trust. I'm building a wall to protect myself. I'm no longer sure I should let him in.

"Hi!" he calls brightly as he comes through the front door. He finds me in the kitchen and kisses me. "Well, thank God that's over."

"How was it?" I ask.

"My barrister was right," says Nick. "In and out, slap on the wrist, that's the end of it."

I leave a pause in case he's going to say any more, but he doesn't.

"Are you okay if I go up and get out of this suit, take a quick shower?"

"Sure," I say. And he heads upstairs.

So, there it is – yet another lie. Nothing about the suspended prison sentence; nothing about the prior conviction. I add it to my mental list of half-truths and deceptions. That's how we're living now – keeping secrets from each other.

I'm overwhelmed by a wave of anxiety. This can't go on. I've been here with Nick less than three months, but it dawns on me that I've made a terrible mistake. I thought the enemy was outside, was Ron. But all along the enemy was Nick, here, *inside the house!*

I have to do something now. If I want something to change, I have to change it myself.

I text Pippa asking if I can come and visit for a few days. I can't let Nick suspect what I'm doing. I sneak around the house, deciding what essentials I need. I find a suitcase and put a few things in it, hiding it far under our bed where Nick won't see it. I haven't told him about me watching him in court, so he has no reason to suspect what I'm planning – that I'm going to leave him.

I need money. I work on the assumption I'll never see a penny of what I've lost in this house. How will I live? I'll just have to start again. I look round my workroom and wonder what I can do about my workbench and tools. I email the craft centre in Manchester to see if there's a unit I can rent cheaply, which is how I started after university. I can work from there until I get back on my feet.

I start looking up Nick's old conviction again, to see if I can learn any more about it. I open a couple of pages, but before I can look properly, a text comes back from Pippa. Dermot is coming out of hospital next week. She's having to make adaptations to the house while he's learning to walk again. Probably best if I don't come to stay for a few months.

Shit. I can't stay there.

The following day, I act as normal as possible. Nick and I have breakfast and chat about nothing, trivia, the weather. He has his big secrets and I have mine.

I go up to the workroom and start completing orders at a blistering pace, hoping I can earn a little cash, in case I need to go to a hotel or something. I make necklace after necklace.

"See you later!" Nick calls from downstairs. Then I hear

the front door slam shut. I listen for the sound of his car engine disappearing down the drive. Then silence. I have no idea where he's going and I realise I don't care.

The house is more peaceful than it's been for a long time. It occurs to me that since Ron and Jackie's hot tub party there hasn't been any building noise. I guess they must have completed the work. There's been the odd sound of films at night, but even that has been quieter. Maybe Ron's new cinema is soundproofed. Even the dogs have been more subdued. I notice the vague whiff of sewage is still there every time I come back to the house. But once I've been home for a while, I don't even smell that anymore. I had a student flat once that was right next to a railway line, but after a couple of months I stopped hearing the trains alto-gether. I guess you can get used to anything if it goes on long enough.

I begin to wonder what it would be like if I lived in the house on my own. Just me and the baby. I'd have some of the view from the garden. It's a bit of a walk on the long route, but I could still get down to the beach. I close my eyes and listen to the sea again, coming in and out, regular, reassuring, reliable. It feels like the whole world is breathing in and out, and for a moment I feel at one with it. Breathe, and move on.

I open my laptop and search, then make a phone call to a local locksmith. He can come in a couple of hours. I hang up. I've done it on the spur of the moment and now I must think the details through. If I'm fast, all the locks will be changed by the time Nick is back. If I'm going to persuade him to leave, he'll need some clothes. I figure I can take my own things out of the case under the bed and put some of Nick's in it and leave it on the front drive.

He's bound to try the locks. He'll think his key is faulty.

He'll go round the back and try the patio door, but the key for that only works on the handles on the inside. He'll try the front door again. He'll work out what's happened. Maybe he'll just take the suitcase and go. Perhaps he'll hammer on the door, and shout, call my name and curse. Maybe he'll be so loud that Ron and Jackie will come out. I'll reason with him through the letterbox – or better, through an upstairs window. Perhaps he'll try to break in. I can barricade myself in one of the rooms, push my workbench against the door, call the police. It might suit me better if he does that, now he has a suspended sentence. They'll put him in prison. I don't know if I want that – but I do want him gone.

While I'm thinking it all through, I hear something. I realise it's the dog at the back of the house. It must be the black one that's usually in the garden. It's whining, but it sounds different to normal. It's like a distressed baby, calling for attention. It's tied up and wants someone to rescue it, but no one's coming.

I go to my workroom and move my chair to the window. I stand up and lean across, pressing my face against the glass so I can see into Ron and Jackie's garden. There's Ron, sprawled on a towel on the grass, baking in the sun, arms and legs splayed out, like he's been dropped there from a great height. I can see the base of the flagpole, with its chain attached. The chain snakes across the grass and disappears behind a section of wall. I can't see the dog, but I can still hear it whining pitifully. It sounds so sad. Why is Ron listening to the dog and doing nothing? How can he just lie there and hear it suffering and not help? I stand up on tiptoes and lean further so I can see what's wrong with it.

There's a sudden shift. The chair beneath me slides sideways with a jerk, its legs making a sharp scraping sound against the wooden floor. I feel my body snap sideways and I topple quickly, a feeling of weightlessness in my stomach like I'm in a car going over a bump. In blind panic, I grab at the window, but there's nothing to get hold of on the thin window frame and smooth glass. My legs kick out, catching on the corner of the workbench and flipping me faster to my side.

My head slams against the floor.

41

CORTICOSTEROIDS

I must have blacked out briefly. I get up from the workroom floor and feel dizzy. I make it to the bedroom and lie down on the bed. I doze a little, and then I hear Nick downstairs. He comes up to find me and is concerned about the bang on my head, which must look bad as he sees it instantly. He wants me to go to the hospital, but I tell him I feel fine, the baby is fine, that I just need to sleep off my headache. He brings me water, closes the curtains, and goes out but leaves the door open.

I doze. At one point I think I hear a knock at the door, then voices. Then silence. I'm snoozing and it's possible it's just the rags of a dream I'm having. I wonder why I can't hear the dog on the lawn anymore.

I wake again and realise I'd drifted into a heavy sleep. I have no idea how long I've been up here, but it's still light. I have a throbbing headache. I put my fingers to my temple and feel a huge lump where my head must have hit the floor.

I remember a dream I was having. I am out in the garden, repairing the septic tank. I'm tearing up Ron and Jackie's

THE WRONG NEIGHBOUR   239

patio, smashing down their buildings with a sledgehammer, ripping up their sundeck. I'm frantic. I'm up a ladder, throwing the decking from their garden over the fence and down the cliff where Dermot fell. Then inexplicably I'm Dermot, falling down the side of the cliff, crashing on the rocks. Then I'm me again, falling from the ladder, smashing onto the decking below, in pain, in agony, rushed to the hospital just like Dermot was, in a wheelchair, relieved to find I can still move my legs – but then discovering to my horror I have lost the baby. Then crying, inconsolable, with Nick just standing there, looking at me.

It's horrible. I'm glad I don't have my dream diary in the room because this isn't something I want to write down and go over again. Awake or asleep, everything is blending into one long nightmare.

I'm thirsty. I reach for the glass of water Nick brought in, but it's empty. I must have drunk it between bouts of sleeping. I pick up the glass and get up to go to the bathroom to get more water. That's when I see it, on the sheets where I was lying.

A small patch of blood.

I LIE on the couch in the ultrasound room, in a paper gown. Nick is by my side, holding my hand. He looks grey with anxiety. I feel completely detached from him. All I can think is that I may have lost my baby, and somehow that will all have been his fault.

A technician who isn't Amina puts gel on my stomach and begins to sweep across me with the probe. It's horribly silent in the room. Then, after what seems like ages, I hear the reassuring whoosh of a heartbeat.

"There's baby," says the technician, "fit and well."

Nick exhales deeply. He squeezes my hand and I instinctively squeeze back.

"Now then," says the technician, "let's see what's going on with you..."

I get a long look over. I give more blood. My head is inspected and dressed. Finally, after a couple of hours, I'm given the verdict. The ultrasound confirms I've had a 'sub-chorionic hematoma', a bleed between the wall of my uterus and the membrane surrounding the baby. It's quite common, I'm told – about one in fifty women have them – and it's nothing to be unduly concerned about. It was probably brought on by the fall and explains the small amount of bleeding I had. The baby is fine, and there aren't any future implications for the pregnancy if I'm sensible. They'll give me regular scans. I must rest. They also think I may have a mild concussion.

"With head injuries, it's best not to be left alone for twenty-four hours," says the doctor. "Will someone be with you?"

"Yes," says Nick. "I'll be there."

So, far from moving out, Nick's now become my nurse.

WHEN WE GET HOME, I tell Nick I'm feeling tired from the stress of the hospital visit and that I'm going to lie down for a bit.

"You go up. I'll make us something to eat," he says.

"Don't worry about me. I'm not really hungry. You make yourself something."

"Okay," he says and kisses me. He's gentle and kind.

Maybe the shock of seeing me like that has switched something in him.

In reality, I want space to figure out what I'm going to do now my plan to move Nick out has been interrupted.

I go into my workroom. My work chair is back behind my bench. Nick must have been in here and seen where it was, tipped up on the floor. My laptop is still on the bench and I suddenly remember the last thing I was looking at. I open the lid and go to the internet page I was reading – the one about Nick's previous conviction. I can't remember whether I left my laptop open or closed. Has Nick seen this? Does he know what I know?

I take the laptop into the bedroom and start to search for other reports about the case. I flick through a couple of sites, reading what I can. Then I come across a news report on Nick's conviction that catches my eye.

Local Man Convicted of Criminal Damage in Pub Car Park

Nicholas Greenacre was convicted of criminal damage in connection with an incident of vandalism that occurred in the parking lot of the Green Oak Pub last month. Greenacre, 22, was arrested at the scene.

According to pub landlord Harold Blackburn, the incident was one of many in recent months. "This is a nice family venue, but attacks on cars parked at the pub are putting off customers and crippling trade," he said.

The owner of the damaged car, who wished to remain

anonymous, described the encounter as harrowing, stating, "I saw the vandal attacking my car in broad daylight. When I confronted him, I felt as though I was staring into the eyes of pure malevolence."

The court handed down a fine of £500, with Mr Greenacre also ordered to undertake fifty hours of community service.

There's one phrase that particularly grabs my attention: *I felt as though I was staring into the eyes of pure malevolence.* It's exactly the wording Ron used in his witness statement. He must have read this article. He looked up Nick's past court case, then talked about him in a way that suggests a pattern of behaviour. Ron was trying to get Nick sent to prison.

"HEY, WHAT ARE YOU DOING DOWNSTAIRS?"

Nick is at the cooker, frying something. He's surprised to see me.

"You need to tell me about this," I say, putting my laptop down on the table, still open on the old news story about Nick's conviction.

Nick looks at it. He bows his head for a moment and I wonder if he's going to come out with another lie. But then he looks straight at me.

"We were just twenty or so," he says. "Our friend Jonnie was going out with this terrible girl, and as a wind-up I sprayed a load of stuff on his car in shaving foam – 'Just Married', and other stupid things. A cock and balls. Puerile, juvenile stuff. I covered it in tinsel and threw glitter all over it. It was a joke. We were in the pub car park. Everyone was laughing, even Jonnie. Then he got a bucket of water from the pub and started washing it off. Trouble was, all the glitter started getting rubbed all over the car and scratched up the paintwork. Tiny scratches, but not good, you know. We had a stupid argument about it and he wouldn't back down in front of the girl. I ended up getting arrested. It was just a bloody stupid joke that went wrong."

There's real regret in his voice.

"I was in the court," I say. "This week. I heard about it. I heard Ron's statement."

Again, I'm expecting Nick might kick off, but he just hangs his head.

"And what about this?" I ask, pointing out the line in the news story that Ron also used in court. *I felt as though I was staring into the eyes of pure malevolence.*

"That must have been Jonnie, twatting about," says Nick. "Who talks like that?"

He looks at me pleadingly.

"I never threatened Evans with a bit of wood. I didn't. *He* threatened *me*. Whatever you think of me, I promise you I'm not that."

I think back to Nick suggesting we kill Ron. He's told so many lies now I'm not sure what to believe.

"Listen, Megan, I won't try to downplay everything I've done. I know I've messed up. But you have to remember the real bad guy is Ron. He's manipulated every opportunity to make things worse. He built his house here and he wants this land – not just his garden, but our garden too, and the bit our house is on. He wants the whole cliff to himself, and he'll stop at nothing to get it."

I nod. That's all true. But I don't tell Nick what I'm really thinking. That things between us are over.

As if he can read my mind, Nick says, "I know you're thinking of leaving me."

"What makes you think that?"

"I found a half-packed suitcase under the bed. And while you were sleeping, I answered the door to a locksmith."

So now he knows all my secrets. I wonder where we go next.

"I also found these," says Nick. He reaches across the worktop and produces all the tablets the doctor at the hospital prescribed. "The vitamins and iron I understand. But what about these?"

He rattles a plastic tub of tablets. I read the label. *Corticosteroids.*

"High blood pressure, I think."

"No, they're not," says Nick. "I looked them up. They're for asthma."

"Oh yes, that's right," I say. I don't tell him about my panic attack, or the asthma story I invented.

"Look, Meg, I know we've hit a really rough patch, and I know you don't really trust me right now, so much so that you're thinking of leaving. But I think there's a reason for that. Hear me out, please. I looked the tablets up. Listen to this."

He takes his phone out and reads to me. "*Corticosteroids. Side effects can include, fatigue, loss of appetite, muscle weakness...*" He looks up from his phone. "That could explain your fall." He continues to read, more pointedly now. "*Problems with mood swings, behaviour, and other psychological effects, such as confusion, anxiety, and, in rare cases, paranoid delusions.*"

He lowers his phone and looks at me.

"I know I've fucked up, but not so much you'd think we're finished. This would make sense of why you felt so strongly about it all. I think maybe you reacted so strongly to me and wanted to lock me out because you were on the drugs. Yeah?"

I think about it. It makes complete sense.

"Yes," I say, "that all adds up. I didn't know about those side effects. But now I hear you describe them, I can completely see how that makes sense."

Nick heaves a massive sigh of relief.

"Thank God," he says, rushing over to me and pulling me into a tight hug. "I couldn't bear it if I lost you, Meg. You're everything to me. You're my entire world. I'd do anything for you. I'd die for you. You know that, don't you?"

"Yes," I whisper to him, hugging him back. "Yes, I know."

He lets go of me, goes back to the counter and picks up the tablets.

"Then let's get rid of these bloody things and get back on track." He throws the tub of tablets into the bin. "We'll work it out, Meg. We will. You and me against the world."

He takes me by the hand. We go upstairs and undress. We slip into bed. I curl up on my side and Nick cradles me, stroking my hair. I listen to his breathing as it becomes heavier, and his hand comes to rest on my neck and he falls asleep.

I think about what he just told me, that my extreme anxiety about him and my lack of trust in him have been caused by the side effects of the tablets. It does make complete sense.

But the tablets are for asthma. I don't have asthma. I made it up. And because of that, I haven't taken any tablets.

Though I won't tell Nick this, my feelings of anxiety and mistrust in him aren't side effects. They are very, very real.

42

SNAP

When I come down for breakfast, Nick is at the kitchen table, staring at a pile of letters. He looks lost.

"What is it?" I ask.

He picks up the pile and shuffles through them.

"It's everything. Invoice from my solicitor, bill from the council for work on the cliff, notice of legal action if we don't do something about the sewage leak." He drops the letters on the table and sighs. "Jesus, Meg, we're completely fucked."

Since our heart to heart yesterday, Nick seems completely confident we're back as a team. He's gone from hiding everything to sharing everything.

"I've been trying to get work," he says ruefully, "but no one will touch me with a barge pole on this sodding island. Ron must have put the word out. The bastard's really got it in for us."

"We knew that."

"I know, but I'm so bloody angry with myself making it so easy for him. Every wrong choice there was to make, I made it. It's like I've handed him everything on a plate."

"We'll work it out," I say. Though in truth, I can't see any way we can work it out.

"I just spend all my time fuming about it," says Nick. "I have all these fantasies about what I'd love to do to him. How to get revenge."

He catches himself.

"I don't mean being violent to him, like that joke I made the other day you took the wrong way. I want to smash his house up. I think about seeing his car somewhere and keying it. I want to rip the electricity out of his stupid cinema and piss in his hot tub and kidnap all his dogs."

He's a mess of pent-up emotions.

"Don't worry," he says, "I won't. I'm not going to drop you and little E.T. in it any more than I have already." He gives me a smile. "Besides, I've actually got a job interview later today. I don't think I'll create the right impression with Ron's blood spattered all down my suit."

Nick leaves an hour or so later. He puts on a brave face as he heads to his interview. He explains it's something to do with telecoms marketing, that it could be quite interesting. It doesn't *sound* at all interesting. He acts positive, but I think he's anticipating yet another rejection.

I look out of the kitchen window and wonder how things can have altered so quickly. We moved here only three months ago, and in that short time every element of our lives has changed.

It's early September and the summer is still beautiful. The light is incredibly bright in here and it reflects and amplifies off the white walls. I slide the patio doors open and let the cooling breeze blow in. The sea air diffuses the stuffy sewage smell, and it occurs to me that locking myself inside with the stale air is contributing to feeling like a prisoner.

I grab a yoga book and head out into the garden. Despite what's going on with the house and with Nick, I'm determined not to let it impact my baby. I look at some of the stretches and breathing exercises in the pregnancy section and realise that I know quite a lot of this stuff already from my classes with Tiffany.

I close my eyes and feel the sun on my face. I put the flat of my hand gently on my little bump and focus on what's going on in the moment, feeling connected to my body. Instead of fretting that my dreams are coming to an end, I get a strong sense I'm at the beginning of something. Maybe this is my big adventure. Maybe this is what's important and none of the other things matter. Maybe it's the baby's hands that are waiting to catch me.

"Nice day for it."

I'm pulled out of my reverie by the sound of his voice. Ron.

I open my eyes and look over to where he's standing, in his garden. He has the fat fingers of one hand clasped around the chain-link fence, grinning at me like a naughty schoolboy leering through the playground railings. I try to ignore him and turn back to my book. I can feel the tension in my shoulders, but I refuse to let him see I'm rattled.

"Nice to see you in court the other day," he says.

I have no idea how he knows I was there, but remember he is mates with the police. He's probably connected everywhere, to everyone.

"Important to see justice being served," he goes on. "I thought he was jammy not to get banged up, but there you go. Then again, he might have liked it in stir. Pretty boy like him could make some nice new friends. Very popular in the showers, if you get my drift."

He jabs one of his fat fingers back and forth through a hole in the fence and roars at his own disgusting joke. I refuse to listen to any more of this. I get up to go inside.

"Hang about, luv," he says. "I only come over to give you something from Jackie. She got a present for you, seeing as you're up the duff."

He picks up a plain paper carrier bag and reaches inside. He brings out a small plastic doll. He cradles it in his arms as if it's a real baby.

"I think she might have wanted her own kids," he says. "She's interested enough in yours. She dotes on them dogs like they sprung out of her own fanny. I never wanted them though. So that's that."

Not for the first time, I imagine what it must be like for Jackie, living with Ron, subjected to this, day after day. I look at him, like a gargantuan chubby baby himself, rocking the doll in his arms. It's dressed like a newborn. Seeing him hold it makes me uncomfortable.

"Maybe this wouldn't be so bad though," he says. "Once you've popped it out, you could drop it round ours and we could babysit if you fancy a night out. Let the little fella meet his uncle Ron."

He tosses the doll up and down in the air as if it's a toddler. I watch it arc through the air. I can't help thinking of Ron tossing rabbits onto his lawn for the dogs.

"Or I could come to yours," he says. "I'm just next door. It's easy as pie for me to come over and get hold of him. Ain't that right, little fella?"

He grins at the doll in a cheesy way and gives me a wink.

"Of course, if you sell me the house, it won't be as easy for me to visit you, will it?"

The blatant threat in what he's saying chills me to the bone. I make to go inside.

"Don't forget this," Ron shouts behind me. I turn to see him loft the doll in the air. It flies over the top of the fence, wheeling through the air. I try to catch it, but don't get there in time and it crashes down on the lawn by my feet in a splayed heap.

WHEN NICK COMES HOME, I'm in the living room holding the doll and the ultrasound scan of our baby. He starts telling me about the interview, that he hasn't got the job. I can hear he's wound up, but I don't take most of it in. After a moment, he spots how upset I am and asks what's wrong. I tell him all about my encounter with Ron, and the way he implicitly threatened our baby if we don't sell him the house.

Before I know it, Nick's thundering across the room and out of the front door. I don't know what he's planning, but it can't be good.

I leap up as well and fly out after him. Nick is already a long way down the drive, striding purposefully, almost running. I have to break into a trot to follow. He gets to the fork in the path and kicks out violently at Ron's *PRIVATE* sign. There's a loud snap as the post breaks, the wood splintering and falling to the ground. He keeps marching ahead, turning up Ron and Jackie's drive and out of sight behind the hedge.

As I get to the sign I look down. There's exposed cable, where the post has snapped near the base. The cable runs up the length of the post and to the top of the sign. It's not just a sign, but has a small security camera fitted as well. *That's how Ron knew when Nick wasn't in the house.*

Then it dawns on me. He knows Nick is on his way now. He's ready for him. This is exactly what he wanted.

"Nick!" I call in warning, but Nick doesn't stop.

He's twenty feet from Ron's house when the front door bursts open. I expect Ron to come charging out. But it isn't Ron who's waiting to greet Nick.

It's the dog.

"FASS!" shouts Ron as he appears in the doorway. The black dog thunders forward like a bullet, and before Nick has a chance to slow down, the dog leaps at him, hitting him full-force. Nick is knocked backwards and lands on the ground hard. His instinct is to put his hands up to protect his face, but the dog follows its training and clamps its vice-like jaws onto Nick's forearm.

Nick gives a scream of pain. He's yelling and crying, clearly terrified and in agony. The dog is making horrifying snarling sounds and shaking him like a rag doll. I don't know what to do. I want to help, but I know I can't. It's awful, but I can't look away. I want to cover my ears so I don't hear the sound, but I know Nick will still be yelling.

I hear a horrifying snap, like the one where Nick kicked down the sign, except I know this time the dog's jaws have snapped Nick's arm. Nick gives a high, piercing scream. It's the worst sound I've ever heard.

Ron has walked slowly out of the house to where the dog is savaging Nick on the ground. He looks on, grinning.

"That's right, son, you shout out. If it's not hurting, it's not working." He just stands over them calmly as he watches the dog rip away at Nick's shattered arm.

"Lass es!" Ron calls finally, and the dog immediately lets

go and steps back, moves to Ron's side, looking up at him. I can see the dark blood around its black mouth, its jaws open. The dog is panting with the effort it's put into the attack, its teeth red. Nick rolls onto his side, cradling his tattered arm, moaning. Ron looks at me.

"You probably want to phone an ambulance, luv. I wouldn't be surprised if that smarts a bit."

And with that, Ron and the dog go back into the house.

43

PADLOCK

Now I'm the one waiting at the hospital while Nick gets treated.

The damage to his arm is so bad they hurry him into emergency surgery. Someone finds me in the waiting room a few hours later. He's out of theatre and in the recovery room. They've had to pin the broken arm, and repair severed tendons and arteries. He lost a lot of blood. There's significant muscle damage. They've managed to save the arm at least, they say, inadvertently making it clear just how bad things might have been. Only time will tell what sort of recovery he makes and whether he gets full movement back.

They suggest I go home for the night and come to see him tomorrow. I drive back, making a diversion on my way to a hardware shop where I buy some bolts and padlocks, a screwdriver and whatever other tools I might need. It's dark by the time I reach the house. At the fork in the path, my headlights catch the *PRIVATE* sign, which has been repaired. I guess that must mean the camera has been repaired too. Ron will know I'm home.

Pulling into the driveway, I spot something on the step of the house. When I get to the door I see it's a bunch of flowers. I pull the tiny envelope out of the bouquet. It has Nick's name on it. I open it and take out a card.

Get well soon, Nick. Best wishes, Ron and Jackie.

I put the flowers and the card in the rubbish bin.

When I get inside, I take my coat off and set about fitting the extra locks. I turn on as few lights as possible so I'll be harder to locate from outside. I can get that locksmith back in the next day or two to do a better job, but for now I fix a couple of bolts to the front door and a couple to the patio door. I push the bolts across and attach heavy padlocks to them.

I go up to bed, using the torch on my phone to navigate the stairs. I wash and get undressed, then slip into bed with my phone next to me. If Ron tries to get in, he'll have to smash glass and I'll hear him. I set up one of the buttons on my phone as a shortcut to dial 999.

I lie there for ages, convinced I won't sleep, but I must nod off eventually, because the next thing I know a thin light is bleeding through my curtains. It's just before 6 a.m. I lie there, piecing together the memory of the dream I just had. It's more of a feeling than a memory, a heavy blanket of anxiety that lies over me. None of it makes sense logically, but there's a mix of related images. I'm standing in the garden, looking at where the baby has fallen over. He's not moving, and his limbs are twisted at odd angles. I pick him up and tell him he'll be okay, even though I know he won't. There's a patch of blood on the grass where he was lying. I take him upstairs and put him in my bed. I lay him down and sit with him, but watch as a puddle of blood begins to radiate out from his body. I don't know what to do, so I try to find Nick. He's not in the house, so I go outside to look for him, but all I can find is a large patch of bloodstained gravel on the driveway. I know this stain is all that's left of Nick and I'm on my own.

I go downstairs feeling incredibly sad. I find my dream journal and dream interpretation book, but I don't write the dream down. Instead, I put them in a drawer. I find my yoga books, with all their stoical, mindful, accepting platitudes and put them in the same drawer. I've struggled for months to make sense of things and bring order to the chaos, but it hasn't worked. None of these methods and philosophies are any use. If I was in one of Tiffany's classes now and she told me about accepting the reality of suffering, I'd tell her she didn't have a fucking clue about the real world. How can anyone just accept this stuff and not go mad? I'm miserable and furious all at once.

I call the hospital to check on Nick. Incredibly, they're discharging him today. I look at the padlocks and think again about my plan to shut him out. But he was injured instinctively protecting me and our baby. Whatever the future holds for us, I can't abandon him like this.

I go to the hospital and find Nick awake on a side ward. He looks deathly pale and is very tired. Until his arm heals and the work from the surgery begins to mesh, there's not a lot else they can do. He has a bag by his bed with pain medication, a timetable of visits to have dressings changed, and a list of light exercises to encourage mobility. He'll need physio across the next six months. While I'm there, an occupational health worker comes in and explains she'll visit

Nick at home in a month or so to see how he's functioning around the house.

Everything has changed.

We drive home. Nick's quiet in the car. At one point I hear him sniff and turn round to see him crying. I pull the car over and hug him as best I can, careful to not to press on his injured arm. He must be in shock. I imagine how traumatic it must be to have a wild, powerful animal tearing away at your body, causing you incredible pain, with no idea if it's ever going to stop. I picture Ron's face, smiling as he stood over Nick and the dog. I can't comprehend the sheer cruelty inherent in that moment.

We get home and as soon as we're inside, I slide the bolts and close the padlocks. I help Nick upstairs to rest. Even the simplest movements around the house become next to impossible with only one arm. Getting upstairs safely. Cleaning his teeth. Getting undressed. Eventually, we manage to settle him in bed. I sit with him while he falls asleep. He looks so vulnerable. I've spent the last few weeks thinking that I'm the victim of Nick's bad choices, but at this moment he couldn't look more like a victim himself. He whimpers slightly in his sleep. Maybe he's dreaming about the dog attack. He sounds like a sad dog himself. He looks helpless, and I get a wave of what it will be like to be responsible for a tiny baby.

I go downstairs.

We haven't discussed the incident at all. On one hand, it's a clear result of Nick's destructive impulses, a behaviour I've seen too much of in the past couple of months. But on the other hand, I think about Ron in the garden, goading me with that doll, his security camera tracking our movements. Nick has been completely set up.

That feeling only gets stronger later when there's a knock at the door and it's the police. I assume they're here to talk to Nick as the victim of a dangerous dog attack, but very quickly it becomes apparent that they want to interview Nick as a suspect, as he's breached his injunction to stay away from Ron. Their tone makes it clear they believe Nick's trespassed next door again and Ron has been forced to defend himself. I say Nick's asleep, too ill to talk to them. They don't push it, and ask that Nick comes to the police station in the next couple of days for a full interview.

When the police leave, I lock the door again and think through what options I have left. I stare into space, trying to think of something, but no ideas come. We're painted into a corner with nowhere to go. Ron now holds all the cards.

I can't go on like this. It's no good for me. And it's no future for the baby. Something's got to change.

Quietly, so as not to wake Nick, I undo the padlocks, slip out through the back door, and go to see Ron.

44

SUCK IT UP

I can hear music playing at the rear of Ron and Jackie's house as I exit onto our decking. I cross to the fence and try to peer into the garden to see who is out there. I can't see anyone, but I can hear voices. I work out it's Ron, in his hot tub, talking on his phone.

I'm terrified, but I don't want him to know that. I have to look strong, confident and in control. I close my eyes and take a few deep breaths, trying to calm my nerves.

I'm ready.

"Ron!" I shout. I feel awkwardly familiar, saying his name.

"Alright. Megan, is it?" he calls back cheerfully. "How's your fella doing? That arm looked quite nasty. He's had a bit of a shock, I expect."

I try not to let him rile me. "I want to talk to you."

"Hang on a minute, doll," he says.

I hear him muttering at his phone before he hangs up and yells out to me again.

"You'll have to go the long way round, luv. Jackie's out. Hywel'll let you in."

I see the thin boy from the first dog attack scamper across the lawn towards the house.

"Oh, and don't worry, luv," Ron adds gleefully. "The doggies are all in their cages."

I walk back across my lawn and up the side of the house, then down the gravel path and towards Ron and Jackie's. I feel like I'm walking out to a firing squad.

Hywel opens the side gate to me as I come up the drive. He's gauche and awkward and barely makes eye contact. I'm relieved not to go inside the house again. He strides across the lawn ahead of me towards the fence.

I can see the work that Ron and Jackie have done on the garden now. Trees have been lopped down to create a huge open space. There's a vast paved area in the middle of the lawn, with a huge wooden dining table and chairs, and a lot of elaborate adjustable umbrellas, the sort you see outside restaurants and bars abroad. Other areas have chintzy wrought iron tables and chairs, set out under archways with the beginnings of trailing plants climbing up them. Jackie's princess pergola is finished, a grotesque mash-up of Disney palace, garden shed and bus shelter. None of it makes any sense. The whole thing looks more like a garden centre than an actual garden.

The building by the fence is enormous. The breeze blocks have been rendered on this side in cream-painted cement. There's a crude-looking shower block that could be from a prison camp, not much more inviting than the shelter that's been built to house the dogs. Next to this is a covered area with the hot tub.

Ron is lying back with the bubbles blasting away. He's

naked from the waist up, and his large spongy body pokes above the surface of the water like a vast fleshy island. A row of opened beer cans sits on the side of the tub. He's wearing dark sunglasses so it's impossible to see his eyes.

"I hope you brought your costume, luv," he says, grinning. "I assume you're coming in? You can borrow one of Jackie's if you like, but I'm not sure you're the same size."

"I'll pass, thanks," I say.

"Sorry you had to go the long way round the security fence. We've had a bit of trouble with the neighbours, you see."

I try not to let him get to me, and say nothing.

"You're not going to try anything silly, are you?" asks Ron. "Only if you do, I'll have to let Hywel loose on you. He's thin, but he's wiry."

I look at Hywel. He's staring at his feet, grinning slightly. I can't work out whether he's smiling at his boss's joke to flatter him, or he genuinely is amused by the idea of attacking me. Ron must have his reasons for keeping him around; maybe he is dangerous. Hywel is wearing a t-shirt and I can see the makeshift cast has been removed from his arm. The forearm hangs at an odd angle, where it looks like the bone hasn't been set straight. The skin is horribly scarred, red and angry, and there are a few indentations where the flesh has been bitten away. I wonder if this is what Nick's arm will look like.

"I want to talk about your offer for the house," I say.

I see this gets Ron's attention. He turns off his music.

"Hywel, go and feed the dogs," he says.

Hywel scampers off across the grass and into the dog pound. Pretty soon, whining and barking goes up. It must surely be traumatic for the boy to be in there, feeding the animal that nearly ripped him to shreds. I wonder if the cruelty of it has even crossed Ron's mind.

"So," says Ron, "you here to accept the offer?"

"Perhaps," I say. "I have a few conditions."

"You're hardly in a position to negotiate, luv," he laughs, "but go ahead. Fill yer boots."

"That's where you're wrong," I say forcefully. "You've overplayed your hand. You've pushed us too hard. You've left us with nothing, so we've got nothing to lose in fighting back."

He's staring at me and I hold his gaze. I fight my instinct to back down. Everything rests on my ability to see this through.

Ron stops the jets bubbling. He stands in the water and walks with difficulty up the steps of the tub. He's naked, but thick folds of flesh hang down like a curtain around his waist, obscuring his penis. His body is red and blotchy from the heat of the water, like Hywel's scarred arm. He hefts himself over the edge of the tub and onto the wooden decking below, then reaches over to a chair and pulls a white sail of towelling robe around himself. He walks towards me and comes to a halt, legs splayed apart to support his weight.

"Let's say you're right," he says. "Let's say you have got the bollocks to front it out. What d'you want?"

"We'll sell you the house," I say, "but we want two hundred thousand more than you offered us."

Ron snorts derisively.

"It's more than you want to pay," I say, "but it's a lot less than we paid."

Looking at the excessive work Ron has done to his house and his garden, I'm guessing he has money to burn. No one has dogs like that without being up to something shady. He must have the money, even if he won't be happy about spending it.

"I don't think so," says Ron.

"You can keep driving us into the ground," I say, "but don't you just want us gone? Is it really worth your time just to save a bit of money?"

He looks like he's considering it seriously.

"They say the sign of a good compromise is where all parties are equally disappointed," I say. "Agree to pay us, and we'll be gone in two weeks."

Ron steps towards me. Have I pushed too hard and pressed his stupid macho buttons? He thrusts his hand forward, and for a second I think he's going to hit me. But then I realise he wants to shake my hand. I put out my hand and it's swallowed up in his.

"Deal," he says.

BACK AT HOME, I sit in the kitchen sipping water. My hand is shaking. I'm terrified. But I'm also exhilarated. When Nick gets up from bed, I tell him what has happened. We are leaving – no ifs, no buts. Nick hates losing the money and hates having to back down – but I'm adamant.

"We'll all just have to suck it up and move on."

I have a deal. A way out. I'll be gone from here in a fortnight.

45

YUMMY YAPPERS

I expect Nick to drag his feet about the house – and for the first day, he does just that. He's sulky and petulant and huffs about the place like a child who's been told off. I know he's in pain from his injuries, and I know he feels he's lost face to Ron. Nick has had a bad streak of losses and it's smarting, probably more than his arm.

I'm more pragmatic about it. What's the point in putting energy into things we can't change? I wish things were different – but they aren't. I'm keen to put the past in the past and get on with the future, whatever that will be.

"Are you okay if I go out for a bit?" asks Nick. "I think I could do with a walk, clear my head."

"Sure."

I go upstairs and start making arrangements for us to move. I look into storage facilities for our belongings while we work out where we're going to live, apart or together. I research places to rent. I assume, for now, we'll head back to Manchester. I don't know what the future holds for Nick and me, and whether our relationship will survive this, but we need to leave together, and quickly. Once we're away from this toxic environment, we can see if we have anything left to salvage.

I haven't told Nick anything about this part of the plan – that this might all be a prelude to me leaving him. That's the biggest secret between us now, and I feel impossibly guilty about it. Maybe I'm the bad one.

I'm upstairs a couple of hours later when I hear the front door close. Nick comes into my workroom, where I'm looking at rental properties on my laptop. He leans down and kisses me on the side of my neck and runs his hand through my hair.

"It's going to be okay," he whispers. "We're going to be okay, the three of us."

Something about the walk has done him good. For the rest of the afternoon, he's upbeat. He gets clothes out of drawers and packs them in suitcases, and puts books in cardboard boxes, working at a steady pace that someone with only one functioning arm can achieve. We don't talk much as we go about our tasks, but to my surprise I feel a sense of shared purpose with him.

I imagine he must be struggling to unfold the flattened cardboard boxes, so I go to help by putting a few together. They're in the utility room, where we've been storing stuff we haven't found a place for. We've been in this house just under three months, and here we are, packing everything up again. I move a couple of flattened boxes, which reveal a small, completed box behind them. I almost don't notice it at first, thinking it must be something we haven't unpacked yet.

Yummy Yappers. Meaty Treats for Waggy Woofers.

It's a small box, about a foot square, wrapped heavily in brown parcel tape. We might have brought it with us, but I don't remember it. And where would we have got an empty box of dog treats?

I know exactly what this is. I'm furious. Nick has snuck off to Ron and Jackie's and stolen something insignificant, hoping to score some feeble victory, like a man who's been sacked from a job and steals pencils from the office. It's pathetic. Can he not just leave things alone and walk away?

"WHAT'S THIS?" I ask in an angry tone, putting the box down on the kitchen table. I hear myself sound like a weary schoolteacher or scolding parent.

"Why the hell have you got that?" says Nick in a blind panic. He flies across the room and looks at the box, inspecting it to see if it's been opened. It's not at all the reaction I was expecting. Instead of underplaying his stupid prank, he's acting like I've brought an unexploded bomb into the room. I look again at the box.

"Nick, what *is* this?"

Nick sits at the table.

"Sit down," he says in a grave tone. I do.

"I went for that walk today. I really was planning just to clear my head. I'm pissed off about what's happened here. It sticks in my throat. It makes me feel ill to think about it. But I know you're right. I know we've got to make the best of it and walk away. I was telling myself all that, getting my head in the right place to come back and help you. I made my peace with it. I was walking back up the path when I met him coming the other way down his drive."

"Ron?"

"Yeah, Ron." Nick heaves a sigh. "I promised myself I wouldn't say anything to him. I realise how much I've messed things up for you and now you've found us a way out I don't want to mess that up too. I really wasn't going to say anything."

There's a pause. "But?" I ask.

"*He* spoke to *me*. He asked me about my arm, as if he genuinely cared about it. Then some bullshit about how he'll be sorry to see us go. He has this way of getting in your head, making you feel stupid and angry all at the same time."

"And?"

"He was talking about you, how you'd sorted the problem that I hadn't managed to solve. The way he talked about you made me feel small and pathetic. It reminded me of all the ways I've let you down. He said it was a shame we'd lose so much money on the house, and he could stretch to an extra ten thousand if I did him a little favour."

Nick goes quiet. I follow his eye line to the box on the table.

"What have you done?" I ask him. I'm not sure I want to know the answer.

"He said all I have to do is deliver this box to an address. He told me not to open it. He didn't say what's inside it, and I didn't ask."

"Well," I say, the anger rising in me, "it won't be bloody dog treats, will it?"

"I shouldn't have taken it. I know I shouldn't. But I've no idea when I'll work again, and we've lost so much, and ten thousand is a lot of money."

"Why would he pay *you* all that, just to deliver a box? He's got people working for him. That boy he has would do it for nothing. It must be bad."

"To humiliate me. Make me his errand boy. Show me he's won and rub my nose in it."

I stare at the box.

"You think you're winning, getting extra money from him. But you're not. You're doing what he wants you to do. *He's* winning."

"But Meg –"

"No, Nick. Who knows where it ends? Do not fuck this up for me. Know when to walk away."

Nick's silent for a moment. Then he looks at me.

"You're right. You're right. I'll take it back."

Nick picks up the box awkwardly with one arm. "I'll do it now. Can you get the door for me?"

I open the front door, and he walks down the driveway and out of sight round the corner of the hedge. I sit at the kitchen table and wait, still not certain what Nick will do. I feel the chances of him and me making a go of it slipping further away from us. Whenever he has the opportunity to do the right thing, he always does the opposite. Eventually, after what seems like ages, he comes back into the house. He no longer has the box.

"I told him he could shove his ten grand up his fat arse. I told him to get someone else to do it."

"What did he say?" I ask.

"He wasn't happy about it, but what can he do?" Nick comes and sits down next to me. He takes my hand in his. "That's it, Meg. It's over."

FOR THE NEXT couple of days, things are much better between us. I feel guilty about not telling Nick I still think our relationship might be over, but that's a complicated conversation I park for now. We make arrangements to leave Anglesey. We put a deposit on a flat to rent. We arrange a storage facility in Manchester for most of the furniture. We calculate what money we have, and where we might be able to afford something half-decent. We talk to a solicitor about selling this house to Ron. Nick makes jokes about visiting Pippa and Dermot, him pushing Dermot around in a wheelchair with his one good arm. We laugh. It all feels surprisingly normal.

I keep waiting for something to happen, but nothing does. We don't see or hear from Ron. Their house is unusually peaceful. The dogs are quiet.

Nick has gone out to get his dressing changed. We're expecting a removal firm to come and look at our stuff and give us a quote, so I stay in for them and Nick gets a taxi to the surgery. The post arrives, and I can see it's from our solicitor handling the sale to Ron. I should wait for Nick to go through it together.

But then a thought strikes me. Nick might still somehow have his deal about that box in place with Ron. Quickly, I open the envelope and look at the contract. It's only when I see it names the sum of money I was expecting, and not ten thousand extra, that I finally accept Nick really has told Ron he's not delivering the box. I'm relieved. Soon this will be over.

I'm in my workroom a couple of hours later when the removal men knock. I go downstairs to let them in. I'm excited, because taking my things out of here will be the first concrete moment I start to leave for real. But when I open the door, it isn't them. It's the police. The instant I see them, I know Nick must have done something else, something bad he hasn't told me about, embezzled someone's money or something. I'm furious. The bloody idiot. I was right not to trust him.

"If you're looking for Nick, he's not here."

"Megan? Can we come in?"

The solemn tone feels all wrong. A feeling of dread washes over me.

"I'm very sorry, Megan. It's Nick. He's dead."

PART 5

46

TOAD IN THE HOLE

I sit on the sofa in a daze. I feel numb. The police left some time ago and I'm on my own. Apparently there was an altercation in a pub car park which Nick was involved in, and he got stabbed. By the time the ambulance arrived, he was dead. The police ask all kinds of things — whether Nick was there for any reason, whether I know if he was planning to meet someone. I can't tell them anything. It doesn't make sense. I explain that he was just going out to see the doctor.

Now they've gone, my mind is racing. Nick's previous conviction was over a fight in a car park. Could this have any connection to that? That makes even less sense – it was years ago.

Ron. Ron went to prison over a fight in a car park. He attacked that man and nearly blinded him. Attacking people in car parks is what he does. Nick refused to deliver Ron's box for him, and Nick said Ron was pissed off about it.

It's Ron who's done this. It must be.

There's a knock at the door, and I go to answer it on autopilot. When I open it, Jackie is standing there.

"Oh Megan, I saw the police car and I've just heard the news. Poor luv, you must be in bits."

Am I in bits? I'm not crying, and I haven't cried since the police arrived. It suddenly strikes me as odd that I haven't cried.

"I'm worried about you alone in this house," Jackie continues. "Have you got anyone who can come and sit with you? Anyone you can call? You shouldn't be on your own."

"I'm fine," I say. I can't be fine though, can I? I still feel numb. It's like I'm sleepwalking. I almost wonder whether this is another of my terrible nightmares, but the moment I have the thought, I know this isn't a dream. This is very real.

"I can come in for a bit if you like," says Jackie. "Let me make you a cup of tea – or something stronger. You could probably do with some gin for the shock." She sounds concerned. But it's too much. I can't deal with someone's concern. I need to be left alone.

"No, really, I'm fine," I say. I'm aware I've kept my hand on the open door, my arm braced across the doorway like a barrier. I don't want this woman in here. This distracting, noisy woman. This woman whose husband has just killed Nick. I can't concentrate. I need to be alone, to think.

"I have some friends coming," I lie.

"Alright, well, I'll go then," says Jackie. "But if you need anything at all, luv, you know where I am. Any time of the day or night. You've got my number. Okay?"

"Yes."

"Oh, and I brought you this." She hands me a rectangular object covered in foil. "It's a toad in the hole. It's all I had in the freezer. You've got to eat, luv, even though I'm sure you don't want to. Get something down you. You've got to look after yourself and baby."

Jackie leaves. I put the dish on the kitchen counter and sit at the table. I should do something, but my head is in a fog and a mass of half-formed thoughts whirl around, refusing to link up into anything coherent. There's a pile of papers on the table that are due to go into the recycling. I lift the one on the top, a brochure about a septic tank. My eyes scan across the words, but I don't take anything in. I don't know what I should do next, so I don't do anything.

I've no idea how long I've been sitting here. It could be a couple of hours. I hear a car on the drive and think it must be Nick, home at last, but I realise his car is already on the drive, that he can't drive with just one arm. Then I remember it can't be Nick because Nick is dead, and the shock of the thought jumpstarts me into consciousness.

There's a knock at the door and when I answer it, Niall is there.

"Niall," is all I say, and I feel a massive rush of emotion, as if seeing a friendly face is a safety net and I can finally let go of whatever it is I've been holding on to. He steps forward and pulls me into a hug and I let him support me. I bury my head in his shoulder and let go, and the strongest thing I feel is relief.

I'M NOT sure what the time is when I wake up. There's a small table lamp on in the corner of my bedroom, and I can see there's no light coming through my curtains. It's dark outside.

I get up and go downstairs and find Niall at the kitchen table, working on his laptop. He turns as he sees me and closes the lid.

"How long have I been asleep? What time is it?"

"It's ten," he says. "You've been asleep for about four hours. It's the shock. It's good for you to rest."

He makes us a drink and we talk. He was working at home when a friend of his, another journalist, got a call about a story. He'd recognised Nick's name and made the connection to Niall and phoned him. Niall immediately tried to call me, but I didn't answer. I realise I have no idea where my phone is; since the police arrived I haven't looked at it. Anyway, when Niall couldn't get through to me, he decided to get in the car and drive here.

"What about your girlfriend – Maya, isn't it?"

"She's fine about it," says Niall. "She understands."

Of course she does. Anyone who knows Niall knows he's the sort of person who'll be there for you in a crisis. I guess that's what this must be: a crisis.

"I haven't cried," I say, knowing this is bad and hoping he will explain what's wrong with me.

"That's the shock too," he says. "You will."

"No. I don't think so," I say. "I mean, there's a bit of me that isn't surprised this has happened."

I begin to tell Niall all the things I haven't told him so far, everything that has led to this moment. The stuff with Ron and Jackie. The garden fence, the septic tank, the meeting with the planning officer and the weird stuff about the boundary line and rezoning. I tell him about Peter and Gavin dropping us in it. I tell him about Ron, and the threats and the pathetic offer he's made for our house, which we were forced to accept.

Then I tell him the hardest stuff of all. About Nick. Nick messing up on the survey, him being sacked from work, his stupid temper and the court case, and being attacked by the dog, and the box of dog treats. I don't tell him I was thinking of leaving Nick. I'm aware, as I list all these instances of Nick's failures, Niall must be wondering why I left him for this man.

As I hear myself say all these things about Nick out loud, I realise the reason I haven't cried is because I know I have fallen out of love with him. It's the thought I haven't allowed myself to express all this time, and now I have, I feel so incredibly sad about it, and the tears begin to flow – for Nick, and for Niall, and for my baby, and for myself. I cry and cry.

Once I've pulled myself together, I need to think about something else for a while, to clear my head. We chat about other stuff, about him. Niall tells me about Maya, who sounds nice, and I'm happy for him. I show him the spare room, and then I go to bed. I listen to the sea for a while and vaguely remember something Tiffany said about joy and sorrow both being transient. Nothing stays the same. Even the sea, which seems permanent, has changing tides and currents and storms. My mind drifts. I think about the sea levels rising and the cliffs crumbling. The world as we know it coming to an end. I imagine it all like a sandcastle as the tide comes in, washing us all away. I'm sure I haven't remembered it right, but I can't figure it out. I hear the rhythm of the tide coming in and out, and I fall asleep.

IN THE MORNING, I see Niall's overnight bag by the front door. Niall is sitting at the kitchen table, at his laptop.

"I have to leave this morning. Is that okay? Will you be okay? I can come back tomorrow if you're not."

"No," I say. "I'll be fine. I really think I will. But I'll call if I'm not. Thanks, Niall."

"Listen," he says, "sit down. I've done some digging."

I pour myself some coffee and sit at the table.

"This Ron Evans," Niall starts, "he's not a good guy. Those three months he spent in prison, that's the first time he's been locked up. But it's not the first time he's been in court. He's quite the regular there. None of the charges have stuck before. My guess is, witnesses will have been intimidated. I mean, he's connected, this guy. Everything points to him being part of some organised crime gang, quite high up from the looks of it. That box he wanted Nick to drop off, that'll almost certainly be drugs or cash. Have you thought of telling everything to the police?"

"I think he's *in* with the police," I say. "He has them round at his parties, with all his other thug mates."

"Hmmm," is all Niall says. He doesn't seem surprised.

"As for that house of his, none of that makes sense. They shouldn't have been able to build. Land doesn't just get rezoned for housing like that. I've got a friend in planning in Manchester; I want him to take a look at it."

"Okay. Thanks."

"Weird thing is," says Niall, "that guy you saw in the planning department..."

"Mr Menzies?"

"Yes. He's married. His wife has a son from a former relationship. The son is called Russell Povey."

Something about that name sounds familiar.

"Russel Povey is the boy Evans was convicted for beating up. Maybe that's the way he influences planning laws."

"Jesus."

"Also, I've looked at this contract." Niall holds up some papers. "I hope you don't mind. It was on the table. It's your agreement to sell the house to Evans. That's a stupidly small amount of money. Are you sure you should do it?"

"I don't know. I don't think I have any other choice if I want to get away."

"Don't do it yet," says Niall. "Hang on a couple of days. Stall. Let me do some more digging. And think about talking to the police. But don't do anything until you talk to me."

Niall kisses me on the cheek and hugs me warmly at the doorstep. The hug lasts for ages. I feel safe and don't want to let go, but I do.

"I'll call you later," he says, and drives off.

I go inside. Now what do I do? There's all my stuff I was packing. There's all Nick's stuff. What will I do with that? I have no idea what to do right this moment, let alone for my future.

And what am I going to do about Ron?

My eyes scan around the room and land on something on the work surface. It's Jackie's toad in the hole. That's one thing I know what to do about at least. I get up, go over, and scrape the lot of it in the bin.

47

CONTRACT

"Oh, you didn't need to do that. I'd have washed it."

I'm standing at Jackie's front door, holding the empty Pyrex dish.

"It's no bother," I say. "Delicious." I don't tell her every scrap of it went in the bin.

"I'm not exactly a Gordon Blue chef. It was only a few sausages shoved in a Yorkshire pudding. But in your situation the last thing you'd want to do is cook."

She takes the dish and puts her hand on mine.

"How are you doing, sweetheart?"

I look at her hand. Every finger is loaded with rings. I wonder how much Jackie knows about where Ron's money comes from.

"I'm doing okay." I don't want to share my feelings with this woman. I'm here for one reason. "Is Ron around?"

"He is, luv. Do you need something?"

"I need to talk to him about my house."

Does Jackie know Ron's trying to buy us out for next to

nothing? It seems she must at least know about the house sale, if not the price, as she doesn't bat an eyelid.

"He's round the back, feeding the dogs. Do you want to wait? He'll get all antsy if I call him away from the boys. He likes to keep them on a tight schedule."

"It's okay," I say, heading towards the side gate. "I know where I'm going."

Before Jackie can stop me, I'm opening the gate and heading into their garden.

"Alright," she calls after me. "But give him a toodeloo once you're on the lawn. The puppies can be a bit nervous with strangers."

She's right. I don't want to be savaged by the dogs. Though with Ron's security camera at the top of the drive, my guess is he already knows I'm coming. I look up and see if he has other cameras round here, but there aren't any. I assume he wants to know who is coming up and down his path, but doesn't want recordings of whatever he gets up to back here.

As I go round the side of the house and towards the dog pound, I can hear noises from the enclosure – a bit of growling and whining from the dogs, but also the buzz of a power tool. Ron must be building something else inside.

"Hello!" I shout from the corner of the building. "It's Megan, from next door."

The power tool stops.

"Meg!" Ron calls from inside the dog kennels. Again, he uses the shortened form of my name that only Nick ever used. "Come on in!"

I walk towards the kennel. I've never been this close to it before. It's larger than I remember. Its stark grey walls are cold and imposing, the roughness of the breeze blocks adding to its intimidating form. It's about ten feet high and twenty feet long, and sticks out into the garden about fifteen feet. This is a massive structure to house dogs.

The opening has no door, so the interior is always exposed to the elements. I go in.

One side of the room has four large metal cages with thick bars. Two of the cages are on the ground, and the other two are above, at eye level. They look solid and expensive, like something they'd have round the back of the lion enclosure at a zoo. There are wires tacked to the wall coming off the cages that go to some kind of electronic panel by the side, which I'm guessing must be heating for the cages in winter. The dogs are all in their individual pens, lying down but keen and alert.

Most striking of all, though, is a hook in the middle of the ceiling, from which hangs a half-dismembered pig carcass. Cuts of meat have been lopped off its body and tattered fringes of flesh drip blood onto the floor, which is tiled and angled on all sides to meet at a metal grate in the middle. Small offcut chunks of meat glisten and seep on the floor around the drain. The whole thing is like a kennel combined with an abattoir.

Ron is in his usual shorts and t-shirt, but wears a thick plastic apron that sits high under his chin and comes down to below his knees, tied at the back. It's smeared with blood. His feet are in heavy green Wellington boots.

"One minute, luv," says Ron. He fires up a small chainsaw he's holding, then slices away at the pig, hacking through skin, flesh and bone. Rags of meat fly off the carcass to the tiles below. Small spatters of thick, dark blood spray out onto his apron. I press myself back against the wall so as not to get sprayed. The smell of the meat hangs heavy in the air and I can see the dogs getting twitchy. A large hunk of pig falls to the floor with a dull slap and Ron stops the chainsaw. He picks up the oozing lump of flesh in his bare hands and lobs it into an enormous open chest freezer against the other wall, leaving a pile of smaller chunks where they've fallen, muscle and sinew.

"I'm particular about what I feed the dogs," says Ron, as he goes to a utility sink and runs the blade of the chainsaw under the tap. He hooks it into a charging point on the wall next to an array of other tools. "You are what you eat," he says, "and these boyos are right pigs!"

He laughs as he goes to the pig carcass and leans against it, sliding it along a track in the ceiling to one end of the room and behind a slashed plastic curtain. Unlike the rest of Ron's house and garden, which is a disaster of clashing styles, this room has been carefully thought through as an efficient, workmanlike space. But he only has four dogs. Does Ron really need to butcher animals so often that he needs his own slaughterhouse? I flash a look at the tools on the wall and wonder if any of Ron's business rivals ever end up in here, hung from that hook, watched with hungry interest by the dogs.

"That's right, my boyos," he says to the dogs. "You can smell that, can't you? I like to make them wait. Feed them not quite enough. Keep 'em keen as mustard."

Ron slams the lid of the freezer shut. He removes his apron and hangs it on a hook. He goes back to the utility sink and rubs the blood off his sausage fingers under a stream of water.

"It's a shame about your boyfriend," he says. "That lad had a pretty bad run of it. Just didn't seem able to keep his nose out of trouble." He turns off the tap and wipes his hands dry on a grubby towel. "It's wrong to speak ill of the dead, but if you ask me, you're well shot of him."

I'm ready for this sort of goading. I steeled myself for it before I left the house. I refuse to let it get to me. I take the contract out of my pocket.

"I've decided I'll still sell you the house," I say. "But I want more for it. I'm on my own now, and I need more. I want more."

He takes the contract and looks at the figure I've written on it. Then he looks at me. "Is that so?"

"And I want you to tell me. I want you to admit you did it. You killed Nick."

Ron looks me up and down. "Are you recording this?"

It hasn't even occurred to me to record the conversation, but now he says it, I can see he might think I would. I've prepared myself for the snide remarks, but I haven't antici-pated this. I'm suddenly scared.

"Are you recording this?" he asks again. "Do I need to search you?"

I think of that hook in the ceiling, that pig carcass.

"I'm not recording anything," I say.

He pauses. "No," he says, smiling, "I don't think you are."

He can read me like a book. I'm so out of my depth. I have no idea what I'm doing. He does this for a living.

"You did it," I say, losing my cool. "You were pissed off because Nick wouldn't deliver your package. He said no to you, and you killed him."

To my surprise, Ron laughs.

"I'll tell you what happened," he says. "Your boyfriend came back to me with my goods and told me he wasn't allowed to do my job. You wouldn't let him. I didn't give a tinker's fart one way or the other. I've got loads of lads who'll do jobs for me. But then he said he could still do it if he left the box with me again and collected it later. He asked if I'd pay the extra money in a different account, so you wouldn't know about it. He begged me. Pleaded. He said he needed the money. I think he wanted to prove to you he could be a man, though he didn't look much like a man, snivelling in front of me. So I let him do it."

What Ron says rings true. Even at the end, Nick couldn't just let things go and walk away.

"I've got a kind heart," he says, "so I let him deliver my box for me. Kept it here and he came and got it. And off he trotted."

Ron pulls out a stool and lowers himself down onto it.

"I'll let you into a secret," he says. "The people your bloke went to visit, they're not very nice men. I'd have sent one of my lads, but I had an inkling there might be a bit of bother. And there was. But still, rather him than one of mine."

He smiles. I can't believe how callous he's being. He seems to delight in other people's misery.

"Your Nick must have messed up somehow and got himself killed," says Ron. Then he looks at me hard.

"But the real shame of it is, that leaves *you* with a little problem. My stuff has disappeared. It's gone and I'm out of pocket. He died, and unlucky for you, you've inherited his debt."

"It's nothing to do with me!" I protest.

"Oh yes, it is," he thunders, straining to get to his feet. He passes me the contract for the house sale. "A deal's a deal. So I won't be giving you any extra for your house, and you need to get me my stuff back, or the hundred grand it's worth, or you and I will be having harsh words."

"Where the hell d'you think I can get a hundred thousand pounds from? Do you think I'd be here if I had that kind of money?"

"I don't know, luv," he smarms as he walks towards me. The room suddenly doesn't feel so big with Ron bearing down on me. He leans in close to my face and speaks in a low and measured voice. The intimacy of it is even more terrifying than his shouting.

"Maybe you could ask that nice fella who came to see you yesterday."

Shit, have I dragged Niall into this now as well?

"Or maybe," he continues, "you could go to the police and see if they found a box next to your one's body. Turn on the waterworks, play the grieving widow and beg for his possessions. Frankly, luv, it's not my fucking problem. It's yours."

He walks past me and over to what I assumed was the heating control for the cages.

"Stand back, pet. There's a good girl."

Before I can move, he turns the key in the panel and doors slide back in all four of the cages. The dogs have clearly been primed for this moment. They leap out of their pens and fly to the pile of meat on the floor by the drain. I step back and press myself hard against the wall. The dogs start lapping at the blood, growling and snapping away at each other.

"Feeding time. Wouldn't want the boys to grab you now, would we?" says Ron. "Not before you've got me what's mine. That *would* be a tragedy."

· · ·

AS I MAKE my way swiftly down the drive and away from their house, I hear their front door open and Jackie calls after me.

"Hope you got what you need, Megan, luv! Don't be a stranger! Come round for a gin!"

I almost break into a run, desperate to get back to the house, away from the threat of those dogs, and of Ron. I rush through the door and run up to the bathroom, picturing the dogs with blood round their mouths, and Ron carving up that pig, and Nick, lying in a pub car park, stabbed and bleeding to death. I think I'm going to be sick, and lean over the sink, gripping the sides of the porcelain hard with my fingers. I retch, but nothing comes up.

I stand up and catch sight of myself in the mirror, white as a sheet and startled eyes, and a tiny drop of pig's blood on my cheek.

What am I going to do?

48

WAITING

Another bland waiting room, another row of uniform grey plastic chairs. How much time have I spent in the last three months in rooms like this, waiting to go in, waiting for good news or bad?

One side of the room has a stretch of windows glazed with security glass. I can see the blurred shapes of police uniforms move behind the green dimples and the thin metal squares. The muffled voices of bolshy criminals or workman-like officers drift in through the open door.

The posters on the wall offer a range of advice. *Know Your Rights. Victim Support Services. Crime Prevention Tips. Emergency Contacts.* They all seem utterly relevant to the situation I find myself in, and at the same time entirely useless to me.

What can I say to the police? I imagine myself crying, talking about Nick, who is never coming back. *I miss him. I can't function without him. I just need to have something of his, so I can feel closer to him.* I run the script of it in my head and it feels crass and stupid and unconvincing, even to me.

I'm not a good enough actor. Besides, Nick has been stabbed and killed. It's a murder enquiry. Do I believe the police are just going to give me the belongings he was found with, all that evidence, three days after he died?

I haven't thought it through, being here. The death is suspicious. Even I've worked out it's over drugs, some bad deal gone wrong. Whatever was in that box, they surely know it's something to do with a bigger crime. And if they have the box, wouldn't they have opened it, looked inside, found all the drugs or money or whatever was in there? If I ask for Nick's belongings, won't they think I'm involved too?

Then it occurs to me. Why would the box even be here at all? If Nick got killed in the middle of a drug deal, the first thing the other people would do is take the box. They're not going to murder someone over a box of drugs and then just leave it behind.

Not for the first time, I feel completely out of my depth. Is Niall right? Should I just tell the police everything I know? Surely now someone's died, they'll have to do something about it, have to arrest Ron if he's involved. Then I picture Ron, standing at his barbecue, laughing with the policemen who came for a party in his garden. If I say something about Ron, will it just get straight back to him?

A new thought occurs to me. Why did Ron suggest I come here and ask for Nick's belongings? If he's got people on the inside, then someone here, some corrupt policeman, may be primed, ready and waiting to give me that box so I can take it straight back to Ron.

My mind is racing at a million miles an hour. I don't know enough. I don't know what the right thing to do is. I must leave, go home, work out what to do next. I stand up and start to put my coat on. But as I do, the door is pushed fully open and an officer in uniform comes through.

"Sorry to keep you waiting. You're here about Nicholas Greenacre?" he asks.

I'm like a rabbit in the headlights. I don't want to look furtive, like I am trying to escape.

"Yes, that's right."

The policeman gestures towards the door. "This way, please. They're ready for you."

49

FEEDING TIME

It's a busy morning. I get up early and head out to the shops, gathering the items I'll need for later. I go over and over things. My brain has been racing with all the different possibilities since I was in the police station waiting room. I think of writing it all down, but decide it's better if I just keep it all in my head, learning it in order, like a formula for a maths exam or a script for a school play.

I come back and get everything ready in my workroom. I'm feeling anxious, and know my temptation is to race at things, so I force myself to slow down and work meticulously. By lunchtime, everything is ready except me. I need to calm down.

I go downstairs and out of the house, take the long walk on the road and go down the public path at the end of the cove to the beach. I take my shoes off and feel the warm sand under my feet. It's mid-September and it's beautiful. The sky is utterly clear of clouds, and vibrant blue. The sea is calm, and I listen to the back-and-forth of the tide. I deliberately slow my breathing to match it. I walk out towards the sea and walk along the dark, flat stretch of sand where land meets water, allowing the fringe of the waves to froth over my toes. I stop and look out to sea. It's a vast, calming expanse of nothing.

This is what I came here for. This view. How this makes me feel. Calm. Centred. Peaceful. I walk back to the house, thinking about my breathing, consciously staying calm. I feel strong.

I go upstairs and back into my workroom. I very carefully ease my workbench a foot or two away from the window. It's heavy, and I'm nearly four months pregnant, so I take it very easy. Having learnt my lesson before with the chair, I open out the small step ladder and place it as close to the window as I can. I go up a couple of steps and deliberately rock it from side to side, checking it's secure and stable. It is. I climb up nearer to the top and press my face against the glass, so I can see the edge of their house, and the stretch of garden and the doghouse.

I wait.

Eventually I see him. Ron. He comes out of the house and lumbers across the lawn towards the kennel block. I've anticipated him being here as it's the same time I was there a couple of days ago. Feeding time.

I grab my things and hurry out of the house, crunching down the drive to the fork in the path, and turn towards theirs. I don't knock this time, just let myself through the gate at the side. I pause for a moment at the corner to slow my breathing again. I close my eyes. I'm ready.

"Ron!" I yell as I come around the side of the house.

"Meg?" Ron calls in a delighted tone from inside the outhouse. "In you come!"

I walk to the kennel and go in. I've got here as quickly as

possible, and Ron hasn't kitted himself up in his butcher's apron and rubber boots yet. The pig carcass is still over in the cooling area of the room, behind its plastic sheet.

"Back so soon," he says. "You really can't stay away, can you? Does the wife know you're here? I don't want her thinking I've got someone else creaming their knickers over me."

Ron does his usual roar of laughter, his own most enthusiastic audience. The dogs are in their cages on high alert. They know the routine and are waiting to be fed. They don't like this interruption. I can see them getting twitchy, circling in their pens, hungry to be let out.

"You're not really my type," I say sneeringly, using the attitude to keep my confidence high.

Ron stops laughing. He looks at the carrier bag I'm holding.

"What's in the bag?"

I put the bag on the ground and lean over to remove the contents. But before I can, Ron stops me.

"I'll have that," he says.

Pleasingly, I detect a note of nervousness in his voice. What does he think I've got in there? A knife maybe. Maybe he's remembered what I told him before, about pushing people too hard until they become desperate. Desperate people are dangerous and unpredictable. I smile at him, and his fear of me makes me feel even more confident.

"No problem," I say. I slide the bag across the room to him with my foot. I step back against the wall by the side of the cages, to give him space.

He leans over cautiously and peers into the bag. His face shifts from wary to delighted. He reaches into the bag and takes out the box of Yummy Yappers.

"How did you get this?" he says.

"The police station. I went, like you suggested. I didn't for a moment believe they'd give it to me, but they did. Nick's wallet, his watch and that box. I assumed it was one of your policeman friends who arranged for me to get it."

"Clever girl," says Ron, not fully paying attention. He's so pleased. He clearly thought he'd never see it again. He's taken the box over to the counter and is slicing away at the parcel tape with a Stanley knife. The dogs are beginning to whine.

"Shut up, you bastards!" He peels back the tape. He chuckles. "Not for you, boyos. This is a treat for Daddy."

Ron opens the lid of the box. His face turns from delight to confusion. He reaches inside and takes out the contents with both hands.

Two limp, dead rabbits.

"FASS!" I shout, turning the key in the control panel. The doors slide open and in a flash the dogs leap out of their pens and across the room to grab the rabbits. The force of four dogs hitting him at once knocks Ron off balance and to the ground, and he drops the knife. He yells, flailing about and flicking a thin spray of blood from the rabbits across the floor. The dogs snap at the rabbits, at each other, at Ron. The more he moves and yells, the harder it is to see in the confusion what is dog and what is rabbit and what is man.

Ron's yell turns to a scream, sickening and high-pitched, like Hywel's, like Nick's. The animals have been trained well, and once they've found their target they won't stop until commanded. Maybe Ron's trying to call them off, but he's not intelligible through his screaming. His arms go instinctively to his face to protect himself, and the dogs follow where his limbs go. They circle him, attacking from all angles, and his screaming gets louder, then becomes muffled, then stops. There's a lot of blood on the floor now. I've seen all I need to see. Keeping my movements slow and steady, I turn and leave.

I walk out through the open doorway and slowly across the garden. As I'm going, the back door to the house flies open and Jackie emerges, flustered, an explosion of colour in one of her usual long, flowery dresses. It's the most glorious sunny day and she's dressed perfectly for the occasion. Her eyes are wild. She's clearly heard the blood-curdling screams and has rushed down to find out what is going on. But now she's in the garden, the noise has died down. It's deathly quiet. Just the sound of insects buzzing about the lawn and the faint rush of sea against the beach.

I keep walking, and as I get to her, Jackie looks at me in pure confusion, her face pleading, wanting to know what's going on and hoping I'll have the answer. I look her squarely in the eye as I walk past.

"You've fucked with the wrong neighbour."

50

KNOCK

I hear vehicles on the path and go to the top room at the front
of the house. Two nondescript dark cars approach, then
disappear along the drive to Ron's. I run to my workroom
and climb the stepladder so I can see what happens in the
back garden. At one point, Hywel and another man come
out at the back of the house, both holding heavy-looking Le
Creuset saucepans. I'm guessing these are improvised self-
defence, as the dogs are running about on the lawn and they
don't want to take chances. Hywel shouts something and the
dogs run inside the kennel building. The other man moves
slowly to the dog pound and leans in through the door. I
assume he's reaching round to turn the key and lock the dogs
in their pens. Hywel comes over, and the two of them stand
in the opening of the kennel, looking inside, at Ron, presumably. After a minute, they head back into the house, taking
their saucepans with them. I hear the dogs bark intermittently. Ten minutes later, the cars drive away.

Then nothing.

About an hour later, more vehicles arrive. This time it's a

police car and an ambulance. Again, I go to the workroom to see into next door's garden. There's a mass of activity this time. A couple of police peer into the kennel, setting the dogs howling and barking. Then one of the paramedics goes in. He comes out a minute later, and they all stand about, talking. The lack of urgency confirms what I expected – that Ron is dead. Another man goes in, in a full protective paper suit and carrying a camera. He's inside for several minutes before he emerges. Meanwhile, the paramedics and the police stand on the lawn, getting dressed in protective paper jumpsuits. It must be a mess in there. Both paramedics go in, wheeling a trolley. They're inside for some time before they reappear with a body covered head to toe in a sheet. That must be Ron – or what's left of him.

I get down from the stepladder and close it up, then move my workbench back into its normal position. I don't want it to look like I've been spying on what's going on, or that I know anything about it at all. I go downstairs. Though it's dinner time, and I haven't eaten all day, I'm too agitated to be hungry. But for the appearance of normality, I start to cook some dinner. I stand in the kitchen, slicing vegetables, boiling a pan of water for some pasta, waiting for the police to knock at the door.

But no knock comes.

I sit at the table, looking at the pasta until it goes cold. I scrape the plate clear and put the crockery and the pans in the dishwasher. I turn on the television, leaving it on whatever channel it was tuned to. I'm not watching. I'm still waiting for the knock at the door.

Still, there's no knock.

When it gets to ten o'clock I turn off the television and head upstairs to get ready for bed. I undress, wash and change into a nightdress. I clean my teeth, slip under the covers and turn out the light.

The room is dark, and the silence is thick and heavy. No dogs barking. No Nick, breathing beside me. No knock at the door. Just the back and forth of the sea.

Then I sleep.

51

MEAT

I wake up and reach for my phone. It's 11 a.m. I've slept for twelve hours. Yesterday was a non-stop workout of emotional intensity and, once the adrenaline stopped coursing through my body, I crashed spectacularly. I feel the baby kick and take it as a demand for food, so I go downstairs and eat toast.

My visit to the police station was as fruitless as I'd feared. Of course they didn't give me any of Nick's things. *What am I going to do without that box? Where the hell am I going to get one hundred thousand pounds?* As I wandered back to the car, my path took me past a butcher's shop. The rabbits hanging in the window felt like a sign. Then I had to drive to three pet shops before I found one that stocked Yummy Yappers. As I worked at home, taping the box up as I remembered it, the feeling of tension was excruciating. Would Ron fall for the replica box?

Incredibly, he did.

I feel exhilarated. Ron is gone.

But what about Jackie? I've never been sure how much Jackie knows about Ron's business, or what he did to Nick and me. She seems less dangerous, more an eccentric than a threat. But whatever she is, she saw me walking out of that kennel where the dogs killed Ron. We can't ignore what's gone on between us. We're neighbours.

I KNOCK on the door a couple of times and wait, but there's no answer. The black four-by-four is parked by the house, so unless Jackie's gone for a walk, or been driven by someone else, she must be inside. I go through the side gate and round the back.

The garden is empty. The patio door on the back of the house is open. There are five or six full black bin bags on the ground outside the kennel, and I walk over to take a better look. As I get closer, I can hear noise from the dog pound.

Jackie is inside. She's standing with her back to me at the open chest freezer, emptying frozen hunks of meat from it into a bin bag on the counter.

"Jackie."

She spins round in surprise and stares at me, as frozen as the pork joint in her hand. I can see she's been crying.

"I'm sorry for your loss," I say, even though I'm not at all sorry.

"They've taken them," she wails. "They've taken my babies away. I don't know where they've gone. They only did what they thought they were supposed to. They're good boys."

She starts crying again, weeping for the dogs that mauled her husband to death. She looks at the empty open cages and sniffs.

"They won't let them come back. I know it. So what am I

supposed to do with this?" She gestures towards the bin bag. "Why did he have to buy so much fucking meat?"

I don't know how this meeting will play out, but I decide to test the water.

"We've each lost a lot," I say. "Maybe it's time for both of us to move on?"

Jackie drops the piece of meat into the bin bag and looks at me. She gets control of her crying.

"How do you mean?"

"I'll be straight with you," I say. "I know how Ron got planning for this land, threatening that man's family. I know your house shouldn't be here. But I'm not going to do anything about that. You can keep your house. And you can have *my* house as well, just like Ron planned. Except, I want a proper price for it. Like I said, I've lost a lot, and I deserve a new start. I think we both do, don't you?"

Jackie smiles at me and gives me an odd look. She has a twinkle in her eye. For a moment I think my suggestion has landed with her, and she'll be glad to be rid of me. Maybe she's even glad to be rid of Ron, and I've done her a favour. Finally, she speaks.

"What, no toad in the hole?"

"What?" I say. I don't understand.

"Well, if you're going to come round here and pretend you're sorry he's dead, the least you could do is bring me a fucking toad in the hole."

I've clearly misjudged the situation.

"Because your fella's dead and mine is too, you think we're even, is that it?" Her grief is turning to anger. "My Ron was fifty times the man that useless ponce of yours ever was."

She takes a step towards me, and I'm suddenly aware of how big she is. She never seemed it before, compared to the bulk of Ron. But here, in this enclosed room, and with her bearing down on me, I'm frightened.

"You think you're so much better than other people, don't you?" she says with a steely coldness. "So much better than us. Well, let me tell you something, lady – you're not. You're worse. Your shit stinks, just like everyone else's."

I have the strangest thought – that maybe Jackie is so upset because she was lonely. She tried to be my friend and I ignored it. Maybe she's just hurt.

"The price for the house stands," she says. "And the contract you had with Ron for the box stands too. You owe me my hundred thousand and you'd better fucking get it or I'll make your life a living hell on Earth, yours and your bastard baby's. Now piss off back to your shit-stinking dump of a house."

Jackie's cut from exactly the same cloth as Ron. It's karma, I guess. Ron destroys Nick. I destroy Ron. Jackie destroys me. There's no escape. Weirdly, at that moment I think of Tiffany, telling us to resist the pull of patterns and habits, let go and break free. But what the fuck does Tiffany know? She never had Ron and Jackie Evans as neighbours.

Jackie has given me my orders and smirks at me with contempt. She's won and we both know it. I'll never be free.

Before I realise, I instinctively take hold of a hunk of meat by the frozen trotter. It's heavier than I was expecting. I swing it with the full force of my body and land a glancing blow against her temple. I've only clipped her, not done the damage I intended. Fuck. Now I'm in trouble.

Jackie staggers back and begins to lose her balance. Once she starts falling she can't stop herself. I remember what Nick said about pushing Ron off a cliff, that his weight would work against him. She topples backwards, loses her footing and tumbles heavily into the chest freezer. Cautiously, I look inside and see she's cleared most of the pork meat out by now, so it's nearly empty, and she's fallen to the bottom. She's winded and dazed, but she'll come to her senses soon enough.

I'm still holding the frozen joint of meat in my hand and think about clubbing Jackie on the head again. But how many times would I have to hit her to kill her? I'm not sure I have the strength for it, let alone the stomach.

I shut the lid of the freezer and look round the room for something to weigh it down. None of the tools on the wall are heavy enough. I race outside to find something and see the bin bags full of pork meat. I try lifting one. It's incredibly heavy. I can't drag it, as the plastic is bound to rip. I lift it millimetres off the ground and shuffle in tiny steps until I have it in the room. It takes ages. Then I go back for another. I'm exhausted and puffing, feeling pregnant and unfit.

I enter the kennel with the second bag just in time to see the lid of the freezer open. Jackie's head begins to poke out and her eyes catch mine. I rush across the room, grab the handle and lift the lid, then bring it down hard on her head with a sickening thump. I wait.

There's no movement. No noise. Nothing.

Maybe I've killed her? I can't take the chance that I haven't.

I begin to unload the hunks of frozen pork onto the freezer lid, from the two bags I've brought in and from the one Jackie has half-filled on the counter. They're huge lumps and heavy to move. I go outside and bring the other bags in slowly, and unload those too. When I'm on my third bag, I hear muffled grunting and thumping from inside the freezer. I can see the lid move slightly, where Jackie must be trying to open it. But it doesn't open. The meat on top is too heavy. Nonetheless, I keep unloading the meat until it's all weighing the lid down. I try to lift it myself, but there's no way I can budge it.

I stand at the side of the room listening to the thumping in the freezer. I'm not sure how long I'm there – an hour maybe – but eventually it stops.

I leave the garden and go home. I'm exhausted and sweaty from the afternoon heat, and I can smell the meat on my hands. I take a shower and change. I look at the weather forecast on my phone. It's the last week of September and we're in a late summer heatwave. The pork will have defrosted tomorrow.

I spend the rest of the evening waiting for the day to end and steeling myself for the task ahead. I'm banking on the fact that none of Ron's criminal mates will want to visit Jackie now the police are involved. I stand at the window at the front of the house and watch for any cars, but nothing turns onto the drive. It gets dark, and I keep watching for lights. Thankfully I'm right. No one comes.

The following day I'm up early. I make my way back to Jackie's house and into the kennel. The meat has defrosted and is already beginning to smell bad. Blood has oozed from it and run down the sides of the freezer. I put on Ron's plastic butcher's apron and begin to heft the lumps of meat onto the floor. It's heavy work, and harder than yesterday now the meat is thawed and slippery. The smell is rich and sweet and nearly makes me gag. It takes me a long time before I'm finished.

Then I open the freezer.

Jackie's frozen body is twisted sideways in the base of the freezer where she's collapsed in exhaustion. A thin frost coats her dress and skin. Her eyes are closed. Presumably, hypothermia must have kicked in and she'll have fallen asleep, then died. I get a screwdriver from the tools on the wall and cautiously poke her, just to check. She's rock-hard.

I go to the wall and take down Ron's small electric chainsaw. I start it up and lean into the freezer and begin to cut Jackie's body up into smaller pieces, like joints of meat. I was right to leave her overnight, as she's frozen solid and there's little or no blood. I pull the rags of her dress and underwear out between cuts, so there's no material in there, just flesh and bone. I'll put the clothes on the fire when I get home.

I see her hands and look at her rings. Were these bought with money from the drugs that got Nick killed? I stop sawing. I don't think I should leave the rings in here too, so I try to get them off, but they're frozen onto the hands, the fingers bent and twisted where she must have been clawing away at the freezer lid, the fat of her fingers expanded round the rings so they won't budge. I start the chainsaw and cut her hands off. I take her hands over to a small patch of sunlight to thaw out a bit while I carry on with cutting up the rest of the body. I'm careful not to saw into the freezer.

What have I become? Is this a mother's instinct, to protect her child at all costs? They say character is who you are under pressure. When my back's against the wall, I guess this is me. I refuse to let the thought get in the way of what I'm doing. But I marvel at how far I've come in three months. I used to be squeamish giving blood.

I take a break while the chainsaw recharges. It's heavy work. I drink a glass of water, then go over to where I've left Jackie's hands. They've thawed enough for me to straighten the fingers, with a bit of a crack, and I'm able to take the rings off. I put the rings in my pocket and put the hands back in the freezer. I continue to cut the body up until Jackie lies on the floor of the freezer in pieces the size of a Sunday roast.

I don't have time to admire my handiwork. I start lifting the hunks of thawed pork back into the freezer, hefting them in until they form a thick layer over Jackie's body. If anyone comes and looks, it'll just look like meat. I close the lid.

I go to the wall and take down the hose, turn on the taps and wash everything down, thoroughly, for ages. I pull on gloves and I scrub everything, rubbing the surfaces as best I can. No one will be surprised to find traces of blood in here, but I do my best to get rid of anywhere I might have left fingerprints.

At last, I'm finished. It's taken the best part of the day, and the sun is low in the sky as I leave the kennel and begin to walk back to my house. Today is the last official day of summer. I pause to look out across the garden to where the sun is beginning to warm orange as it approaches the horizon, spreading a glimmering golden light across the sea.

This really is a beautiful spot.

52

KARMA

"Thanks," says Pippa as I hand her a glass of wine.

I lower myself into a chair on the decking and we sit in silence for a while, watching Dermot push my son's pram over the bumpy grass, talking to Dylan, pointing out seagulls and the lighthouse and ships in the distance. Dylan's only four months old. He can't even see this stuff from the pram, but Dermot chats to him like they're best buddies down the pub.

"He's a natural," I say. "Do you think you'll have any?"

"It was always the plan," says Pippa. "Everything changed when he got injured. But he's making an incredible recovery. Leaning on that pram, he doesn't even need the crutches. So we'll see."

I close my eyes and let the sun warm my face. It's the first really hot day of the year. I look back at Dermot, who's pointing out small flowers, and then at a rabbit which skips out of a hedge near his feet. The rabbits are coming back. Spring is properly here.

"It's weird, being here again," Pippa says. "Weird, but

nice. Dylan's so cute. He looks like Nick." She pauses. "Do you miss him?"

I take a sip of my wine and carefully consider the question.

"I miss what I thought our life was going to be like. We didn't know each other that well, I suppose, and I guess I found out he wasn't what I thought. I miss the person I *thought* he was, if that makes sense. It's hard to believe it all happened. It feels like a bit of a dream, not quite real."

Pippa laughs. "Do you remember us on that night, before it all went wrong, mucking about with that dream book? We did have some laughs. We should look at it later."

"We can't," I say. "I don't have it anymore."

The day after the Jackie incident, I boxed up that book, and all my yoga books, and took them to that shop in Beaumaris. Maybe that stuff is useful for other people, but these days I'm not convinced you can deal with life's curve balls with lessons from books. And it turns out passively accepting things as they are isn't really my thing.

"It's funny," I say to Pippa, "but since Nick died, I don't dream anymore."

"Huh," says Pippa. She goes back to her wine.

Dermot wheels Dylan's pram back up onto the decking. Just as he does, there's a loud crash from Ron and Jackie's side of the fence. We turn and watch as a small digger pulls down another section of the shower block. A vast section of breeze blocks smash to the ground, throwing up a cloud of dust.

"Sorry about the noise," I say.

"You've had your fair share of that, haven't you?" says Dermot.

"This is different," I say. "I'm happy about this noise."

"It was amazing – Niall's story, how that's all worked out for you," Pippa says.

And it is. Niall followed up the stuff he researched on Ron, then did a story for the Western Mail, which got picked up by BBC local news. The whole planning scandal came out and permission for everything Ron and Jackie built was reversed – the outbuildings, the garden, and the house itself. It's all being knocked down now, at the council's expense. The work is due to be completed by the end of June, exactly a year to the day since I first moved here. By summer Dylan and I should have Bae Breuddwyd to ourselves.

I listen contentedly as the workmen smash down another bit of Ron's empire.

"What about Niall?" says Pippa. "Any chance you two might..."

"He's marrying Maya next year," I say. "I'm happy for him."

And I am. I no longer feel the need to chase philosophies or other people to find my happiness. Dylan and I will be happy here. I don't need hands to catch me. I've already landed.

"What about her then?" asks Dermot. "Mrs Punch next door. Does anyone know what happened to her?"

"Jackie?" I ask. "No idea. I guess once the planning story hit the news, she just skulked off somewhere."

That's what I say when people ask. There's a limit to what you should share, even with good friends.

"She's probably out there, under a stone somewhere, waiting to pop up," says Dermot. "Isn't it the cockroaches who always survive the nuclear holocaust?"

"You're probably right," I say. I rock Dylan gently in his pram and sip my wine.

We all look on as the digger begins to go to work on the dog pound, hammering away at one of the corners until two entire walls collapse inwards. Of all the things to get knocked down, this one has a special interest for me. I keep a careful eye on it while I rock Dylan.

"I guess this means you'll be able to get to your septic tank now," says Dermot. "Shame, I used to love that shitty smell." He takes a deep breath as if he's savouring wine.

I watch the man get off the digger and go through the cloud of dust into the exposed kennel. What has he found? I stare at the work, trying to see what's going on. The dust begins to settle, and I see him there, peering at something in the middle of the space. He kicks away a couple of breeze blocks and reveals the chest freezer, propped at an angle on some rubble.

"Will you look at that?" says Dermot. His attention is caught by the chest freezer. Pippa looks too.

"She did clear off in a hurry, didn't she?" says Pippa.

The man from the digger clears away more breeze blocks by the freezer. He gets a shovel and begins to tug at the rubble it's propped up on. Finally, as we all look on, the freezer falls over onto its side with a loud thud, and its lid falls wide open.

It's empty.

"Actually," I say, "I decided not to wait on the septic tank. It was a bit more urgent than that."

In fact, it was the day after I put Jackie in the freezer that I called a firm and ordered a new tank to be installed in our garden. I'd become quite an expert from all my brochures and ordered a state-of-the-art one. Far too big for the house really. But enormous as it is, it won't need emptying for many years. There's ample capacity for the sludge to settle in the bottom, and if anything should accidentally fall in it, like a rabbit or anything like that, or even something much, much larger, the biological processes will completely break down the hair, bones and teeth. It's an amazing chemical reaction and one which you can accelerate if you feed the tank with the correct bacteria, which I regularly do. In about ten years from now, they'll need to drain off the sludge and take it to a processing plant. But any large lumps of organic matter will be long gone by then. It'll all get cleaned up and disappear.

"We're standing on top of it right now," I say, as we walk across the lawn. I think of Jackie, below our feet, hauled over here lump by lump and now slowly rendering down into sludge. It was only her rings I threw into the sea at low tide. Who knows when and where they'll turn up, if at all?

"Talking of building work," says Dermot, "we heard from your old friends Gavin and Peter the other day."

"We haven't spoken to them since we found out how they stitched you up," says Pippa.

"Bastards," says Dermot. "Oooh, sorry, Dylan. Pretend you didn't hear that. Anyway, they called us about the problem we had with our plumbing that time, at the party where you met them, when a load of cement had blocked our drains. Apparently, the same thing happened to them. They need to dig up their entire garden – trees, patio, decking, everything. It's going to cost thousands. What are the chances of that coincidence, eh?"

"What, indeed?" I say with a smile. An advantage of having building work next to my house is that it was incredibly easy to get my hands on several bags of cement. It was a long round trip, and hard work in the dark, but Dylan loves a drive, and it was worth it, I think. One thing I do hang onto from Tiffany's classes is a strong belief in karma, even if you have to take it into your own hands.

"Shall we go for a walk down on the beach?" I say, lifting Dylan out of his pram and strapping him into his carrier.

"Oh, that's a nice idea," says Pippa. "What do you think, Dermot?"

"I might take the stairs this time," he jokes.

We walk towards the end of the garden. Then Pippa suddenly stops.

"Hang on," she says urgently, turning back to the house.

She looks like she's had a terrible thought. And for a moment I get a small chill. Have I given something away about Gavin and Peter? About Jackie? About Ron?

"What is it?"

"The door's open," she says. "Don't you need to lock up?"

Ah.

"No need," I say calmly. "You wouldn't believe how safe and quiet it is round here."

END

THANK YOU FOR READING

Did you enjoy reading *The Wrong Neighbour*? Please consider leaving a review on Amazon. Your review will help other readers to discover the novel.

ABOUT THE AUTHOR

Caleb Crowe is a British writer of psychological thrillers, and is fascinated by stories where extraordinary things happen to ordinary people, and the mundane is transformed into the menacing.

He's afraid of the sea, fearful in the countryside, panicky in large open spaces and terrified of small, confined spaces. He finds eerily quiet villages and bustling impersonal cities equally unsettling. There's nowhere, and no one, that doesn't possess some kind of dark, brooding anxiety just waiting to have the lid prised open and turned into a twisty, suspenseful, nerve-shredding story.

He lives in Manchester with his partner, two children and two cats, who probably have their own mysterious agendas. Whether he's navigating the urban jungle or wrestling with the daily challenges of family life, Caleb draws inspiration from the unpredictability of everyday existence.

Find Caleb on his website: www.calebcrowe.com

ALSO BY CALEB CROWE

The Girl in the Painting

The Wrong Neighbour

Printed in Great Britain
by Amazon

45114254R00189